J.C. FIELDS

THE
MONEY
TRAIL

BOOKS

By J.C. Fields

The Sean Kruger Series

The Fugitive's Trail

The Assassin's Trail

The Imposter's Trail

The Cold Trail

The Money Trail

The Dark Trail

The Virtual Trail

The Ominous Trail

The Manchurian's Trail

The Michael Wolfe Series

A Lone Wolf

The Last Insurgent

A Matter of Payback

Dakota Storm

A Storm Does This Way Come

Vinci Books

vinci-books.com

Published by Vinci Books Ltd in 2025

1

Chapter One

RECENTLY UNEMPLOYED DEFENSE attorney Jolene Sanders was unaware an assassin sat at a Starbuck's table across from her apartment building sipping coffee. Her thoughts were too consumed by anger after being laid off from a six-figure position at Rothenburg & Sandifer, one of the largest and best-known legal firms in Washington, D.C.

Turning left outside the foyer of her apartment building, Jolene set out at a hurried pace. She knew where she was going and, unbeknownst to her, so did the assassin. She did not see him calmly take a last sip of coffee, stand, pick up a small plastic bag and nod at another man sitting at a different table. As she strode down the street, she did not notice him follow her a few moments later.

Tall and slender with short black hair, she was a no-nonsense attorney with an attitude to match. Born two years after her parents immigrated to the United States from Jamaica, she spent her childhood matching wits with five older brothers. After four years at Georgetown Law School and three successful ones with Rothenburg & Sandifer, she had prevailed in the good-old-boy legal network of Washington, D.C.

Until now.

The day before her thirtieth birthday, the firm summoned all the members of the legal defense department to a meeting. A meeting where everyone in the room, except Kyle Sandifer, would be offered a miserly severance package and bid a good life. The only catch to receiving the package was signing a non-disclosure agreement.

Non-negotiable.

She refused.

Furious about the dismissal, she could not appreciate the fact these matters happened all the time and people moved on. She possessed knowledge about certain clients of the firm. Knowledge only Kyle Sandifer and Joseph Rothenburg, the two senior partners, were supposed to know.

Now on a mission she would be meeting, for the third time, a Washington Post reporter at a pre-determined park bench on the south side of Constitution Avenue facing the Washington Monument.

The information she clutched in her left hand would destroy the firm, the reputation of the two partners and several high-profile politicians.

The area bustled with tourists and locals going about their business. Both women believed they were hiding in plain sight.

They were not.

The reporter already occupied the bench upon Jolene's arrival. Sitting next to her, Jolene smiled grimly, "Thanks for meeting me."

"My pleasure," replied Keira Pennington, five years older than Jolene and a ten-year veteran of investigative journalism at the Washington Post. During her tenure, she had already exposed more than her fair share of stories about corruption and greed within the halls of Congress. Today she pursued the biggest story of her career and Jolene Sanders possessed insider information confirming her premise. Their meetings always occurred in public and always during the busiest time of day on The Ellipse.

"Here are my documents."

The attorney handed the small thirty-two gig flash drive to Keira who accepted it and studied the object for a moment. She glanced around their surroundings, returned her attention to Jolene and smiled.

"Everything you've told me is confirmed on this, right?"

She nodded but did not return the smile.

Placing the flash drive in her purse on the bench next to her, Keira stared out over the open space toward the Washington Monument and said, "I know I promised to try to keep your name out of this, but I will have to identify you as my source to my editor or he won't publish."

"I've been thinking about that. Since I haven't signed their ridiculous non-disclosure agreement, I don't see a problem telling him my name."

Turning her head to glance at the attorney, Keira frowned and asked, "What about your severance package?"

Jolene shrugged. "I have some money saved and it wasn't really that good of a package. I'll be fine."

"He will let me call you an unnamed source in the published story. At least he said he would."

"I appreciate it. Thank you."

"What are your plans?"

Taking a deep breath, Jolene stared at the tall monolith 350 yards from where they sat.

"I've been approached by a firm based in Chicago. They have an opening in their Minneapolis office. The offer is good with a clear, definitive path to partnership. Not the pie-in-the-sky crap offered by that scumbag Sandifer."

"Good. Did you accept the offer?"

"No. Too cold there for my taste. I'm hoping for something in Dallas, Atlanta or a big city in Florida." Smiling, she turned back to the reporter. "Regardless of what happens, I'm leaving D.C. at the end of the month. I'll go home for a while until I find the right position. Mom and Dad will be happy."

"Where's home?"

"Orlando."

Pennington smiled. "I'm from Jacksonville."

"Really?"

"Yeah, I hate the weather here."

"Me too."

Neither woman noticed as a tall man walked up to their park bench holding his right hand behind his back as he approached. When he was directly in front of them, he asked with a slight French accent, "Do either of you have the time?"

Startled by the interruption, Jolene looked up at the intruder and gasped.

Keira also glanced at the man and started to say something when she noticed the clear facial mask obscuring his features. His hands wore flesh-colored surgical gloves and in his right hand was a small spray bottle.

The mist from the bottle engulfed both women as the stranger calmly walked away. Passing tourists and locals paid no attention to the women as they struggled to breathe. Jolene lost consciousness first as her head rolled back and her body slumped toward Keira.

Keira's eyes tracked another man as he stepped up to the park bench. She could not move or offer resistance as a gloved hand took her purse. He paused briefly, smiled at her, smoothly dropped the purse into a shopping bag in his left hand and walked away. As she watched him leave, her last thought on this earth was how dangerous the information on the flash drive must be.

Neither woman would hear the scream of a passing tourist from Cincinnati.

Chapter Two

FBI SPECIAL AGENT SEAN KRUGER stood with his arms folded over his chest as numerous agents in hazmat suits entered and exited a temporary hazmat tent surrounding a park bench north of the Washington Monument.

"Who were the victims?"

Special Agent Ryan Clark looked at his notes and answered, "We didn't find an ID on her, but the blonde is Keira Pennington. She's a well-known high-profile reporter for the Washington Post. The dark-haired woman did have an ID: Jolene Sanders, a local attorney."

Kruger frowned. "Jolene Sanders?" He looked at Clark and tilted his head questioningly.

"Yeah, according to the ID they found on her. Why?"

"Ryan, think about it. Isn't that name familiar?

"Ah, shit. She was Robert Burns Jr.'s lawyer."

Nodding his head, Kruger continued to stare at the tent. "Yes, she was. Why was she on a park bench in front of the Washington Monument talking to a Washington Post reporter?"

Clark glanced at his partner. "I don't know."

Kruger shook his head and returned the glance. "The pieces of the puzzle are there. You just need to arrange them properly."

"Okay, how would I arrange the pieces?"

Kruger smiled. "Our first task will be to determine if they were friends. If they were, we have a problem. If she was meeting the reporter as a source, we have a different and more serious problem. Rothenburg and Sandifer sold their law firm a month after the death of Robert Burns Jr. ended our investigation. To whom they sold it has been the subject of speculation ever since. Maybe Jolene Sanders knew the answer and it resulted in her untimely death."

"That's a lot of conjecture without a lot of facts."

"Yes, it is."

"You obviously have a theory. Care to share?"

Kruger gave Clark a grim smile. "Right now, it's not even a theory, more of a hunch. But there's a reason the ex-attorney of Robert Burns Jr. is dead on a park bench in Washington, D.C. along with a Washington Post reporter. We both know Junior was involved with the Russian mob." Clark nodded as he listened and stared at the tent.

"Now we have what appears to be the use of a Russian nerve agent in his attorney's death," Kruger continued. "I don't like coincidences, so this makes me nervous."

Clark shot Kruger a hard stare. "Russian nerve agent? Where the hell did you get that?"

"Iraq."

"Really?"

"Summer of 2008," Kruger nodded. "The case is still classified. But I can tell you it involved the death of several American businessmen. From the pictures I received five minutes ago of the victims over there," he nodded in the direction of the tent, "their appearance is the same as what I saw in Iraq. A-232, a derivative of Novichok-5, was the agent used during the incident we investigated. It's a versatile agent and can be delivered with a variety of methods without diminishing its effectiveness. Confirmation will have to wait for the lab analysis, but at this point, I bet I'm right."

"If you're right, the implications are staggering, Sean."

"Yes, they are."

"So, what now?"

"We find out if Jolene Sanders and Keira Pennington knew each other and were meeting socially, or…"

"If Sanders was a source."

Nodding, Kruger looked at Clark. "Yeah, now you see the pieces coming together, don't you?"

"Unfortunately, I do. Where do you want to start?"

"I think we need to start at Rothenburg & Sandifer."

———

KRUGER STOOD in front of the reception desk in the law firm's ornately decorated lobby. Two attractive young women sat behind a dark mahogany counter. The brunette of the pair was talking into a wireless headset as she typed on a computer keyboard. The blonde was staring wide-eyed at Kruger and Clark.

"Excuse me. You said the FBI?"

Giving her a warm smile, Kruger nodded as both agents held their IDs so she could see, but not reach them. "Yes, Special Agents Sean Kruger and Ryan Clark to see Kyle Sandifer."

After blinking several times, she asked, "Do you have an appointment?"

"No, we're on official business. Please let him know we're here."

"Mr. Sandifer's schedule is very tight. He only sees clients by appointment."

Still smiling, Kruger leaned forward slightly.

"We're not clients. I'm sure he will make an exception for the FBI."

"I'm afraid you'll have to make..."

Kruger glanced at the name plate on the counter as the young woman made another excuse.

"Ms. Griffith, I don't think you understand. I'm not going to make an appointment and come back. We are investigating the death of one of your attorneys. Now kindly call Mr. Sandifer and tell him we need to speak with him."

Her blinking increased as she picked up the handset of a multi-line phone.

Three minutes later, they were escorted into the office of Kyle Sandifer. The attorney stood and walked out from behind an enormous mahogany desk as they entered the office. The desk was cluttered with various files and a laptop computer. He wore a Brooks Brother dark gray suit and white on white shirt with a maroon striped tie. Three inches taller than Kruger's six-foot frame, Sandifer's grip was firm as he shook both men's hands. He was lean, athletic and appeared to be in his early sixties with a regular regime of exercise. His dark tan and lack of wrinkles or facial hair gave him the professional appearance needed for a Washington, D.C., power broker.

He stared at Kruger and asked without preamble, "What is this about the death of one of our attorneys?'

"Jolene Sanders." He paused to assess Sandifer's reaction. "She was murdered this morning on a park bench near the Washington Monument."

Sandifer let his breath out slowly. "Ahh..." He returned to his chair and sat down behind the desk. "She is no longer associated with this firm."

"Really?"

"Yes, Agent."

As another piece of the puzzle fell into place, Kruger kept

a neutral expression. He tilted his head and asked, "When did she leave the firm?"

"Two weeks ago."

"Her choice or yours?"

Sandifer frowned and glared at Kruger. "Hers, of course."

"Careful, Mr. Sandifer. Lying to a federal agent is a felony."

"Corporate decision. We disbanded the criminal defense team."

Smiling, Kruger understood. More pieces of the puzzle slammed into place like a fast-paced Tetra game. "If you don't do criminal defense, what pays the bills?"

"Corporate advocacy."

Chuckling, Kruger smiled. "In other words, lobbying."

"That and other services for our clients."

"I see. So, Jolene Sanders was let go?"

"Yes, unfortunately, we had to let several accomplished attorneys go that day. It was purely a business decision. They were compensated, of course, and there was nothing personal in the decision."

"I'm sure that was comforting for them and their families to hear."

Sandifer frowned when Kruger made the comment.

Clark spoke for the first time to ask, "Mr. Sandifer, why would Jolene Sanders be talking to a reporter for the Washington Post?"

Most men in Sandifer's position were experts at hiding their emotions and thoughts behind a mask of neutrality. Sandifer succeeded, but not before a momentary look of horror flashed across his face. The mask returned and he shook his head.

"I would not be able to comment with any authority. I didn't know much about Ms. Sander's personal life. I knew she was unmarried and ambitious, but beyond that, nothing."

"What about the cases she was handling when you dissolved the criminal defense department?"

"We consulted with each client and transferred their cases to the law firm of their choice. Some of the attorneys who were let go followed those cases to the new firms. I assumed Ms. Sanders was among them."

Kruger frowned. "You don't know?"

Sandifer shook his head.

"I find that hard to believe, counselor."

"Believe what you want."

Clark asked. "May we have a list of cases she was working on before she left?"

"Not without a subpoena."

Smiling, Kruger withdrew a folded piece of paper from the inside breast pocket of his suit coat and handed it to Sandifer. "Goes without saying."

———

"WHAT WAS SHE WORKING ON, RYAN?"

Kruger drove as Clark looked through the file.

"Nothing big. It looks like they stopped taking major cases six months ago. All she was handling, according to these records, was a few DWI, DUI and shoplifting cases."

"That had to be frustrating."

"For someone with her experience, very."

"Go back to the date you indicated. What was she handling before that?"

Flipping back through the pages, Clark stopped on one. "Uh, let's see. Ah, here it is. She was defending a congressman in an aggravated assault charge. At the same time, she was representing an oil company executive on an embezzlement indictment." Looking up from the pages, his eyebrows rose.

"How do you go from defending high-level executives to defending drunk office workers?"

Kruger glanced at him. "Don't know. Never been a lawyer."

"Me neither, but it seems strange. I would think they would give the DUI cases to a junior or rookie lawyer, not someone who had handled the Robert Burns Jr. case."

Thinking back on the Burns case, Kruger felt the same way. Burns was a newly elected Senator from the state of Washington. His father was the thirty-ninth richest man in the world and spending a lot of his wealth on the defense of his son, who was accused of murdering a hooker. When it was discovered he was a serial sexual predator with ties to the Russian mafia, the case got complicated. Jolene Sanders was his attorney.

"What did you think of Sandifer's reaction to Jolene's death, Ryan?"

"Cold and uncaring."

"My thoughts exactly. I think it's time we found out more about Jolene Sanders. Is the crime lab still at her apartment?"

Clark pulled his phone out and sent a text message. Kruger heard it beep thirty seconds later.

"Yes, and they just found something."

Chapter Three

LOCATED three blocks from Constitution Avenue, the Imperial Apartments were within walking distance of the park bench once occupied by the deceased Jolene Sanders and Keira Pennington. Situated in the upscale Foggy Bottom neighborhood, it provided easy access for residents to enjoy a variety of restaurants and night life. Built in the 1930s, a 2013 renovation transformed the interior into a trendy and expensive place to live.

Kruger and Clark showed their badges to a D.C. cop standing at the door of Jolene Sanders' apartment and entered. The place was small, Kruger guessed fewer than 700 square feet and busy with forensic technicians looking for anything that could possibly be associated with her death. Clark proceeded to look for the individual who sent the text message while Kruger took in the room. The apartment consisted of an open living room, kitchen and dining area toward the rear of the space. A small hallway to his right led to the bedroom and bath area. Kruger walked toward the dining area and peered out the window of the far wall. The Washington Monument was clearly visible rising above the roof line of adjacent buildings. As he turned from the window, Clark approached.

"They think someone was here searching the apartment either while Jolene was being murdered, or immediately after. They recovered her cell phone at the scene, but her laptop and an iPad are missing."

"How do they know?"

"Receipts found in a small desk in the bedroom. Plus, the place has Wi-Fi."

Kruger nodded and walked into the kitchen area. "What else?"

Clark's hands were covered by latex gloves and he offered a five-by-seven-inch spiral notebook.

"This was found taped to the bottom of her nightstand drawer. Whoever was here missed it."

Smiling grimly, Kruger pulled two similar gloves from his suitcoat side pocket and slipped them on before taking the journal. As he flipped through the pages, his smile grew. "She suspected someone would steal her laptop, didn't she?"

"Apparently. I didn't read much of it, but after skimming a few pages, she knew something was wrong at Rothenburg and Sandifer. What exactly, she doesn't disclose, but it was the reason she was talking to the reporter."

Kruger paused on a page and read it carefully, then said, "This answers the question if they were friends. They only met a week ago. Jolene reached out to Keira."

Clark nodded, "I saw that."

"Where did Pennington live?"

"House in Manassas. Techs are there now."

"Let's go."

THE NEIGHBORHOOD CONSISTED OF SMALL, comfortable homes well suited for middle-income families in the high-cost Washington, D.C., area. Keira Pennington's ranch-style house featured buff brick on the front façade and vinyl siding stretching around to the back. Yellow tape blocked off the yard and an FBI forensic van blocked the driveway. Curious neighbors stood in their front yards, staring as FBI agents scurried in and out of the home.

Clark parked their Bureau car behind the van and both stepped out. With their badges on lanyards around their necks, they ducked under the crime scene tape and walked to the front door. A familiar face greeted them.

Kruger smiled and shook the hand of a long-time friend. "Charlie, I thought you were in management and too important to be seen at a crime scene."

Charlie Craft, a pencil-thin thirty-something with a slightly-stooped posture from working with computers his entire life, smiled at his former mentor. His rimless glasses and now-thinning hair made him look older than his true age.

"I'm never too busy to help on cases you're investigating, Sean."

"Thanks, Charlie. You remember Ryan Clark?"

Clark shook the younger man's hand and smiled, "It's been a long time, Charlie. Good to see you again."

"Same here, Ryan."

Looking inside the house, Kruger's smile disappeared as he asked, "What've we got, Charlie?"

"House was ransacked before we got here. Neighbor across the street is an elderly woman and said there was a white van from a local plumbing company parked in the driveway from about ten this morning till noon. She didn't see anyone, just the van."

He handed them disposable booties to cover their shoes.

Once inside, Kruger asked, "Is there a husband?"

Charlie shook his head. "Divorced about a year ago. She lived alone. No pets."

Kruger nodded as he slipped on a new pair of latex gloves.

"She was a reporter. Have you found any files or notes?" he asked.

"No, there's a bedroom in the back she appeared to use as an office. All the drawers are empty. The only things left in the desk are a few pens and paperclips in the middle drawer. No computer or tablet. Her cell phone was found at the scene, but that's all we have."

"Same thing for the Sanders woman."

While Kruger and Craft conversed, Clark wandered toward the bedroom to look inside a walk-in closet he could see from the hall. Chaos was the common theme in the house and the closet was no exception. Clothes were ripped from hangers, shoe boxes opened with their content scattered, books tossed about and old suitcases cut apart.

Standing in the doorway, his gaze swept over the mess until it settled on a lockbox barely visible under a pile of sweaters in the corner. When he reached to see if it was open, it moved only a few inches before a steel cable bolted to the floor prevented it from going further.

"Hey, got something here."

Fifteen minutes later, a forensic technician managed to open the box. The contents were a treasure trove of files and information: ten flash drives, three spiral notebooks and fifteen jewel-cased CDs stared back at the investigators.

Kruger smiled. "Wanna bet those are investigation notes?"

Clark nodded, "More than likely." Reaching for one of the notebooks, he flipped it open to the first page. "Looks like some kind of code." He continued to flip through the book.

Looking over his shoulder, Kruger frowned. "Reporter's shorthand?"

"Doubtful. Most reporters record interviews these days. This looks like a code someone like Keira would use to keep a logbook or personal notes."

Glancing at Clark, Kruger grinned as he said, "How would you know?"

"Close friend."

"I heard. How is Tracy?"

"Good. I never thanked you for introducing us."

"My pleasure. Think she could interpret these notes?"

"Won't hurt to ask."

Smiling, Kruger shot a glance at his wrist watch. "Go for it. I have to catch a flight home in three hours. Talk to Tracy and give me a call tomorrow."

All Clark could do was nod as he studied the pages with the strange-looking hieroglyphics.

———

SEVERAL YEARS younger and three inches shorter than Clark, Tracy Adkins wore her dark blonde hair long and assessed the world with dark blue eyes behind black blocky glasses. Conscious of her California good looks, she kept her hair up when working and always wore conservative dark gray, brown or black pantsuits with a white blouse. This kept her interviewees calm and concentrating on her questions, not on her looks or what she wore.

With Clark, she dressed to enhance her figure. Sean Kruger introduced them during the hunt for Robert Burns, Jr. Unbeknownst to Kruger at the time, they started dating, fell in love and were now planning a quiet, private wedding in Panama City Beach, Florida, the follow summer.

She studied one of the spiral notebooks found in Keira Pennington's lockbox.

"It's been a long time since I've seen this particular shorthand so I'm rusty. But I can tell they are notes concerning stories she was working on. These are more background notations versus the actual story." She looked up at Clark to ask, "What else was in the lockbox?"

He held up one of the flash drives. "Nine more of these, notebooks and fifteen CDs."

She nodded and went back to studying the pages.

"What does Sean think?"

"He suspects Jolene Sanders was telling her what was going on at Rothenburg and Sandifer."

"Ryan, there is something about the vice president in these notes."

"Vice president of the law firm?"

She shook her head.

"The United States."

"Ah, geez. What?"

———

KRUGER WALKED into the kitchen from the garage and the first person to greet him was his five-year-old daughter, Kristin. He scooped her up as she squealed, "Daddy's home."

Two-year-old Mikey stood next to his father, bouncing up and down with his arms up, waiting his turn for hugs. Bending over, Kruger grabbed his son and embraced his two children. This was a common occurrence when he returned from any lengthy trip.

Kristin Kruger looked remarkably like her adoptive mother, a quirk of luck rather than genetics. Adopted at birth by her newly-married parents, she had naturally curly brown hair, pale blue eyes and an infectious, gleeful smile. She had her father totally and completely wrapped around her finger.

Mikey Kruger was the natural son of Sean and Stephanie

Kruger. Blonde, blue-eyed and rambunctious, he resembled his father and in contrast, had his mother wrapped around his finger.

After the hugs and kisses, Kruger let both kids down and they scurried away back to whatever activities they had previously been engaged. Kruger smiled as he gazed upon his wife, Stephanie, who stood off to the side watching the homecoming. They embraced and Kruger took in the fragrance of his wife's hair as their hug lasted almost a minute. With each breath, the loneliness of being away from her and their children vanished.

"Glad you're home safe."

"Me, too. I'm back for a while. Clark is handling things in D.C. and I'll be doing what I need to on the internet."

"Good."

Stephanie was a petite woman, seven years younger than her husband. Her curly brown hair was growing longer since the children no longer tugged at it while she held them. Pale blue eyes sparkled as they gazed up at him.

Their meeting was by chance. Kruger had already raised one son as a single parent when he met Stephanie. Her career as a top-level executive with a greeting card company suppressed any thoughts of family until she met Kruger. After buying the neighboring condos in a renovated apartment building west of the Kansas City Plaza, they met during an attempted assault on her by two men in the parking lot. Kruger's arrival on the scene prevented any harm coming to her. Even though their meeting was random, they immediately became friends, fell in love and were totally devoted to each other.

"How were your classes today?"

She shrugged as they walked toward their bedroom so Kruger could unpack. "I've got some really involved students in my marketing class and a few who I don't anticipate will finish the semester."

Kruger chuckled. This was Stephanie's first full year as an instructor at a local university. She was working on her doctorate and teaching a few classes at the same time. With a PhD in psychology, Kruger had spent three years teaching at the same university during a break from his career as a profiler for the FBI.

"It happens," he told her. "You can spot them pretty quickly. The ones who are there to learn and the ones who would rather be anywhere but in class."

As he unpacked his suitcase, Stephanie sat on the bed and watched him. He was tall, just over six feet in height. Still slender and athletic in build, his dark brown hair was growing lighter with each haircut as gray hairs proliferated. She thought of him as the most handsome man she had ever met. However, she refused to tell him so. One day, maybe.

When he came back into the bedroom from depositing his suitcase in their closet, she asked, "Have you spoken to Brian recently?"

Brian was his grown son who lived with his wife about a mile from them.

"No, I got a text message from him. He said he and Michelle wanted to come over this weekend. Why?"

"Remember what I told you in the parking lot the night we first met?"

"You said more than one thing that night."

"I know. But I made one comment in particular."

He smiled. "You mean when you told me it would be a great story to tell our grandchildren?"

She nodded.

Chuckling, Kruger shook his head. "I thought it a strange comment at the time, but I was going to enjoy finding out what you meant. We hadn't even had a date, let alone talked about getting married…" He paused and stared at her. "Wait a minute—no."

"Yes."

"Michelle's pregnant?"

Smiling, she nodded. "Yup. My prophecy will be fulfilled."

Chapter Four

TRACY ROLLED over and put her hand on Clark's chest as she murmured, "I'm the one who normally has trouble sleeping. What's wrong, Ryan?"

The digital clock on his nightstand indicated the time was 2:16 in the morning.

"The vice president's name in Keira's notes."

She moved over and snuggled against him. He automatically put his arm around her to bring her closer.

"I'm sorry I can't read all of them."

"Not your fault. You told me she had her own shorthand."

"Yes, she does. Now what?"

"I don't know. That's why I can't sleep. Investigating a sitting vice president is politically dangerous for the agency."

"And you."

He shrugged. "Yes, but what if Keira discovered something about the vice president and it was being corroborated with information Jolene Sanders possessed? If that's the case, why were they killed with a Russian nerve agent?"

"Well, when you put it that way…" She paused for a second. "Now I don't know if I can get back to sleep." Silence filled the room. "We don't know if Jolene was giving her information about the vice president. Maybe they were discussing something entirely different."

"Maybe." He was quiet for sixty seconds as they lay in each other's arms. Finally, he said, "As Sean has said many times, he doesn't believe in coincidences. I don't either. From what you could read of her notes, it was the only story she was working on. Jolene's notes indicated she reached out to Keira. Why? How did Jolene know to reach out to her? Does that mean her investigation of the vice president involves the law firm of Rothenburg and Sandifer? I would bet it does."

"How are you going to determine if it does, Ryan?"

"With what we have right now, I'm not. The official agency position is Keira Pennington was working on a story someone didn't want published. Jolene Sanders may have been collateral damage. There are fifty agents trying to determine who that someone is. I think they're wasting their time."

"Why?"

"They're looking at it the wrong way. Jolene is the key. She knew something and was telling it to Keira Pennington."

"Don't you need to mention this to the agency?"

He shook his head. "Not until we can prove it."

"How do you do that?"

"Keira's notes are the key. Can you keep working on them?"

"Yes, I was thinking the same thing. If this is what you think it is, her investigation needs to be completed. I'll talk to my editor."

"Good, just don't get too specific."

She chuckled slightly. "Not my first rodeo, Ryan."

"I know, but you need to be careful. The fewer individuals who know the direction we're taking, the better."

Clark felt her nod.

"I'll talk to Sean in the morning."

"JR?"

"Yeah, JR."

"SO THAT'S MY THEORY, SEAN."

Kruger was quiet as he sat in his home office listening to Clark's reasoning. At the end of the summary, he said, "I think you're onto something, Ryan. It makes more sense than statements the agency is making about the two women's deaths."

He lapsed into silence again. Clark let him think.

Finally, he said, "If someone wanted Keira Pennington out of the way, they could have done it quietly and made it look like an accident," he mused. "This was a show, a production to draw media attention. It worked. The agency has their collective underwear in a wad about it and the news media can't go five minutes without speculating about their deaths."

"Kind of what I was thinking. What are our next steps?"

"Has Tracy given up on interpreting Keira's notes?"

"No. After we talked last night, she's going to keep working on them."

"Good."

"Is JR able to help?"

"Don't know. I'll have to ask him."

WHEN KRUGER MET JR DIMINSKI, he and Mia lived on the third floor of a three-story building in the downtown region of Springfield, MO. His business occupied the second floor, with storage and administrative functions on the first. With the birth of Joseph Sean Diminski, the couple sold the building, bought a house across the street from the Krugers and moved the business to a two-story structure in a multi-use development in the southwest part of town. JR's business had grown from a one-man operation to a nationally-known computer security firm employing sixty individuals. He let others run the day-to-day operations while he met with clients and did the programming.

His private sideline business and first love remained the art of hacking.

Before being known as JR Diminski, he was a computer software analyst for a large privately-held software company. The owner of the company decided to bring in new investors to help expand his business. The new investors, through stock manipulation, suddenly owned a majority of the outstanding shares. They proceeded to fire the entire analyst team and outsourced their jobs to India. Within a year, they dismantled the company and sold each piece separately, reaping millions for the new investors.

After being dismissed, JR hacked into the laptop of the new owner and found multiple files outlining illegal activities. He copied the information and tried blackmailing the man, thus finding himself in the company of two men who intended to end his life. JR managed to escape, but in the process, killed one and wounded the other. He became a fugitive, fled to the center of the country, changed his name and started over. Now seven years later, with the help of Kruger and a man named Joseph Kincaid, he operated a successful business with no need to hide. He also aided his friend, Sean, on occasion.

Kruger parked his dark gray Ford Mustang GT in a visitor's slot in front of JR's office building. When he walked in, Jodi Roberson, Vice President and General Manager, was talking to the receptionist and made a bee-line toward him. After a quick I-haven't-seen-you-in-a-long-time hug, she smiled.

"What's it been, Sean, six months since you visited us last?"

"At least. How've you been, Jodi?"

"Busy. Trying to keep JR on task is exhausting work."

"I'm sure it is. Where is he?"

She pointed toward the ceiling. "Second floor, same cubicle. I got here at seven and he was already engrossed in something. No telling how long he's been here."

Chuckling, he walked toward the stairs. Kruger was proud and amazed at how his friend's small one-man company had grown.

As he approached JR's cubicle next to the glassed-in conference room on the far side of the cubicle farm, he saw his friend's head swiveling as he surveyed three flat-screen monitors in front of him. Stopping at the table behind JR, Kruger looked at the Mr. Coffee machine he had bought for JR almost a year ago. It looked well used, but he did not see any coffee for it.

Without turning and looking at him, JR said, "Everyone uses it when there's coffee. But they all think it's someone else's duty to buy the coffee. If you want a cup, you'll have to use the Keurig."

Shrugging, he picked a coffee pod, placed it in the Keurig and started a cup. So far, JR had not diverted his attention from the monitors. When the coffee was done, JR finally turned to look at him.

"Make me one, too."

Kruger placed his untouched cup in front of JR and waited for a few moments.

"You're welcome," he announced.

"Excuse me, what?"

"I said, you're welcome."

"Uh, okay. Uh—thanks, I guess."

Chuckling, Kruger returned to the machine and replaced the used coffee pod with a new one. When the blue light started flashing, he pressed the button to start another mug of coffee. While the water was forced through the pod, he leaned against the table.

"What're you working on?"

"New client. Their system got hit with ransomware. Creeps wanted a million dollars to release their data. I did it for fifty thousand and now the client never has to worry about it again. I've got an idea of who did it and now I'm looking for them. Why?"

"That was TMI."

"Huh?"

"Too Much Information."

JR chuckled. "You asked."

Kruger took a sip of his coffee, grimaced and returned his attention to JR. "The reason I asked was to determine if you might want to work with me again."

JR stopped typing, turned to look at his friend and said, "I always enjoy working with you. You don't need to ask. What's the project?"

"There are two parts." Kruger outlined the investigation of the reporter's and attorney's murders and how the vice president's name became involved.

"The second part is a continuation of the Robert Burns Jr. investigation I was asked to do six months ago, but never started due to other priorities popping up. I think the two are related."

"How?"

"You remember I had a meeting with Dmitri Orlov in Paris, right?"

JR nodded.

"After I gave Paul my report, he asked me to look into Orlov quietly, without using official FBI assets."

Silence was the response. Kruger knew his friend and allowed him to process the information.

"Interesting." JR took a sip of coffee and stared at a point on the far wall. After several moments, he turned his attention back to Kruger. "Why do you think they're related?"

Shaking his head, he took a deep breath. "A feeling."

"I've found your *feelings* are generally correct, Sean. Care to explain?"

"We know Orlov was trying to gain influence in Congress by compromising senators."

"Yeah."

"What we don't know is how successful his efforts have been. We know Robert Burns Sr., during his time as a senator in the early 2000s, was successful in getting various banking laws rescinded so Orlov's banks could make more money."

Nodding, JR sipped his coffee.

Kruger continued, "Those changes in banking regulations indirectly led to the Great Recession of 2008. The unintended consequences emboldened Orlov. What if the vice president is as compromised as Burns Sr. was? What then?"

"Scary."

"Yeah, it's scary. I spoke to Paul on the way over here. Looking into Orlov and the VP is now my top priority. He agrees with me about the two events being related."

JR turned back to the computer and started talking to himself. "Hmmm... I'll first need to look at the VP's social media presence before he was a politician and see where that takes us."

Kruger knew his friend was now in a zone and would be non-communicative for a while. He walked into the conference room, closed the door and started making phone calls.

Thirty minutes later, Kruger saw JR turn in his chair and motioned for him to join him at the cubicle. When he opened the conference room door, JR said, "Pull up a chair. You're not going to like what I've found."

Chapter Five

"EVER HEAR of a 501(c)(4) corporation?"

Kruger nodded, "Yes, they're non-profit organizations."

"Yes, but they also have another identifier. Non-profit social welfare organizations."

"So?"

"They can act like Political Action Corporations or Super PACs in political campaigns with no need to reveal who their donors are. By law, they have to keep a list of donors who give over $5,000, but not those who give below that amount."

"Okay. Again, so?"

"That means it is completely legal for overseas contributors to give them money for the purposes of contributing to politicians."

"Yeah, but $5,000 is chump change in today's political atmosphere."

"Yeah, but if 1,000 donors give $4,999 dollars, that's five million dollars, which is definitely not chump change. Plus, if you have more than one 501(c)(4) giving money to the same candidate and each has a thousand donors, you're talking serious money."

Kruger didn't respond.

JR continued, "When Donald Pittman was elected governor of Virginia, he had five of these organizations giving him money for his campaign. Two of those organizations were legit. Three were dubious, at best."

"Okay, you've got my attention. Can you trace the money?"

Shaking his head, JR said, "Not now. But I was able to find the campaign report showing huge sums of money spent on things like postage, meals and a variety of generic disbursements during those years. Plus, I found the name of the LLC the campaign claimed provided security for the candidate."

Kruger frowned as he said, "I thought the state provides that."

"But the candidate is also allowed to provide additional security if he so desires."

"What are you trying to say, JR?"

"I'm not trying to say anything, Sean. I'm merely pointing out a possibility. One that seems to be more reality than speculation. To be positive, I need more than thirty minutes to confirm any of it."

"Okay. What's the name of the LLC providing security? I can have them checked out."

"No, you can't," shaking his head, JR turned back to his keyboard. "The Virginia Secretary of State's office shows the company did not renew its charter after the election." He pointed to the left screen of his three monitors.

With pursed lips, Kruger drummed his fingers on the cubicle's desk. After a dozen seconds, he asked, "What happened to all the money left in the PAC's?"

"Numbered account in Dubai."

"Shit."

"There's more."

"What?"

"It got worse when he became the VP candidate."

"How much worse?"

"Twenty million dollars."

"Take whatever time you need, but this may be what Keira Pennington was trying to confirm."

"Do you think Jolene Sanders had confirmation of any of this?"

Once again, Kruger did not respond immediately. After taking a few moments to stare at the computer screen, he returned his attention to JR. "That is something we need to find out."

———

THE SECOND-FLOOR CONFERENCE room in the southwest corner of JR's building began as a normal glassed-in meeting room. Now, after the installation of specially-designed windows comprised of two independent glass panes with a vacuum in between and acoustic ceiling tiles, the room was soundproof. This served two purposes: it prevented conversations from being monitored on the outside and kept the sounds of the second floor from intruding on meetings. JR regularly met with clients about their computer security and remained paranoid of others listening to those conversations. In addition, on occasion, he held meetings with Sean Kruger concerning investigations. These discussions always occurred within the confines of the room.

He sat across from Kruger as both men stared at the Polycom VoIP Conference Phone sitting in the middle of the conference table. On the other end of the call was Director of the FBI Paul Stumpf, Assistant Director Alan Seltzer and Ryan Clark at the Hoover Building, with Assistant Attorney General Brian McAlister at the Robert F. Kennedy Justice Department Building.

Kruger finished outlining JR's findings about the vice president and waited for a response.

The Polycom unit only emitted silence.

Finally, Stumpf cleared his throat and asked, "So, you believe Vice President Pittman is compromised?"

"Sir, what I believe is immaterial," Kruger replied. "But evidence suggests Pittman was heavily financed by Dmitri Orlov during the time he ran for office in Virginia. Ryan, have you discussed your findings?"

"Not yet," Clark answered.

Everyone on the conference call at the Hoover Building focused their attention on Clark. Stumpf nodded at him, "Go ahead, Ryan. The floor is yours."

"Some, but not all, of the notes found in Keira Pennington's home were transcribed from their original shorthand late yesterday." He paused for a few moments as he took a sip from a bottle of water sitting in front of him. "The reporter was investigating the members of an economic steering committee Vice President Pittman chairs. They meet on a weekly basis at the VP residence at Number One Observatory Circle on the grounds of the United States Naval Observatory. She found evidence linking three of the members of this committee to banks with ties to Dmitri Orlov. All three are on the Boards of Directors of these banks. An investigation concluded by Agent Kruger and myself last year suggested Orlov was seeking influence within the US government to make policies friendlier to the Russian government."

Director Paul Stumpf was in his early 60s. At one time a dedicated marathon runner, he still maintained a lean body. But after having both knees replaced, he was starting to add a few pounds to his five-eleven frame. His hair was dark brown, perfectly styled, with the first appearance of gray around his temples. Rimless glasses sat on an unremarkable nose in front of arctic blue eyes. During Stumpf's rise within the FBI, he and Kruger worked together a few times in their early careers. Now decades later, he was the director, thanks in part to an investigation Kruger solved four years earlier.

The director's demeanor remained neutral as he tapped his lips with an index finger.

"Can you substantiate the links or is this a coincidence?" he asked.

"We can substantiate the links, Paul," Kruger answered. "The information is solid."

Stumpf nodded and remained quiet for a few moments. "Brian, what is the DOJ's position?"

"After hearing your preliminary evidence, I believe I need to take this to a grand jury."

This was the response Kruger was hoping for. "Sir, we'll summarize our findings with the collaborating evidence and Ryan Clark will do the same with what he has. You will have it by the end of the day."

Clark nodded in agreement and Stumpf stood.

"Gentlemen, this information is disturbing I can't emphasize this enough: be detailed with your evidence, document where it was obtained and throw out anything you are unsure of. The person being accused is the vice president of the United States. Once it's presented to the grand jury, if there is any hearsay, untruths or holes in your evidence, it will come back and bite you and the FBI in the ass. Make sure that does not happen."

He walked out of the conference room, leaving Alan Seltzer and Ryan Clark staring at each other.

AFTER DISCONNECTING THE CALL, Kruger smiled and looked at JR.

"So how do we disclose how our information was found

without admitting to you hacking into various government and private computer systems?"

"You worry too much. We tie it back to the investigation of Joel Moody."

Nodding, Kruger was quiet as he thought about the case that brought him back from a self-imposed retirement of teaching at a local university to being an FBI agent again. The cold case was almost two decades old when an incident with a local graduate student reminded him of his old investigation into the disappearances of six college women. Unhappy teaching, he returned to the FBI to reopen the case. The original investigation never produced a person of interest, nor did it result in finding the women. But with JR's assistance, they took a different approach and discovered a possible suspect: Joel Moody.

He was a former Seattle vice cop working as the head of security for the thirty-ninth richest man in the world, former Senator Robert Burns. As the investigation progressed, they learned Moody had a financial arrangement with certain groups of Russian criminals importing women from Asia to work as sex slaves on the west coast. How the financial arrangement came to be was never truly proven. But Kruger and his team discovered why the college women disappeared and why their bodies were never found. The son of Moody's employer, Robert Burns Jr., became the person of interest. Unfortunately, his death brought the investigation to a premature conclusion.

During the inquiry, JR traced money paid to Moody via a number of foreign-owned banks with branches in the United States.

Now, those same banks, with hidden ties to both Russia and a Russian criminal organization operating in New York City and Washington, DC, had members of their boards serving on the vice president's economic council.

Emerging from his funk, Kruger stood.

"Outline the steps you took following the money trail and I'll review my case notes. I want an airtight case summarized by this afternoon."

JR smiled. "Does this mean I'm working with you again?"

"Yes, my friend, it does."

"Good. I've been bored."

Chapter Six

VICE PRESIDENT of the United States Donald Pittman sat behind his desk and wiped sweat from his upper lip with a white handkerchief. He listened as President Richard Bryant screamed at him over the phone. Pittman's Chief of Staff, Colin Rector, stood in front of the desk, a concerned look on his face. Rector could hear the president's angry voice, but the words were unintelligible from where he stood.

"Why are these men on your advisory council, Don?" The president's words were harsh and accusatorial. He took time for a calming breath. "Care to tell me why all three of them have ties to a Russian oligarch, who, by the way, has a direct link to the Russian president?"

"I was unaware of their connection. Their reputation within the financial community is well established."

The president's voice rose ten decibels.

"Bullshit, Don. According to a briefing given to me this afternoon by FBI Director Stumpf, they are unknown outside the European market and have direct ties to Moscow. Two of them don't even have a background in banking."

"But they are on the boards of their respective banks, Mr. President. They offer a diverse view of world economics."

"Oh, for gawd sakes, Don, they're figureheads at best. If you say anything like that to a reporter, you and this administration will be crucified by the media. The Attorney General is taking all of this information to a grand jury. Were you aware of that development?"

Pittman paused and took a deep breath. "No, sir."

"Well, he is. Be in my office at 7:30 a.m. tomorrow. We have damage control to do."

The call ended abruptly without any pleasantries.

"Sir, I could hear him this far from the phone," Rector said. "He sounded angry. Is there a problem?"

Pittman waved his hand and replied, "A misunderstanding. I'll straighten it out in the morning."

"I hope so, sir. This sounds serious. Do I need to be there with you?"

"Not necessary."

"Are you sure? I can clear my schedule."

"Positive." He glanced at his wristwatch. "It's late, Colin. Go home, be with your family and get some sleep. Tomorrow might be a long day."

Rector stared at the vice president and after an awkward half-dozen seconds, replied, "Very well. You sure you're okay?"

Smiling, Pittman stood and walked around the desk to put his hand on the younger man's shoulder.

"Yes, Colin, I'm fine. There is obviously a major misunderstanding."

As soon as his Chief of Staff closed the door to Pittman's office, the vice president walked to a credenza. He opened a door in the middle and extracted a bottle of Jack Daniels and a short crystal glass. He poured two fingers and downed them in one gulp. He poured two more fingers and returned to his desk with the bottle and glass. After sitting down and taking a sip of the bourbon, he opened the lower left-hand drawer of his desk. At the bottom of the drawer, under a thick stack of bound reports, resided a black metal box with a numeric lock. After extracting the reports, he punched in a six-digit code. When the box popped open, he withdrew a Glock 26 with a full clip next to it. He studied the gun for several minutes, then slowly loaded the ammunition and chambered a round. He twisted it left and then right in his hand. While he stared at the gun, he took several more gulps of his drink. Without thinking, he poured more of the amber liquid into the glass.

Finally, after downing the rest of his third drink, he took a deep breath and let it out slowly.

Placing the barrel of the pistol under his chin, he closed his eyes and pulled the trigger.

———

SEAN AND STEPHANIE strolled hand in hand, barefoot on a beach. The sound of waves coming ashore could be heard. A gentle breeze rustled her hair and he felt the sense of warm sand between his toes. The distant sound of a cell phone made itself present as he turned to her, "Do you hear a phone…?"

The impression of holding her hand dissipated as the persistent sound brought him out of the dream. Glancing at the digital clock on the nightstand, he groaned. A call at 2:36 a.m. could not be good news.

He grabbed the phone and croaked, "Kruger."

"Sean, it's Ryan. Sorry to wake you."

"What happened?" The sound of a siren could be heard in the background. "Why the siren?"

"I'm running Code 3 to the Eisenhower Executive Office Building."

"Oh, shit."

"Yeah, from what I was told, Pittman committed suicide at his office desk. Cleaning crew found him about an hour ago."

Kruger heard the beep of another incoming call. He took the phone from his ear and glanced at the caller ID. Paul Stumpf's personal cell phone number showed on the screen.

"Ryan, I've got Stumpf calling. Get back to me after you know more at the scene."

"Got it."

Kruger answered Stumpf's call. "I just heard."

"Clark?"

"Yeah, he's Code 3 heading to Pittman's office. I can catch a plane in the morning and be there by noon."

Though Kruger couldn't see the expression, Stumpf smiled. "Not why I called. I think you can be more helpful where you are."

"Oh?"

"Yes, I want you and JR to dig deeper into Pittman's finances. I believe it will take someone with JR's talent to find the truth. Someone of Pittman's stature doesn't blow his brains out over having three Russians on a study group. I briefed the President yesterday with what you provided. However, I did leave the account in Dubai out of the conversation. He indicated he would discuss the advisory board members with Pittman. There's something else there, Sean. It may be the money or it could be something totally different. I want to know."

"JR's already on board."

"Good. Put him back on retainer. He can dictate his terms. I really don't care what it costs."

"He'll be reasonable."

"Like I said, I don't care. I need you two working as a team again."

Kruger chuckled, "Consider it done."

The call ended and he laid back down, all thoughts of getting back to sleep gone as his mind raced on to next steps.

Stephanie rolled over and put her arm over his chest. "That didn't sound good. What happened?"

"Vice President Pittman committed suicide in his office."

"Oh, dear. You're not going to Washington?"

Smiling, Kruger put his hand on her arm.

"No, I'm staying here for a while. Paul believes there's something in Pittman's past that resulted in his taking this way out. I agree with him. JR doesn't know it yet, but he's just become one of those men in black suits he used to complain about."

Stephanie snuggled up to him and his arm automatically embraced her. She said, "Irony can be humorous sometimes."

"Yes, it can."

———

MOST MORNINGS FOUND JR at his cubicle next to the conference room on the second floor of his building by 6 a.m. Today was no exception. While the Keurig spewed coffee into his mug, he turned on the three flat-screen monitors on his desk and started the process of bringing his computer terminal out of sleep mode. He was the only person in the building, or so he thought.

As he turned to get his coffee, he saw Sean Kruger navigating the cubicle farm comprising the second floor. His presence did not surprise JR. The FBI agent possessed his own security access code to enter the building. And like JR, Kruger's name and phone number were registered with the local police department as a contact to call should there be a break-in or emergency.

JR sipped his coffee and then tilted his head at Kruger. "You here at six in the morning can't be good."

"It isn't. You're on retainer again. Director's orders."

"Huh."

"VP Pittman ate a bullet in his office last night. The director wants to know why."

"Huh."

"You're beginning to sound like me."

"Annoying, isn't it?"

Kruger ignored the jab and continued, "Stumpf doesn't believe someone like Pittman would commit suicide just because he got caught with three Russians on a committee. I agree with him. There has to be something more in his background besides the money."

Staring at a point on the far wall without blinking, JR sipped his coffee again. Kruger had seen this look before. JR was deep in thought. He walked past his friend to make his own cup of coffee.

"Where's the Mr. Coffee?"

"Inside the credenza. No one except you cleans it and I got tired of looking at it."

"Huh."

Kruger picked a coffee pod, placed it in the Keurig's receptacle and pushed the flashing blue light for a large cup of coffee.

JR turned to watch his friend. "We missed something, didn't we?"

Kruger nodded without comment as he watched his coffee mug fill with the dark liquid.

Sipping coffee again, JR sat down at his now-awake computer. Setting his mug aside, his hands flew over the keyboard.

With the coffee mug full, Kruger took a sip, grimaced, turned and leaned against the credenza. He watched as JR did his magic.

"What're you thinking?"

"Let's start with the three Russians."
"I think that's an excellent idea."

Chapter Seven

ROY GRIFFIN'S office resided on the third floor of the Hart Senate Office Building. Despite his wife's distaste for Washington, she was responsible for its décor and appearance. Natural wood, leather and black steel composed the main features of the senator's work space, making it comfortable and inviting to visitors and his fellow senators. More than a few legislative proposals were negotiated on the two leather sofas facing each other in the center of the room.

Approaching fifty, Roy stood a bit over six feet tall. Male model handsome, he wore his blond hair longer than current fashion, causing certain pundits to proclaim him to be the next John F. Kennedy. Even by California standards, he was wealthy. Keenly aware his looks and money were the reason he now occupied a United States Senate seat, he strived to make a difference for the citizens of California. His rise to the Senate was meteoric. Originally elected by his image-conscious Northern California district as a member of the House of Representatives, he was drafted by his party to unseat the previous junior senator from California. After being caught taking numerous overseas trips, paid for by a huge California defense contractor, the previous senator lost in a landslide to Griffin. Now in his fourth year as a senator, he held several chairmanships, including the Homeland Security and Government Affairs Committee. With this responsibility, he became privy to information most senators were not.

The phone rang on his desk as he looked over the schedule for his committees in the coming weeks. Glancing at the caller ID, he frowned and picked up the handset.

"Good morning, Mary."

Mary Stewart was the president's scheduler and a frequent caller to his office.

"Good morning, Senator. The President has requested a meeting with you. How soon could you get to the White House?"

Griffin was old fashioned and liked a written calendar more than a computer generated one. He glanced at the printout for the day and replied, "Looks like I have an hour mid-afternoon."

"Uh…" She hesitated for just a second. "The President would like to meet with you now, Senator. Is that a problem?"

"Why, no. Tell him I can be there in thirty minutes. Will that be soon enough?"

"I'm sure it will. Thank you, Senator."

Frowning, Griffin stood and retrieved his suit coat from a wooden coat tree his wife picked out. As he entered the reception area of his office, he turned to his young assistant, Jerry Fender, who looked up as Griffin appeared.

"What's wrong, Senator?"

"Emergency meeting with the president. Reschedule my morning appointments and tell our Chief of Staff what happened. I have no idea what this is about or how long it will take."

"Very good, sir." He half-smiled. "Have fun."

Griffin shook his head. Fender knew his boss hated meetings with the president. They were usually long and unproductive.

Thirty-five minutes later, Griffin sat across from President Richard Bryant in the Oval Office. Shorter than Griffin by an inch, Bryant's age approached the beginnings of his eighth decade of life. He possessed a solid head of silver hair, a feature he cultivated as that of a wise and caring man. In public, he wore contacts; in private meetings, he wore rimless glasses sitting on a noble nose in front of hazel eyes. He was not heavy, but he could lose a few pounds and be healthier.

A steward poured coffee for Griffin and the president. When finished, he exited the room and the president took a sip from his mug.

"Roy, I have a problem and I need your help in solving it."

"I hope that I can, sir. What's the problem?"

"As you know, the Vice President's funeral will be private with only family in attendance."

"Yes, sir. I heard."

"Not a fitting way for this to end, is it?"

"No, sir."

The President smiled slightly. "I need a new vice president."

Griffin stalled by reaching for his coffee. After taking a sip, he replied, "I'd be more than happy to chair a search committee for you, Mr. President."

"Not what I was thinking, Roy. I want you to be my new vice president."

Clearing his throat, Griffin stalled again. Finally, after setting his coffee cup down, he looked the president in the eyes.

"I am sure there are individuals far more qualified for the position than me."

"Maybe, but the 25th Amendment allows me to choose a new VP. I get to pick anyone I want and I pick you."

"I'm flattered, sir. But I'm just a first term Senator. You need someone with more experience."

"Bullshit," chuckled the president. "I need someone who will help me get re-elected in two years. You're that someone."

Griffin was silent as he prepared another rebuttal.

"Roy, Pittman's death was a blessing in disguise for this administration. He was an embarrassment, forced onto our party's ticket by hardliners and I didn't want him as my VP. I knew too much about him and it wasn't good. But he brought in support we needed to get elected."

"Still, Mr. President, I'm not sure I fit your needs."

"Listen, Roy, I've already addressed this with leadership in both houses. You will be confirmed on the first vote. You are the only person in the Senate, or the House for that matter, who can be confirmed quickly. Your reputation is spotless, you're well-liked by the public and your peers, plus you get shit done. Who else in this town has those qualification? Besides, I know you are thinking about running for president after my second term is up. So, don't be coy with me. Accept my proposal so we can get this Pittman mess behind us."

Griffin stared out the window behind the president's desk. He remained silent for a while. Finally, he turned back to look at the president.

"Very well. I accept."

Bryant stood and offered his hand. Griffin followed suit and shook it.

"We're going to make a great team, Roy. Plus, this will assure your election for President of the United States after I'm out of office."

"We'll see."

KRUGER'S CELL phone vibrated as he walked back to his Mustang after spending the morning with JR. Glancing at the caller ID, he accepted the call.

"Kruger."

"Sean, it's Roy Griffin."

"How are you, Roy?"

"I need your counsel."

Kruger paused. He had never had a phone call from a sitting senator asking for advice.

"Uh, sure, what about?"

Five years earlier, Kruger and Clark saved the lives of Griffin and his wife during an attempted assassination. They had both stayed in touch with the senator over the years and each felt loyalty to the man and considered him a friend. Griffin felt the same way.

"Are you out of town on an investigation right now?"

"No, why?"

"I would prefer not to discuss it over the phone. Cheryl and I are taking the weekend off and would love to visit you and Stephanie. Would you two be available?"

"By all means, we'd love to see you two as well."

"Good, invite JR and his lovely wife."

"I will."

"Sean?"

"Yes, sir."

"The location of our meeting will have to be secluded and away from the media."

"Uh-oh."

"I'll explain when we see each other. You know where Joseph's place is, don't you?"

"Yes, Steph and I have been there on numerous occasions."

"Good. Saturday afternoon at four."

"We'll be there."

KRUGER DROVE his wife's Jeep Cherokee. It offered higher ground clearance and four-wheel drive versus the Mustang's low ground clearance and rear wheel drive. Joseph's property was rural, very rural and the Mustang did not play well with off-the-beaten-path roads like the one leading to Joseph's. JR sat next to Kruger in the front passenger seat with Mia and Stephanie chatting away in the back seat. The children were under the watchful eye of Kruger's oldest son Brian and his wife Michelle. It was a rare treat for the two couples to be together without kids.

JR turned to Kruger and asked, "What do you think this secluded meeting is all about?"

Shrugging, Kruger shook his head. "No idea. Like I told you earlier, he wouldn't talk about it on the phone."

"Huh."

Kruger shot a glance at his friend and grinned. "There you go again."

As he said it, they cleared the trees on the one lane road leading to the rural property.

Joseph's home sat on a sprawling parcel of land in Christian County five miles south of Sparta and a half mile west of Fairview Road. To the north, Fork Bull Creek ran through the property. Trees were the main feature of the twenty acres behind the house. The only access to the structure was by a single one-lane dirt road barely accessible by anything other than a four-wheel drive vehicle.

As they emerged, Kruger and JR said in unison, "Uh-oh."

The house was a modern rustic log structure with two stories and a wrap-around wooden deck with a massive front door as the main feature. Rock pillars supported the deck with rough-hewn railings. From previous visits, Kruger knew the sleeping quarters were on the second floor with the living and kitchen areas on the first. A gazebo-like structure containing a breakfast nook featured prominently on the right side of the house.

Parked in the circle drive in front of the home were Joseph's dark gray Land Rover and the reason for their comment, two armor-plated black Chevrolet Suburbans with heavy smoke tinted windows.

JR spoke first. "I thought it was just Griffin and his wife meeting us here. Since when does a senator get Secret Service protection?"

"They don't." Kruger pursed his lips as he parked the Cherokee two car lengths behind the rear Suburban. "Something's happened. Something we don't know about. It may be the reason we're meeting him in this secluded spot."

Mia spoke from the rear to ask, "Do you suppose he's been asked to take the VP position?"

No one responded as a tall slender man in his early seventies emerged from the front door, stood on the front deck and waved. He wore a navy blazer, white button-down oxford shirt, khaki cotton pants, shiny loafers and boldly colored socks. With his broad smile, he bore an uncanny resemblance to the actor Morgan Freeman. Joseph Kincaid was a lifelong friend of Kruger and the reason he became an FBI agent. He was also an equally good friend of JR. His past remained a mystery to most people, except them.

The two couples emerged from the Jeep and approached the deck. Kruger pointed to the Suburbans with a questioning look. Joseph nodded and said, "Roy will explain. Come on in."

As they entered, Roy Griffin and his wife, Cheryl, smiled. Both were dressed casually and standing in the living room waiting to greet the newcomers. Four men stood off to the side watching every move Kruger and JR made. Stephanie squeezed her husband's hand and whispered, "That's creepy."

Kruger mumbled under his breath, "Yep, it is."

Griffin offered his hand to Kruger, who shook it and then made the same gesture to JR.

"Thank you all for coming. I don't remember if Stephanie and Mia have ever met my wife, Cheryl?"

Stephanie and Mia shook their heads as they were introduced. Cheryl Griffin stood as tall as her husband, slender with long blonde hair and blue eyes. She possessed a California tan and a beaming smile.

"It is so nice to finally meet you two," Cheryl said. "Your husbands helped save Roy's and my life a few years ago. We owe them a lot."

Stephanie smiled and glanced at her husband. "Don't brag about him too much, he'll get a big head."

Everyone chuckled.

Kruger turned to Griffin and asked, "What's the big mystery and why do you have Secret Service protection?"

Taking a deep breath, Griffin let it out slowly. "Because I've been asked by the president to fill the vacancy left by the death of Donald Pittman."

Silence filled the room.

Chapter Eight

"I KNOW, it shocked me too when he asked," Roy explained. "He wouldn't take no for an answer. A vote in both chambers of Congress is scheduled on Monday. The Senate Majority Leader told me late yesterday there would no opposition in either the Senate or the House."

"Makes sense," Kruger nodded. "You aren't a controversial individual like Pittman."

"No, I guess I'm not."

Joseph interjected, "Roy has a proposal for us."

JR's eyebrows rose and Kruger smiled. "Kind of figured he would."

A tall woman with curly black hair emerged from the kitchen area. "Joseph and I have a wonderful meal planned for everyone. Let's adjourn to the back deck and enjoy this lovely Saturday in the Ozarks."

Mary Lawson's heritage was Jamaican, French and for attitude, a bit of Louisiana Cajun. After graduating in the top ten from Columbia University Law School, she had spent her entire career at the Justice Department. Having met early in their careers and falling in love, they pursued separate paths, she with the DOJ, he with the CIA and later as a recruiter for the FBI, CIA and DEA. Now retired from her position as deputy director of the Office of Violence Against Women, she and Joseph were inseparable.

As everyone followed Joseph toward the back deck, Stephanie and Mia lagged behind and exchanged hugs with Mary. Stephanie glanced at her friend's left hand and smiled. Pointing to the simple gold band on Mary's finger, she asked, "When?"

Returning the smile, Mary replied, "While we were in New Zealand this past winter."

Mia chuckled. "It's about time."

"I know. Joseph told me we weren't getting any younger and needed to do what we should have done a long time ago."

"Glad he came to his senses," Mia's smile intensified.

Mary hugged both of her friends again. "Me, too."

When they arrived on the deck, Griffin, Kruger, Joseph and JR were huddled in the corner on the western side. Two Secret Service agents were to the right and two to the left of the group, all out of hearing range and staring off into the tree line behind the log structure.

Joseph frowned, "I've never met the man, Roy."

"He's a pure politician. The only reason he chose me is because I can be confirmed by both houses of Congress without any lengthy hearings."

"At least we got lucky this time." Kruger shook his head.

"Agreed." Joseph grinned.

JR crossed his arms over his chest. "So why the secluded meeting to tell us all this, Roy? We'd eventually hear it on the news."

"Very astute, my friend." Griffin looked at each man with a grim smile. "We need to find out why Pittman committed suicide."

Kruger stared at the newly appointed Vice President, "Stumpf's already requested an investigation."

"I know, he and I spoke. Another reason to have this clandestine meeting." He glanced at Joseph. "We need your old team looking into it. Paul and I are concerned the official version coming out of the White House will be tainted. Our commander-in-chief is not interested in the truth, only what will make him look good. This country needs to know the real reason a sitting vice president committed suicide." He looked at Kruger and then JR and asked, "What do both of you think?"

JR shook his head. "Don't know enough to even make a guess."

Kruger crossed his arms over his chest. "I agree with JR. What little we do know doesn't explain why he took his own life. There has to be more."

Griffin nodded. "Paul told me about his little nest egg in Dubai. Do you think the money is related to having Russians on his committee?"

With a grim smile, Kruger said, "Too early to tell, but if I were to guess, I'd say, yes."

Looking out over the tree line, Griffin remained silent for several moments. Turning back to Kruger, he said, "How can we be sure?"

"During our investigation of Robert Burns Jr., we learned he and his father had ties to the Russian mafia here in the states. His attorney during that time was murdered along with a Washington Post reporter by a Russian nerve agent a few weeks ago."

"I heard that. Is it related to Pittman?"

"We found notes at Keira Pennington's home suggesting she was investigating him. At this point, we can't determine why because her notes are in her own shorthand. Ryan Clark is working on getting them translated."

With his arms crossed over his chest, Griffin stared at Kruger, "Care to speculate?"

"I don't like coincidences. But if I were to speculate, I'd say the attorney, Jolene Sanders, knew something about Pittman and was providing confirmation to Pennington. Because of it, both women were murdered. The method used to kill was so flamboyant, I believe it was meant as warning to Pittman."

Joseph frowned. "How so?"

"Someone was basically telling him to keep his mouth shut. If he talked, he would be facing a horrible death." Kruger paused for a brief moment. "He took the easy way out."

JR joined the conversation to ask, "If Jolene Sanders knew something, where did she discover it, Sean?"

Kruger gave his friend a sly smile. "Think about it. She'd just been let go at Rothenburg and Sandifer. My guess is someone at the law firm represented Pittman at one time. Heck, it might have been Jolene for all we know. But the answer may be hidden in their files."

Griffin frowned. "Gaining access to those files could be difficult."

"I agree, Roy." Kruger looked at JR. "Unless..."

"Hey, don't look at me, I still have some scruples."

"Don't worry, JR," Griffin chuckled. "We'll figure something else out." Turning to Joseph, he grew serious. "Paul wants you to come out of retirement to put your team together again. Financing's already been appropriated."

Pursing his lips, Joseph took a deep breath and said, "I have one condition."

"Okay, what?"

Joseph continued, "Once this is over, I go back to being a consultant."

"Agreed."

"Then, yes, I'll get the team back together."

"Gentlemen, thank you for your support. I don't know

what the future holds and I'm trying not to be paranoid, but my fear is our government and way of life are being attacked externally and more importantly, internally, by forces we can't identify."

Kruger took a deep breath and let it out slowly. "I don't know if you read the official report about the Robert Burns Jr. case or not."

Griffin shook his head.

"One fact was left out, mainly because we didn't have corroborating evidence. However, we did determine the Russians were blackmailing Robert Burns Sr. while he was in the Senate back in 2004 through 2007. They put pressure on the senator to introduce and help pass several bills in Congress easing restrictions on banks and financial institutions. The consequence of those changes led to the Great Recession of 2008."

"How did they know those restriction would cause a recession?" Griffin's eyebrows rose as he spoke.

"They didn't. They wanted the restrictions eased to help them make more money with their banks here in the states. The recession was an unintended consequence. Once they determined they could exert influence on our government with legislative connections, their efforts intensified. Robert Burns Jr. was elected with the help of funds provided by a man named Dmitri Orlov. We suspect, but can't confirm, other politicians may be compromised as well."

"How do we find out?"

"We have to look at Dmitri Orlov."

Griffin stiffened. "Sean, I can't authorize any overseas trips for the FBI. Paul would have to do that."

"We wouldn't have to. Besides, it would raise too many red flags. When we discovered how involved Robert Burns Jr. was with the Russian mafia, Clark and I worked with an Interpol agent named Sergey Brutka. He's from Ukraine and is fluent in English, French and German, plus his Russian is good."

Joseph nodded. "That would work. Is he trustworthy?"

Kruger smiled. "Extremely."

Griffin's mood lightened. "How would you get in touch with him?"

Pulling his cell phone out of the back pocket of his jeans, Kruger held it up. "We've kept in touch since his last visit to the states about six months ago. He seems to think going to Silver Dollar City and Bass Pro Shop would be the event of a lifetime."

Griffin crossed his arms and brought his right hand up to this chin. Tapping one finger on his lips, he was quiet for a while, then said, "Invite him to visit as soon as possible. I'll personally pay for his trip."

Kruger nodded.

Turning to Joseph, Griffin asked, "Would you allow him to be your guest here, Joseph? I would prefer his visit to be as invisible as possible."

"We'd be delighted."

———

EVENING FELL and the night sky above Joseph's home seemed on fire with the Milky Way. Kruger never tired of standing on the back deck and gazing up into the sky. Discussion of political and investigation matters ceased long ago as the old friends feasted on steaks, freshly caught grilled trout, Caesar salad, roasted root vegetables and hand-turned home-made ice cream. Wine was plentiful and the laugher and conversations satisfying. Kruger made himself a small glass of Glenfiddich single malt scotch and retired to the back deck. The stresses associated with his FBI career always melted away when he stood on the deck of Joseph's retreat and stared skyward.

"I've never seen the night sky like this."

Kruger turned and saw Roy Griffin standing beside him. Two Secret Service agents stood respectfully by the door, their eyes sweeping the area for threats.

"There are a lot of places in this part of the country with a view like this. Unfortunately, most aren't as civilized as Joseph's property." He raised the Glenfiddich and smiled. "I like it here."

"As do I." Griffin raised his glass and the two friends clinked them together.

Returning his attention in the direction of the North Star, Kruger pointed, "See the bluish bright smudge above the north star?"

"Yes."

"That's the star Vega. The Lynid meteor shower will be visible in its direction." Kruger paused as he saw a streak appear where he was pointing. "We got lucky this year. The moon isn't in the way."

Griffin remained silent as he studied the area Kruger pointed out. After a few more streaks of meteors were visible, he spoke without looking at Kruger.

"Sean?"

"Yes."

"I've been blessed with your friendship over the years. My wife and I owe you more than you can imagine."

"No, you don't."

He nodded in the dark. "We do. I wish I had a crystal ball to see if I'm making the right decision."

Kruger remained quiet, knowing Griffin was thinking out loud.

"Cheryl and I had been trying to decide if I should run for

President after Bryant's two terms. We had decided not to, but Pittman changed everything. She still doesn't like Washington, but understands how I feel about serving the citizens of California."

Kruger let the senator talk and sipped his scotch.

Taking a deep breath, Griffin sipped his drink as well. "Once I'm Vice President, my duty is to serve the entire country. If, for some reason, and I hope this doesn't occur, something happens to Bryant, I'll be president. If that happens, I will need a lot of support."

Kruger nodded, but remained quiet. He knew Griffin was building up to something.

Looking at Kruger instead of the night sky, Griffin said, "Joseph doesn't want to lead his old team after this Pittman business is resolved. I want you to take it over."

"And do what?"

"I'm the chairman of the Homeland Security and Government Affairs committee. We see more top secret matters than most other senators. Some of the information scares me to death. Our country is under siege from all angles, politically, financially, cyber and internally. The problem is no one is taking it seriously. Bryant has his head in the sand because he would have to make decisions his base wouldn't like. Congress doesn't want to address it because no one can agree on a spending bill to cover the cost. When was the last time Congress approved any huge expenditures?"

Again, Kruger remained quiet.

"The answer is not for a very long time. So, they won't be any help. We need individuals like you and JR to start chipping away at these threats."

"Roy, I'm not sure I'm the right person to lead that kind of program."

"Yes, you are. I'm a good judge of character and you and JR fit the bill."

"He won't like it."

"Why?"

"He's spent the last seven years keeping under the radar. He doesn't obsess about it like he used to, but he still feels he needs to hide from the so-called men in black suits."

Griffin chuckled.

"I'm serious. You're asking him to become one of them."

With a broad smile, Griffin put his hand on Kruger's shoulder. "Karma can be a bitch sometimes."

"Yes, it can."

Returning to quiet contemplation of the heavens, both men stared at the sky. After several minutes, Griffin asked, "Where do we start, Sean?"

"I've been thinking about it. First we have to determine if Orlov has any other politicians in his pocket."

"How?"

"Something's not quite right at the law firm of Rothenburg and Sandifer."

"What makes you think so?"

"Too many connections. First, they represented Robert Burns Jr., which at first seemed innocent enough, but then they were bought by an undisclosed corporate entity. Who was it? Next, Jolene Sanders and the reporter are murdered with a Russian nerve agent." He paused and looked at Griffin. "I don't like coincidences like that."

"I see your point. What can you do about it?"

"I'll talk to Paul in the morning about putting video surveillance on the law firm's building. Let's see who comes and goes for a while. JR can utilize his facial recognition software to monitor the video feed without costing the Bureau any manpower."

Griffin nodded and stared out into the night.

"I'll get Paul the funds for the monitor."

Kruger smiled. The investigation was starting.

Chapter Nine

SERGEY BRUTKA READ the plaque under the portrait of the Indian Chief.

"Your American Indians have a lot in common with my country, Sean Kruger."

Smiling, Kruger looked at his guest. Brutka was tall for a Ukrainian and the two men stood at eye level with each other. A massive calloused hand traced the words on the plaque. The Interpol detective wore Levi jeans, a beige cable knit turtleneck sweater and an oversized corduroy sport coat. With disheveled dark brown hair and an untrimmed drooping mustache, he was a throwback to fashion of the early 1980s. As he spoke, his bushy eyebrows danced with delight. He was staring at a portrait of Chief Seattle in the Bass Pro Shops World of Wildlife museum.

"How so, Sergey?"

"We both have been the subject of an oppressive government during the last century. Germany twice and the old Soviet Union after World War II."

"Yes, but your people were not driven from their land and given false promises that were never fulfilled."

Brutka smiled grimly in reply, "A matter of opinion. We were promised a lot, but those promises were empty."

"I see your point."

Nodding, Brutka walked further down the passage as they navigated the one and a half miles of trails within the WOW museum and aquarium.

"While I appreciate your invitation to visit what you call the Ozarks, I question the motive. Nothing is free, Kruger."

He pronounced the name with an emphasis on the last syllable, turning the 'e' into a hard 'a'.

"No, it isn't."

Brutka stopped and read another plaque. "I love learning about this vast country of yours. Its history is colorful." He paused and turned to stare at Kruger. "So, why was I invited?"

"I thought I explained it when we spoke on the phone."

"You might have. I stopped listening when you said someone else would pay for my trip."

Kruger chuckled. "As an Interpol Agent, we would like for you to join an international task force."

"International?"

Nodding, Kruger gave him a grin. "The United States and Ukraine."

Brutka laughed out loud as other visitors of the museum gave him a strange look.

"Now you have my attention. What is this *task force* supposed to do?"

"Find out how deep Dmitri Orlov has penetrated the US government and either put him behind bars or, you know…"

Another laugh. Brutka slapped Kruger on the back.

"Nothing would make me happier. But first, I want to immerse myself in this World of Wildlife."

———

JOSEPH STOOD on the front deck of his home in rural Christian County watching a dark gray GMC Denali crunch its way over the long gravel driveway. He was glad these two individuals arrived first for the meeting. They were the apex of his team, retired Special Forces Major Benedict "Sandy" Knoll and retired Seal Team Six operator Jimmie Gibbs. Both were now FBI agents attached to a Rapid Response Team on loan to Special Agent Sean Kruger.

He raised a hand in greeting as the Denali parked behind his Land Rover in the circle drive. Weariness washed over him as he steeled himself to the task ahead. After fifty years in the field running covert operations for four presidents, Joseph Kincaid was ready to put his own priorities ahead of making sacrifices for the country. There was a reason for spending more time here at his remote log home. He could get away from the chaos of the outside world.

The driver of the Denali stepped out and raised a hand to return Joseph's greeting. He was a large man with bulging biceps, stretching the sleeves of an untucked black polo shirt that hung over faded blue jeans. Dark blond hair cut short displayed the beginnings of gray streaks above his ears. His handsome weathered face was permanently tanned from too many tours of duty in Iraq and Afghanistan. Mirrored Ray-Ban sunglasses shielded the gray-blue eyes from the afternoon sun. This was Sandy Knoll, a long-time friend and colleague of Joseph.

The smaller man stepped out of the passenger side of the vehicle. While Knoll was built like a body builder, Jimmie Gibbs' swimmer physique provided a sharp contrast to Knoll's bulk. Swimming was a passion for Gibbs and he still held several Seal Team records for endurance and distance.

After retiring from Seal Team Six, he allowed his black hair to grow long and kept it in a ponytail extending past his shoulder blades. As a native Southern Californian, his usual dress was surfer casual, cargo shorts, linen shirt and sandals. Today was no exception. Blue eyes rounded out his handsome features and contributed to the tales of his womanizing, which he claimed was more urban-legend than reality. Knoll prized Jimmie's poise and level-headedness during missions, especially when events turned sour for the team. A broad smile appeared on the face of the smaller man.

Joseph took a deep breath. Seeing these two men helped erase some of the tension he felt about his current task.

As the two ex-Special Forces men approached the steps leading to Joseph's house, Knoll spoke in his gravelly voice.

"Good to see you again, sir."

"Good to see you, too, Major Knoll."

Gibbs stepped onto the deck and shook Joseph's hand and said, "Heard a rumor you and Mary tied the knot in New Zealand. Any truth to it, sir?"

Joseph just smiled and nodded once.

"Well, congratulations, sir."

"Thank you, Jimmie." He paused briefly. "Gentlemen, we have a lot to discuss. Come on in."

———

JOSEPH STOOD behind the breakfast bar and poured another cup of coffee as he concluded his summary of Kruger's investigation. Jimmie Gibbs pursed his lips as he stirred his own cup. He stared at the dark liquid as his spoon created a whirlpool. Sandy Knoll stood at the sliding glass door leading to Joseph's back deck, his hands behind his back as he watched a hawk soar above the tree line behind the house. Silence permeated the room as each man processed the task ahead of them.

Gibbs was first to speak. "What's the official story about the vice president's suicide?"

"Depends on who you talk to." Joseph sipped his coffee,

placed it on the breakfast bar and crossed his arms over his chest. "The president's press secretary made a comment yesterday about Pittman's deteriorating health. No one's taking it seriously."

Gibbs nodded.

"Someone needs to go to Europe, don't they?" Knoll asked. "Jimmie's fluent in German and Russian, he'd be the perfect choice."

Smiling, Joseph shook his head. "It might not be necessary."

Knoll tilted his head. "Oh?"

"Sean is asking Sergey Brutka."

Gibbs asked, "Who's he?"

"He's with Interpol. I had never met him until yesterday. Sean likes him and trusts him."

"What else does he bring to the party?" Knoll asked.

"Years of investigating Dmitri Orlov's organization."

Frowning, Gibbs stared at Joseph. "Years?"

His answer was a nod.

———

"WHEN DID you decide to buy a Jeep Wrangler? Thought you only liked inconspicuous vehicles."

JR glanced at his friend as he steered the new Jeep over the rutted access road to Joseph's property.

"The same day the Camry got stuck and cost me two hundred dollars to have it towed out of here. Not to mention what it was going to cost to have it repaired. Besides, everybody seems to have a Wrangler these days. Last week I was at a stop light and the guy next to me was in a red one, the woman behind me had a four-door gray one. So, it is inconspicuous."

Kruger laughed as he held on to the grab-bar above the

front passenger door. He turned in his seat and spoke to the passenger in the back.

"What do you think of rural Missouri, Sergey?"

Brutka's face displayed a slight smile as he stared out the passenger window in the back seat. "Makes me homesick."

"Really?"

"Yes, very similar to where I grew up. We have real mountains, but the trees are the same."

"Huh. Didn't know that."

"You should visit my country, Sean Kruger. You would enjoy it."

"I hope to someday."

JR parked the Jeep behind Knoll's Denali and set the parking brake.

"Guess Sandy and Jimmie are here." He turned to Kruger. "Does Sandy drive anything other than a Denali?"

"Not if he can help it. He told me one time it's the only vehicle he feels safe in, other than a Humvee."

Smiling, JR climbed out of the Jeep and waited for his two passengers to exit. Once they were out, they walked toward the front deck where Joseph stood, a grim expression clouding his face.

Kruger immediately knew something was wrong.

"What's wrong, Joseph?"

"You haven't heard, have you?"

Chapter Ten

BRIGHT LIGHTS and swirling colors greeted Richard as he opened the kitchen door leading to the back-yard of his childhood home. He could hear his mother and father arguing about how to stretch their paychecks until the end of the month. He looked back and saw himself, crying, sitting at the kitchen table across from them. He was hungry. He was always hungry growing up.

Glancing at his image in the back-door window, he saw a seventy-two-year-old man staring back. The concept of being old and looking back on himself as a nine-year-old child confused him. A young teenage girl walked through the kitchen and kissed him on the cheek. It was Linda, his girlfriend when he was a sophomore in high school and the first girl he ever kissed. His eyes followed her as she walked out of the door and disappeared into the swirling colors.

Still standing at the back door, he turned and was suddenly in the middle of his small college dorm room. Jennifer, the woman to whom he lost his virginity, stood next to him smiling and naked. She gave him a hug and whispered in his ear.

"You should have stayed with me."

As he reached for her, the image dissolved as the swirling lights engulfed him.

He emerged inside a hospital room were his wife handed him their newborn daughter. He turned and lowered the now two-year-old girl into a coffin. With tears rolling down his cheeks, he looked up and saw his seventeen-year-old son score the winning touchdown at his senior homecoming game. He started to clap, but the scene dissolved into standing on the Capitol steps facing a tall man dressed in a black robe, an over-sized dark hood obscuring his face.

The bony hand of the figure offered him a Bible to hold. He then told Bryant to raise his right hand to recite the words for his oath of office as President. Before he could say the words, his knees buckled as a searing pain overwhelmed him.

President Richard Bryant woke suddenly from the images of his dream. An agonizing headache engulfed him as he sat up. Bile rose to the back of his throat, causing a gag reaction. His skin felt clammy and sweat dripped from his forehead. A crushing weight on his chest brought his right hand up to cover his heart as the first twinge of fear crept into the back of his mind.

On the verge of panic, a feeling foreign to his psyche, he swung his legs over the side of the bed. A severe pain shot down his left arm as he reached for the phone on his night-stand with his right. Just as he raised the handset to his ear, blackness engulfed him as his now-unconscious body collapsed onto the bed.

The sound of the First Lady screaming reached the ears of the Secret Service agent sitting outside the First Couple's bedroom door. He rushed into the room without hesitation.

CHIEF OF STAFF Carl Wood took a deep breath as he watched the resident EMTs work on the President of the United States with the White House crash cart. Both looked grim as they attended to the unconscious president. He heard one whisper to the other, "I'm not getting a pulse, are you?"

His companion replied with only a shake of the head.

"Let's get him to Walter Reed."

"Call them and tell them we are 10-45C with POTUS. Use your cell phone, not the radio."

"Got it."

Wood watched as they wheeled the gurney out of the bedroom and down the hall toward the elevator. His next duty involved making a call on a secure line to the Vice President and then the leaders of the House and Senate, calls he knew would be some of the last duties he performed as President Bryant's Chief of Staff.

Griffin answered on the fourth ring, his voice groggy with sleep.

"This is Roy."

"Mr. Vice President, this is Carl Wood."

"Yes, Carl." Griffin paused, suddenly fully awake. Receiving a call from the President's Chief of Staff at 4:36 a.m. could only mean one thing. Something bad occurred somewhere in the world. "How can I help you this morning?"

"Uh…" He hesitated before continuing. "Uh—sir, the President had an episode this morning and we need you to come to the White House immediately."

"What kind of episode, Mr. Wood?"

"Medical."

Griffin closed his eyes. "How bad?"

"We don't know, sir. But I think it would be a good idea for you get here as fast as possible."

"I'm on my way."

Cheryl Griffin rolled over in bed, leaned up on one elbow

and placed a hand on Roy's back as he sat with his hand still holding the receiver.

"What's the matter, Roy?"

"Don't know. The president's had a medical episode. From the tone of Carl's voice, it doesn't sound good. I have to get to the White House immediately."

She sighed, lay back down and closed her eyes. "Great. Just —great."

Griffin forced a smile. "He'll be fine, Cheryl. They are always overly cautious with the president."

He did not receive a reply.

———

AT 6:03 A.M., Washington time, Roy Griffin was sworn in as President of the United States by Chief Justice Simon Becker in the Oval Office. Richard Bryant had been pronounced dead on arrival at Walter Reed Hospital, having suffered a massive heart attack. An autopsy would later discover a ruptured aortic aneurysm caused massive bleeding and a stroke at the same time. President Bryant was technically dead before he fell back on his bed. The White House Physician would later be dismissed after he was charged with neglect and incompetence.

A shocked nation heard the news of Bryant's death at 6:43 a.m. Eastern Daylight Time and by 6:57 a.m., still pictures of the solemn swearing-in ceremony of the new president were released by the White House. By 7:03, all the cable and internet news services were falling over themselves as they rushed reporters and staff to the White House to cover developing events and an official announcement from newly sworn in President Roy Griffin at 8:00. Washington was in a dither, enemies of the deceased president began plotting, supporters grieved, conspiracy mongers spun their theories and indifferent individuals remained indifferent. The rest of the country took a collective deep breath and wondered, "Oh, good grief, now what?"

———

KRUGER SILENTLY WATCHED the CNN talking heads summarize the events of the morning for the fifth time since he started watching. JR stood next to him and sipped a mug of coffee. Joseph watched both of them from behind the breakfast bar as he made another pot of coffee. Gibbs stood off to the side with his arms crossed over his chest, while Knoll talked to Brutka on the back deck.

Glancing away from the TV, Kruger looked at Joseph. "I'm not sure if we should congratulate Roy or feel sorry for him."

Joseph nodded. "I was wondering the same thing. It's a good thing for the country, but…"

"Think this has something to do with what we've been asked to investigate?" All eyes turned to stare at Gibbs as he watched the TV.

Kruger responded first. "Good question, Jimmie. I certainly hope not."

JR returned his attention to the events on the TV. After a few moments, he said, "Guess we need to get busy." He looked up at Joseph and Kruger and added, "Don't we?"

———

AFTER A HECTIC DAY, Roy Griffin and his wife returned to Number One Observatory Circle late. It would remain their residence until President Bryant's widow could be moved out. Griffin demanded she be given time to grieve before she was, for lack of a better term, evicted and hustled out the door.

As they were preparing for bed, Cheryl walked up to her

husband, placed her arms around his waist and laid her head on his shoulder.

"Roy?"

He returned the embrace and leaned his head on hers. "Yes?"

"What now?"

"Our life has forever been changed."

"I know. That's what scares me. I liked where we were before you became the Vice President and now…"

"We have a huge opportunity to help this country, Cheryl."

"What if it doesn't want the help?"

He raised his head and frowned. "What do you mean?"

"What if the dysfunctions are so engrained no one can fix it?"

"I refuse to believe that."

"You said it yourself when you became a congressman that this town lacked a soul."

"It was a figure of speech."

"Yeah, but you did say it."

Taking a deep breath, he let it out slowly. "I know."

"What about Carl Wood?"

"I don't care for him. But, for now, he'll stay on as my Chief of Staff until I can find a new one. At least he has the experience I need right now."

"Keep him at a distance, Roy."

"I will."

"What about the Cabinet?"

"Every single one of them offered their resignation today. I didn't accept any. Yet."

They were both silent as the embrace continued.

"I need someone outside this town who can give me a clear vision of what's going on. Not someone whose judgement is clouded by how to get to the next sound bite on Fox, MSNBC or CNN."

"We were at his house a week ago."

Griffin was silent for a few moments.

"Yes, he'd be perfect."

She raised her head and looked him in the eyes. "Would he do it?"

"Don't know. Won't hurt to ask."

Chapter Eleven

"WHAT DO we know about this Roy Griffin?"

Dmitri Orlov stood with his back to his guest as he stared out the window of his office, his hands clasped behind him. His gaze fixed on a tourist boat traveling northwest on the River Seine past Notre-Dame Cathedral.

Boris Volkov stood in front of Orlov's desk and read from the screen of an iPad in his hand.

"He's from northern California. Law degree, served as a prosecutor for a few years in San Francisco, then started an internet company, sold it, invested the money and now he's rich. Started out as a congressman in the House of Representatives, elected to the Senate in a special election and when Pittman killed himself, well, you know what happened."

"Yes, yes. What about the man?"

Volkov slid his finger across the tablet and read for a few moments.

"He is in his early fifties, married to a woman he met in college, no kids, handsome. And hates being a politician."

Orlov smiled and turned to look at Volkov. "Interesting. What else?"

Volkov swiped again before speaking. "Media declared him the next John F. Kennedy when he was elected to the Senate. No scandals, has never cheated on his wife, only drinks wine, but never in public. Considered a conservative Democrat, even though he is from California. There was an assassination attempt on him when he was a Congressman." Volkov read this part carefully, smiled and raised his head. "Guess who prevented the assassination?"

"No games, Boris. Tell me."

"FBI agent Sean Kruger."

Orlov whipped his head around and stared at the big man with the tablet in his hand. After a few moments, he nodded. "Interesting. Go on."

Another swipe.

"His confirmation as Vice President was approved over-whelmingly by both houses of Congress. The vote was considered historical as there were only a handful of no votes in each chamber. Most of the no votes were by individuals who felt slighted they were not chosen for the job."

Orlov shook his head and returned to staring out the window. "Are any of those individuals approachable?"

"Possibly."

"Okay, go on. What else do you know about Griffin?"

"American cable news commentary seems to believe he is a *reluctant warrior* and the American public looks at him as a *white knight* riding into town to save the day."

"Hmmm. Anything else?"

"Not really. The media continues to speculate about why Pittman committed suicide, but the theories proposed so far are not even close."

Orlov was quiet for a few moments. "Tell me about the theories."

"The most common one concerns a woman who came

forward after his suicide. Her attorney claims she is pregnant with Pittman's child. The woman is not his wife."

"Americans can be so provincial. What else?"

"The FBI found bank accounts in Dubai and Hong Kong that Pittman never declared when he was vetted to be Vice President. My informants tell me the source of those funds have yet to be discovered."

"Can they be traced?"

"Eventually, but not to you, sir."

"Good."

"Anything else?"

"Lots of conspiracy theories, but nothing close to the truth."

Orlov nodded again. His eyes tracked an attractive Parisian woman as she hurried down the street below his office. He turned, sat behind his desk and looked up at Volkov.

"Boris, the loss of Pittman was a major setback to our president's plan. He was not happy about the loss of the Burns family. Now with the planning and resources spent on Pittman also gone, he is furious."

Volkov nodded, but did not comment.

"Where is the Algerian?"

"We do not know. He refuses to reveal his location."

"Understandable. Could he get to Griffin?"

"Doubtful. He is now the most protected man in the world."

The Russian oligarch responded with a thoughtful nod. "The men who voted against Griffin intrigue me. Since the Algerian is being paid on a standby basis, tell him we need background on these individuals. Our president's patience has limits. He wants contingency plans made on how we can proceed without Pittman. Maybe there will be one or two individuals disgruntled enough to help us out."

Another nod from Volkov.

Orlov drummed his fingers on the desk and stared at a blank spot on the wall behind his assistant. "What have you heard from the hacker in Mexico City?"

"We have the information you requested and will proceed when you are ready."

"Very well, move forward with it."

With a slight smile, Volkov kept his attention on his boss. "Anything else, sir?"

"Why don't you plan a trip to the US? It is time to cash in on one of our investments."

———

"SO, what did you find on the three Russians, JR?"

Kruger sat across from JR in the glassed-in conference room. JR smiled and raised a flash drive in response.

"It's all right here."

"Give me the executive summary."

"Our initial premise was correct. They are not legitimate bankers. All are ex-KGB operators who worked for Orlov when he was a section chief. When the KGB disbanded, these three moved over to the SVR while Orlov transitioned to banking."

"What did they do for the Russian Foreign Intelligence Service?"

"All three worked out of embassies in Western Europe and North America. Mid-level diplomatic work, which gave them the cover they needed. Now they work for Orlov's banking empire."

Kruger was silent as he tapped the flash drive on the table. "Are they still considered employed by the SVR?"

JR nodded.

"So, their roles as so-called bankers, that's a ruse too?"

Another nod.

"How'd you find this?"

"Let's just say one of them clicked on a link in an email he shouldn't have."

Returning to silence, Kruger turned to look out the conference room windows. Now tapping the flash drive on his lips. "Why? Why would Orlov want three SVR agents in constant contact with the Vice President? To me, it would be easy for the CIA, FBI, or anybody to determine who these guys are."

"One would think so, but they didn't. Sean, you have to be looking for something to find it. They were businessmen and he was the vice president involved in a boring study group. No one was looking."

"Apparently." He paused. "Any hints about Pittman in what you learned?"

"A little. There were a few emails referring to a source deep within the Bryant administration. The source was not named."

"You think it was Pittman?"

"I don't analyze data, I just collect it."

"Bullshit."

JR chuckled. "Yes, I believe all the data points we have right now point to it being Pittman."

"I would agree."

"One other thing, Sean."

"What?"

"Since Bryant's death and Roy's swearing in, email traffic from Orlov's laptop has increased by a factor of three. I traced one to the Kremlin."

"Can you read the emails?"

"Most are encrypted, but some aren't."

"Can you get into any of those servers?"

JR just smiled.

———

JOSEPH KINCAID STEPPED out of Knoll's Denali and buttoned his suit coat. He was greeted by several Secret Service agents and escorted into the White House. After being shown into the Oval Office, the door closed behind him. President Roy Griffin stood behind the Resolute Desk and smiled.

"Thank you for coming, Joseph."

"You're welcome, Mr. President."

Griffin's smile turned grim as he stepped out from behind the desk and the two men shook hands.

"Wish it was under better circumstances."

A nod of Joseph's head was his response.

"Please, sit down."

They sat across from each other on the sofas in front of the President's desk.

"I'm sure you are wondering why I called you all the way to Washington, D.C."

"I'm sure you will tell me, sir."

"That's unnerving, Joseph."

"What, sir?"

"Calling me sir."

"Sorry, you are the President."

Taking a deep breath, Griffin let it out slowly. "Yes, a fact I am struggling to deal with."

"How can I help?"

"By becoming my National Security Adviser."

Joseph's eyes widened and he stared at the newly sworn in president. He chose not to say anything immediately.

Griffin continued, "I know I asked you to head up your old team again, but that was before current circumstances changed. I need your insight and experience. Plus, I trust you."

"I'm honored, Mr. President."

"Then your answer is yes?"

Another deep breath.

"I don't know, sir. Mary and I…" He paused and looked out the window behind the president's desk.

"I understand your hesitation, Joseph. Trust me, I understand. But I need someone with your experience, plus, you won't have a hidden agenda to cloud your judgment."

"I just don't know, sir."

"What if you agree to the position for at least a year? Help me get my feet on the ground. You and Mary can rent an apartment while you're here."

"I'd have to ask her. She left Washington and didn't look back."

"Good. Let me know as soon as you can."

———

"YOU TOLD HIM YES, didn't you, Joseph?"

"No, I wanted to talk to you first."

"That was sweet, but you can't tell him no."

The call was being made on a secure satellite connection from the White House to his place in Christian County."

"What about our plans?"

"We can wait a year. Besides, this is a wonderful way for you to end a distinguished career, Joseph. Plus, I've never been married to a National Security Adviser before."

Chuckling, Joseph realized he was the only one hesitating about accepting the position. "Will you join me in Washington?"

"Of course. We can plan on being here at our place once a month. The year will go by fast, Joseph."

"Thank you."

"For what?"

"Being you."

Although he couldn't see it, Mary smiled.

Chapter Twelve

JR SHIFTED his view from the rightmost screen to the leftmost screen as he finalized a bid for a new client. An instant messaging notation appeared at the lower right-hand corner of his middle computer monitor.

Call for you on line 3

He stood and entered the conference room, shut the door and accepted the call on the Polycom phone on the conference table. "This is JR."

"Mr. Diminski, my name is Dennis Greene. I'm an attorney with Barnes, Hickman and Holmes. How are you today, sir?"

Frowning, JR shook his head. "What's this about?"

"Mr. Diminski, we represent a large investment firm that is interested in purchasing your company."

"It's not for sale."

"You haven't heard their offer yet."

"No, and to be honest with you, I don't need to hear it."

"Sir, they are offering a very generous purchase price and a long-term retainer for your services."

"Okay, I'll play your game. Tell me."

Dennis Greene told him.

JR was silent for a few moments. Finally, he shook his head. "Mr. Greene, that's very generous, but this is an unsolicited phone call. I have no idea if you are who you say you are, or if this is even a legitimate offer."

"I understand, Mr. Diminski. With your permission, a certified letter will be sent with the details. At that time, you can have your own attorney contact our office and review the offer. Once you attorney is satisfied, you can get back to us. Is that agreeable?"

"You can send the letter. Whether it is agreeable isn't part of the discussion right now."

"Very well. I'll follow up with you in a few days. Good day, sir."

———

"WHAT DOES MIA THINK?"

JR frowned and looked at his friend. "She says it's up to me, but thinks if the offer is legitimate, we should look at it very closely."

The two friends sat on Kruger's back deck enjoying a beer and discussing the events of the morning.

"Wise counsel," Kruger grinned. "It is your company, JR. You built it from scratch and now…"

"I know."

"What do you want to do?"

"I don't know. Part of me wants to sell and the other part is worried about my clients and the employees. What happens to them?"

Kruger smiled and sipped his beer.

JR stood, walked to the railing of the deck and leaned against it as he looked out over Kruger's treed backyard.

"The incident in New York City keeps me thinking about

how much it hurt the employees when Tony sold the company. I don't want to do that."

"But…"

"Yeah, there is that."

"Are you tired of running the company?"

"No…" There was silence. "Maybe." He studied the grain on the hand rail. "I enjoy the coding and problem solving."

"Go on."

"I don't like the minutia of managing cash flow, dealing with employee issues, sales budgets, or the constant stress of having to increase business each quarter."

"I thought that was what Jodi did?"

"It is, but she feels I need to be involved. Besides, I never get to do the things I like to do anymore."

"Such as?"

"Hacking other computers."

Kruger laughed out loud.

"Don't laugh. It's saved your butt several times."

Covering his grin, Kruger stifled another guffaw. "Sorry. Yes, it has and I appreciate your talent. However, I didn't know that was your favorite pastime."

"It isn't, but…"

"You enjoy it."

JR nodded.

"Do you think you could get a guarantee about your clients and employees?"

"It will mean exactly zilch. My clients are independent. Some will stay, others will get pissed at me for selling and find another company to work with. Same with everyone who works for the company. Some will stay, others will move on. The essences of the company will change and become something unrecognizable."

"Little high on yourself, aren't you?"

"Nope, it's just the way it works."

Kruger nodded. "So, what are you going to do?"

JR was quiet.

A thought occurred to Kruger and he stiffened. Standing, he walked to a position next to JR and leaned on the wood railing.

"How many offers have you received for your company over the years?" he asked slowly.

"I don't know, several, why?"

"Were they worth pursuing?"

"Nope."

"Why now?"

Frowning, JR turned to stare at Kruger.

"What do you mean, why now?"

"Just what I said, why now? If you've never had a lucrative deal until now, why?"

His attention did not divert from his friend, who stared out over the yard. After a few moments, JR smiled slightly. "Yeah, why now?"

"What do you know about the company trying to buy you?"

"Not enough. Looks like I need to get on a computer."

———

IT WAS mid-morning the next day before Kruger saw JR again. He was busy at his cubicle as the Keurig pressed water through a coffee pod into Kruger's cup. He turned to JR, who had not acknowledged his presence. "Any luck?"

Silence was his answer for about five seconds.

"Maybe. You were right to ask the question of why now."

Remaining quiet, Kruger sipped his coffee.

JR turned to look up at the FBI agent and said, "It's a large holding company that owns numerous IT companies in Europe, the Middle-East, China and a few in the US."

"Okay, no law against it."

"No, there isn't." He paused for a few seconds. "It's the same holding company that owns the anti-virus and internet security firm known as Kaspersky Labs. Ever hear of them?"

Nodding, Kruger sipped his coffee. "Yeah, the name sounds familiar. What about them?"

"Kaspersky is based in Moscow."

"Oh boy."

"Yup. Homeland Security banned the use of Kaspersky products on any government computer in September of 2017."

"Huh."

"I've always been aware of the company, just didn't need any of their products."

Taking a moment to collect his thoughts, Kruger hesitated before he commented. "We both know I don't believe in coincidences. Do you think this could be one?"

JR's response was a deep breath and a hard stare at Kruger.

"Okay, JR, let's assume it's not a coincidence. That raises two questions. How did they know about you and your company? And, secondly, how did they know you are involved in our investigation?"

JR shook his head. "I don't know and I don't like it."

———

JOSEPH SAT QUIETLY as JR and Kruger summarized the events of the previous day and their discussion of the morning. He sat quietly keeping his comments to himself until they completed the story. When they finished, he gave JR a slight smile and said, "Don't sell the company, JR. Turn down their offer. Simple."

"That's not the point, Joseph. How did they know about me?"

"JR, your company has clients in all fifty states and a few in the UK, if I remember correctly."

"Yeah."

"It's profitable and therefore becomes a target for investment companies. I don't see anything sinister with the offer."

"What about the Kaspersky Labs connection?" Kruger asked.

"What about it? The holding company is based in the UK. That's probably how they found out about your company, JR."

Silence fell over the conference room. JR studied his coffee mug as he turned it clockwise and then counter-clockwise.

"Put that way, my initial paranoia about the offer seems silly, he said."

Joseph shook his head. "Skepticism is healthy, don't stop asking questions." He took a sip of his coffee. "What are you going to do, JR?"

"Mia and I discussed it last night. She agrees with you, don't sell. So, we decided to reorganize into an employee stock ownership plan, my attorney called it an ESOP. That way if something happens to me, the employees aren't hurt. Plus, it gives everyone an incentive to keep the company profitable."

Both Kruger and Joseph nodded.

"This whole episode helped me see I need to step back from managing the day-to-day operations and do what I do best. Jodi will become the new president and CEO. Mia and I together will still own the majority of the stock, but I'll only be chairman of the board and Mia will be over new products."

Kruger chuckled. "I thought Jodi already managed the day-to-day operations."

"She does," JR smiled. "Her title doesn't acknowledge it. Now it will."

Joseph also smiled. "Good. Glad you're making changes. You're going to need more time to help Sean."

Both JR and Kruger stared at their friend. Kruger spoke first. "What's that supposed to mean?"

"Mary and I are moving to Washington for a year."

JR's eyes widened. "What the hell for?"

"Roy asked me to be his National Security Adviser. We're going to rent an apartment and live there temporarily."

The room fell quiet again as Kruger and JR stared at Joseph with questioning expressions. Kruger broke the silence. "I take it you won't be heading up the task force Roy asked us to start?"

"Correct. You, FBI Agent Sean Kruger, were promoted to the position by the president. You now only report to him, no one else."

"Not even Paul Stumpf?"

"No, Paul's on board. He and the president worked out the details yesterday. You will have autonomy to choose your team and what resources you require."

Joseph turned his attention to JR.

"You, Mr. Diminski, are now classified as a member of the FBI Cyber Division assigned permanently to Sean's task force."

JR closed his eyes and shook his head. "Don't suppose I have any say in the matter, do I?"

"Nope. It's a done deal."

JR folded his arms in front of him on the conference table, leaned over and rested his head on them.

"Great. I've just become one of them."

Kruger smiled. "Yep, you are now officially one of the men-in-black-suits."

Joseph and Kruger laughed. JR muttered, "I don't find it funny."

The laughter got louder.

After Joseph explained his plans, JR looked at him and asked, "What about your place?"

"Good question. Jimmie Gibbs is going to move in and keep an eye on it while we're gone."

"Just how long do you think you'll stay in Washington, Joseph?" Kruger's expression remained questioning.

"I didn't want to commit to the job until Roy suggested I take it for a year. By then, he'll have his feet on the ground and can find someone less..." Joseph pursed his lips, "... Unwilling."

Kruger nodded, finally understanding why Joseph accepted the position. "When are you two moving?"

"We aren't really moving. Mary's in D.C. right now finding a furnished apartment. I'm leaving tomorrow to join her. Jimmie rented a U-Haul van and is driving. He should arrive this afternoon. His lease was up and he jumped at the opportunity. Apparently, he likes it here."

"What about all of his stuff?"

"Storage. I don't think he has much, or at least, it didn't sound like it. He only rented a small transit van."

Chuckling, Kruger nodded. "Sandy told me he's been kind of a nomad since he left the Navy. He doesn't even own a car. When he was home, he drove one the bureau assigned."

Joseph nodded but did not respond.

Tilting his head to the side, Kruger asked, "Do you know something I don't know about Jimmie?"

Taking a deep breath, Joseph nodded again. "When Jimmie was working with you on the missing college student's case, it brought back memories of a dark chapter in his life."

Kruger frowned. "Care to elaborate?"

"Very few people know about it, but I think you need to. Jimmie's sister was abducted when she was fourteen. It didn't end well. Both of his parents died not too long afterwards, his mother from cancer and his father's grief drove him to commit suicide. Jimmie's been on his own since. I think he'd like to get out of California and start a new chapter."

JR bowed his head and stared at his hands while Kruger nodded slowly.

"He told me he was looking forward to working with you two again."

Kruger smiled.

Chapter Thirteen

THE LARGE MAN threw his carry-on bag into the back seat of the white Chevy Malibu, closed the door and slid into the passenger seat. As soon as his door closed, the car accelerated away from the passenger pick-up curb at Montréal's Pierre Elliott Trudeau International Airport.

Looking at the driver, Boris Volkov smiled and said in Russian, "Good to see you again, Yuri."

Yuri Popov returned the smile and answered in the same language. "Everything is arranged. We will cross the border as businessmen."

"Excellent." Volkov paused as he stared out the front windshield. "Dmitri is concerned about his plans in Washington. Pittman committing suicide was totally unexpected. He believes that one event pushed everything back five years, maybe more."

Popov shot a glance at Volkov. "Unless?"

"Yes, unless we can convince Kyle Sandifer to do a favor for Dmitri."

With a smile, Popov nodded. "Do you think he will?"

"Yes. Without Dmitri's help last year, Sandifer would be a

poor man. Now he will help us find the next Pittman. Plus, we have to find a way to disgrace the new president and undermine his reputation. If we don't, he will be elected on his own in two years and then…"

"Why not just assassinate Griffin?"

"Too messy, and it raises too many conspiracy theories. Look at the last assassination of a US president. They are still debating about how many individuals shot JFK."

Popov grinned. "Yes, one of those theories is actually correct."

Chuckling, Volkov nodded. "Yes, but all the players are dead now. We have to be subtler about getting someone into a position of power in D.C."

Silence returned to the interior of the car as both men stared ahead. After a few minutes Popov reached behind him and retrieved a tan envelope from the back-seat floor. He handed it to Volkov.

"These are for you."

Taking the envelope, the larger man undid the clasp and extracted a passport, Canadian driver's license, a Platinum American Express card and $10,000 in US dollars.

"Who am I?"

"You are an agricultural consultant for the Ukrainian Embassy in Toronto working on the exportation of Canadian wheat to Ukraine."

Volkov chuckled. "I know nothing about wheat."

"You don't have to. All you need to know is that Canada exported more wheat last year than the United States."

With narrowed eyes, Volkov glared at Popov. "You are kidding, of course."

With a shake of his head, Popov glanced at the big Russian. "No, it is true."

Silence returned as they drove toward the US border. As the border crossing loomed ahead, Popov broke the quiet.

"You have an appointment with Kyle Sandifer at nine tomorrow morning. I will be available to drive you."

"Good."

———

KYLE SANDIFER OFFERED his hand to the large man who had just entered his office. His visitor was dressed in a gray pinstripe Brooks Brother's wool suit with a white-on-white shirt and a red and light-gray striped tie. Dark brown hair was thinning on top and cut short. He wore rimless glasses on a broad nose in front of pale blue eyes. His bicep muscles stretch the material as they shook hands. The name on his business card introduced him as Illya Tokar, a resident of Toronto working for the Ukrainian embassy.

Sandifer looked at the card and said, "It's nice to meet you, Mr. Tokar. I understand you need assistance in negotiating wheat contracts here in the states."

Volkov did not respond immediately. He studied Sandifer for a few moments, then shook his head.

"No. I am here to discuss a matter of great concern for the firm's owners."

With his patented lawyerly neutral expression, Sandifer said nothing. Crossing his arms over this chest, he tilted his head. The two men stared at each other. Finally, Sandifer broke the silence.

"How is Mr. Orlov?"

"Upset."

"Oh? Why has he not contacted me about his concern?"

With a slight smile, Volkov looked around Sandifer's office. He saw numerous pictures of two young boys in baseball uniforms, the same two boys in tuxedos standing next to women in wedding gowns, small children and a picture of Sandifer standing next to a woman his same age.

"He is not upset with you or this firm. He is upset about a situation and you can help."

Sandifer nodded as his stomach tightened. He pursed his lips as his mouth felt like cotton.

"Excuse my manners. Please sit down so we can discuss how we may be of assistance."

Volkov recognized the action as stalling for time and silently he approved. Once both men were settled, Sandifer in his desk chair and Volkov in a high-back, leather wing chair in front of the desk, the Russian explained what Orlov required Sandifer to do.

When Volkov was finished, Sandifer blinked several times before commenting. Finally, he spoke.

"That would violate more than a dozen US laws, Mr. Tokar. Is Mr. Orlov aware of what he is asking?"

"He is very much aware of what he is asking. You will be compensated for your efforts."

"I understand, but the risks to this firm outweigh the financial rewards. For the good of the firm, I can't in good conscience allow that to happen. The actions you are requesting could risk his investment."

Volkov leaned forward in his chair and spoke in a voice just below a growl.

"If I were you, I would be more worried about your risk before worrying about his risks."

The response from Sandifer was a few moments of rapid blinking. Finally, his neutral expression returned and he asked calmly, "Are you threatening me, Mr. Tokar?"

"Not at all, just explaining about risk." Volkov smiled grimly as he directed his gaze to the pictures on Sandifer's credenza. "You have a nice family. I take it both of the boys are married now. How many grandchildren do you have, Mr. Sandifer?"

The full realization of his situation caused bile to reach the back of Sandifer's throat. He swallowed hard, but remained quiet as Volkov continued.

"I'm sure a compromise can be reached for this firm to accommodate Mr. Orlov's requests. Don't you agree, Mr. Sandifer?"

The attorney glared at Volkov as he said, "Yes, I'm sure something can be agreed upon."

Volkov stood suddenly.

"Excellent. I will let Mr. Orlov know you have agreed to his request. Good day, sir."

The large man walked to the office door and turned before opening it.

"Don't change your mind, Mr. Sandifer. It would be unhealthy for you and your family."

After the man Sandifer knew as Illya Tokar left the office, the lawyer stared at the now closed door, his hands shaking. He sat unmoving behind his desk as he finally understood

why Dmitri Orlov paid more than market value for the firm. He realized his greed allowed him and his partner Rothenburg to be played by a master manipulator. Only Rothenburg had the good sense to take his money and leave the company. Sandifer hoped his mistake was not a fatal one.

He opened the top drawer of his desk and extracted a bundle of business cards held together with a rubber band. The cards were important enough to keep, but not important enough to be readily available.

Removing the rubber band, he searched the bundle for the card he wanted. Halfway through the stack, he found it. Holding it between his thumb and forefinger, he studied the name on the card then began tapping it on his desk as he turned his head to stare out the window. The tapping continued.

Ten minutes later, he turned back to face the desk. Replacing the rubber band around the remaining stack of cards, he returned the bundle to his top drawer. Hesitantly, he reached for the handset of his desk phone, looked at the card and started to punch in the number. Halfway through, he stopped and returned the phone to the base unit.

Keeping his cell phone in the top right-hand drawer of his desk during business hours kept distraction down. Now he reached for it but hesitated before punching in the number. The stupidity of calling the number on a cell phone struck him as a very bad idea.

Opening his laptop, he waited until it booted up before placing a 32-gig flash drive in one of the USB ports. He copied a large file to the small device and watched as the progress bar increased in size. When completed, he closed the laptop, removed the drive and placed it in his pocket.

After locking his desk, he retrieved the business card from the desk top, placed it in his wallet, stood and left the office. Not making the call was probably the smart thing to do at this time.

He was wrong.

Chapter Fourteen

MOST DAYS, JR arrived at his cubicle on the second floor no later than 6:30 a.m., sometimes earlier.

Today he was late.

Jodi Roberson's normal routine included climbing the stairs to the second floor to check with JR about any new projects needed by their clients and to give him any financial updates she deemed necessary. She always arrived at 7:30 a.m. and this morning was no exception. When she found the second floor dark and JR's cubicle unoccupied, a hint of concern tugged at the back of her mind. But having worked for JR for six years, she quickly dismissed it.

By 8:00, JR was still absent. At this hour of the morning, the building was humming with activity as other associates began their day.

When 8:30 arrived without JR making an appearance, Jodi thought about calling his cell phone, hesitated and decided against it.

At 10:12, JR and Mia walked through the front door, holding hands, both smiling broadly. He stopped at Jodi's office and asked her to join him and Mia in the conference room upstairs.

When all three were settled with fresh cups of coffee at the conference table, JR stood and shut the door. After he was seated again, he smiled and said, "Jodi, Mia and I have some news for you and the company."

The current vice president returned the smile and took a sip of coffee.

"Good or bad news?" she asked.

"Good news."

She nodded, but did not comment.

"Mia and I have been at the company attorney's office this morning. We've decided to make a few corporate changes."

Jodi raised her eyebrows but maintained her silence.

JR continued, "We started the process of turning the company into an ESOP this morning. Which means each current associate will receive stock in the company. Mia and I will hold equal shares amounting to fifty-six percent. You will be the next largest shareholder and will become CEO and company president."

She had raised her coffee cup halfway to her lips, but stopped as her now-wide eyes stared at JR and then at Mia. Returning the cup to the table, she blinked several times.

"What about you and Mia?" Jodi asked.

"Mia will continue her role as Director of New Products and I will be stepping back from my normal day-to-day activities. I'll be more of a consultant than anything else."

"But…" Jodi continued to look back and forth between the two people on the opposite side of the table. "But…" She closed her eyes and shook her head. In a quiet voice she said, "I don't have the first clue about being a CEO or president."

"Nonsense," JR chuckled. "You're doing it right now. Your duties won't change, only your title and salary."

Her look changed from shock to confusion, back to shock and finally settled on suspicion.

"Okay, JR, I know you. What's going on? Why now?"

JR shrugged.

Jodi looked at Mia and said, "Since he won't tell me, will you?"

Mia smiled. "JR wants to insure the longevity of the company and make it a more desirable place to work. Plus, he'll be working with Sean Kruger more in the coming months and years."

After a slow nod, Jodi smiled.

"I want a conference room built on the first floor," she said. "You'll have this one tied up."

"Agreed," JR smiled. "Figure out where you want it."

———

KRUGER STARED AT THE MONITOR. The video feed frozen as the three men studied one of the FBI's electronic surveillance recordings of the front entrance of the Rothenburg and Sandifer law firm.

"That's Boris Volkov," Sandy Knoll said, his arms crossed as he stood next to Kruger.

"That's what I thought, too. When was this recorded, JR?"

JR turned and looked up at Kruger. "Yesterday morning." Returning his attention to the monitor, he pointed at the figure walking toward the front entrance of the building. "Watch the time stamp." With a click of the mouse, the recording jumped ahead thirty-two minutes and started playing.

The image of Boris Volkov exiting the building appeared.

"Meeting lasted around thirty minutes. Now watch who picks him up."

A white Chevy Malibu pulled to the curb and Volkov opened the front passenger door. A face appeared in the driver's side window as it checked for oncoming cars before pulling out into traffic. JR froze the video with the face visible. He looked up at Sandy Knoll to ask, "Recognize him?"

A slight smile appeared on Knoll's face.

"I'll be damned. Yuri Popov. How'd those two SOBs get into the country?"

Kruger leaned forward to study the image, "I haven't heard anything about them since our meeting in Paris with Orlov. Both are on an FBI watch list, which raises several questions. How did they get into the country? And, why is Volkov meeting with Sandifer?"

Not taking his eyes off the monitor, JR said, "Wait, watch this." He clicked the mouse again and the time stamp jumped forward another forty-three minutes. As the motion started again, Kyle Sandifer hurried out of the building, turned left and walked out of camera range.

Sandy turned to Kruger. "Should I head to Washington?"

"Not yet. I'll ask Clark to speak with Sandifer about this little encounter."

Knoll nodded and returned his attention to the computer monitor as JR replayed the sequences.

An instant message appeared on the middle monitor: *Call for you on line 1.*

JR stood and motioned for both Kruger and Knoll to follow him as he headed for the conference room. As Kruger shut the door, JR plugged his laptop into a USB port on the side of the Polycom phone unit occupying the center of the conference table. When he was satisfied the two were connected, he hit the button for line one.

"This is JR."

"Mr. Diminski, this is Dennis Greene. How are you today, sir?"

"Mr. Greene, I told you during our last phone call, the company is not for sale."

As he spoke, his fingers danced on the laptop keyboard.

"Yes, you did mention that, but you also agreed to look at our offer."

"I did look at your offer and the company is still not for sale."

"I see. My client will be most disappointed. They don't like being disappointed."

"They'll just have to get over it."

"If we increased the offer, would you reevaluate your decision?"

"Mr. Greene, I don't know how to be clearer than to say the company is not for sale, period. Regardless of your offer."

The only sounds in the room were JR typing on the keyboard and the hiss of air forced through the ventilation ducts as they waited for the caller to reply.

"Very well. I have been authorized to make the following amendment to our original proposal, Mr. Zachara."

JR stopped typing and his head jerked up. His eyes widened and Kruger saw his friend take a deep breath and bring one hand to his forehead.

"I beg your pardon," JR said slowly.

"You heard me. We know who you are and what happened after the sale of CWZ Software."

Kruger started to say something, but JR raised his left hand and shook his head rapidly. The FBI agent stayed silent.

"What do you propose to do with this information, Mr. Greene? I will assume that is not your real name."

"Very astute, Mr. Zachara. When you agree to sell your company, we will remove your resume from our records and things will return to normal."

"If I refuse?"

There was a slight chuckle on the other side of the call.

"Use your imagination, John. If we know your real name, your association with CWZ Software and the truth about what happened to Abel Pymel, think about what else we might know."

"Is that a threat?"

"Take it for what it is. An additional incentive to sell your company."

"How long do I have to think about it?"

"I'll call tomorrow at this time. Have your attorney in the room so we can finalize the deal."

The call ended.

JR looked over at Kruger and Knoll, who were now sitting across from him. Knoll tilted his head and asked, "CWZ Software? What was that all about?"

JR took a deep breath. "It's the name of the company I helped form with Tony Chien and Steve Wilson after college. We were all computer nerds. Tony and Steve wrote code and I debugged it. The company was Tony's idea. He asked Steve and me to join him. Thus, CWZ Software. Those first few years, we'd work till two or three in the morning, crash and start all over again at nine or ten the next morning. We had a blast.

"After our first program was released, Tony stopped programming and became our one-man sales department. Within six months, we had twenty people working for us. Steve was the genius behind all of the different products and I was the guy who simplified the code and kept the programs working. We made a good team.

"About a year after we started, Tony had a meeting in Albany and bragged about me to some New York state senator. Not long after the meeting, I was asked to consult on the redesign of the state's revenue and licensing software."

Kruger turned to Knoll and added, "That's how he was able to delete his New York driver's license file."

Knoll smiled.

JR continued, "Everything went great for the next nine

and a half years. We grew to about a hundred employees. Tony was a great individual to work for. He paid well and shared the profits with his associates. We all had shares in the company, like an ESOP, but not quite. My company is transitioning to a true ESOP structure. Back then I had chosen not to get into management, so the number of shares I owned didn't equal Tony's or Steve's.

"One day, Tony gathered ten of the individuals who had been with the company the longest and had a meeting. Since Tony owned the majority of the stock, he made most of the decisions. He would consult with Steve, myself and a few others, but generally he had the final say. To start the meeting, he took a bottle of champagne from a small refrigerator and passed out plastic cups. He poured us all a small glass and said, 'We have just made the big time. P&G Global has agreed to invest in our company.' Steve shook his head and said, 'Why are we celebrating? I've heard about them. They'll destroy this company.'

"Tony shook his head, 'I have it in writing. They plan to leave current management in place and provide needed funding for our next expansion.'

"It was probably thirty days after that little meeting when all the employees were called into the company's food court for a conference. When I got there, everybody was either sitting or standing around talking. We all grew silent when three guys in dark, expensive suits walked into the room. Tony was with them, but he wasn't wearing a suit and did not look happy. Everyone grew quiet. One of the suits was Abel Plymel."

"I know the story from there," Knoll nodded. "Thanks for the background, JR."

Kruger pointed at the Polycom unit and asked, "Where did the phone call originate, JR?"

"With a cursory trace, it would appear to be New York

City. But…" JR displayed a small smile as he spoke, "…it didn't."

"Where then?"

"You're not going to like this."

Rolling his eyes, Kruger shook his head slightly.

"WHERE, JR?"

"An office building in Paris."

Knoll and Kruger stared at JR, both realizing what he was telling them.

Kruger said, "Let me guess. The office building where Dmitri Orlov is located."

JR nodded slowly. "Another piece of the puzzle falls into place, doesn't it?"

"It would appear so."

"Apparently you two see something I don't," Knoll frowned. "What?"

"Abel Plymel was a sleeper agent planted in the United States during the Cold War to disrupt our financial markets." Kruger took a sip of his coffee. "When the Berlin Wall fell and his handler died of a heart attack, he disappeared into the maze of Wall Street, believing no one in Russia knew about him. He amassed a fortune as a merger and acquisition specialist. As you know, Sandy, his real name was Alexei Kozlov."

JR took up the narrative: "My guess is since Orlov was with the KGB, he knew about the sleeper agents in the US and probably knew that Kozlov was posing as Plymel."

"They've been at this for a while, haven't they?" Knoll crossed his arms over his chest and leaned back in his chair.

Kruger nodded. "Yeah, it would appear so." He stood and walked to the end of the room and back. Stopping behind his chair, he placed his hands on the top of it. "I don't see how Orlov could know of our association, JR. Do you?"

Shaking his head, JR pursed his lips. "With these guys, anything is possible."

"I know he blames me for exposing Robert Burns Jr."

Both JR and Knoll nodded.

"And it's public knowledge I was involved with exposing Plymel as Kozlov. So why, all of a sudden, are you involved, JR?"

"I don't know, but we're avoiding the real question here."

Both Knoll and Kruger looked at JR. Knoll said, "What's that?"

"How did they know my birth name?"

Chapter Fifteen

KRUGER STARED at JR for several silent moments.

"You're right, too many coincidences. There has to be a relationship somewhere."

Knoll pursed his lips, "There's another question we haven't discussed."

Both JR and Kruger answered in unison: "What?"

"If they know where you are, do they know about your family?"

JR jumped from his chair, went to his cubicle and brought back his cell phone. He touched an icon and pressed the phone to his ear. The call went unanswered. Turning his back to his friends, JR wrote a short text message to Mia and sent it. He closed his eyes and said a silent prayer.

A minute later, the phone chirped. JR wasted little time answering it.

"Where are you?"

"Joey and I are at the grocery store, why?"

JR looked at Knoll, who nodded and stood. JR returned his attention to phone.

"Which one?"

"The one across the highway from your office. Why? What's up?"

"Sandy is heading that way. Stay in a crowd until he gets there."

"JR, you're scaring me. What's going on?"

"I'll explain when I see you. Stay on the line. He'll be there in less than five minutes."

Looking at Knoll, JR said, "She's across the highway at the grocery store. Can you go get her?"

"My pleasure. We'll be back in a few."

When the big man was gone, JR returned to talking to Mia. Four minutes later, he heard the distinct sound of Knoll's voice over the phone.

"Mia, I'm ending the call. Do what Sandy says."

"Okay, JR."

With Mia in safe hands, JR stared at Kruger and said, "I need to leave town for a while."

"What about Mia?"

"She and Joey can stay at Joseph's. They're leaving soon and Jimmie will be there. Mary's due back from Washington today to do some packing."

"I've seen your paranoia before, but never like this. What are you thinking?"

"Sean, you more than anyone else know how completely I deleted all public records of my prior life when I came here seven years ago."

"Yes. The only thing left was a top-secret Army file even the FBI couldn't get to. But I also know President Osborne pardoned John Zachara of all criminal charges before he left office two years ago."

A small smile appeared on JR's lips as he said, "My old life holds nothing but bad memories. It's as dead to me as the name John Zachara. I am JR Diminski."

He stood and did something Kruger had never seen

him do.

He started pacing.

"JR, think about it for a few moments. There has to be a connection somewhere. How in the world could Orlov know you were involved with Kozlov?"

JR stopped and stared at his friend. "There is only one way. The hacker in Mexico City."

"The one who arranged for the body to be found?"

A small nod was Kruger's answer.

"What do you know about this hacker?"

"Not much. He keeps a low profile on the internet and only frequents a few chat rooms. Why?"

"Could he also work for Orlov?"

JR was quiet as he started pacing again. After taking a deep breath, he let it out slowly. "I didn't think about that. I guess it's possible."

"I think it's more than possible."

"Then I have to find him."

"How?"

"I'm going to Mexico City. He's the only possible link. There is no other way for Orlov to know who I am."

"Does this person in Mexico City know who you are?"

Silence returned to the conference room.

"I don't see how, but…"

"It's possible."

"He's good, maybe as good as I am. As Sir Arthur Conan Doyle said, 'Once you eliminate the impossible, whatever remains, no matter how improbable, must be the truth.' It's the only explanation."

"You're not going by yourself."

"I can take care of myself."

"Yes, but you can't speak Spanish."

JR didn't answer.

"Jimmie can go with you."

"I thought he was going to make sure nothing happened to Mia and Joey?"

"I know a few local FBI agents who will be more than willing to help while we're gone."

"We?"

Kruger nodded.

A smile came, once again, to JR's lips.

———

GIBBS SAT ACROSS FROM JR, a mug of coffee in his hand. Sandy Knoll sat next to him. They were situated at the kitchen table in Joseph's Christian County home.

"What did you want to talk to me about, JR?"

Looking up from his laptop, JR pursed his lips and sighed.

"How familiar are you with Mexico City?"

Gibbs gave JR a slight smile and asked, "By familiar, do you mean I know my way around, or I know where the place is?"

"The former."

"I can tell you were the good bars are located and which tourist bars to avoid. Why?"

JR glanced at Knoll, who nodded slightly.

"I'm searching for someone I believe lives there. But, without eyes and ears physically in Mexico City, I won't be able to pin him down."

"There's nine million people in Mexico City," Knoll frowned. "How do you propose we find him?"

Jimmie chuckled slightly, "Like we found Trinh Huy?"

Nodding, JR closed the laptop.

"A little more difficult than Huy. But, yeah, the same concept."

Trinh Huy was a Vietnamese ex-pat living in Bangkok who was responsible for financing Islamic terrorists in Malaysia. He was the money man behind a series of planned attacks in the United States against targets in twenty different cities by immigrants from Vietnam and Malaysia. JR had been instrumental in uncovering the plot, allowing Knoll and his team to intercept the attackers before they could act. He also helped find Huy in the busy city of Bangkok. The team was able to find him because Huy, being over confident about his security, never changed cell phones and frequented the same restaurants.

Sipping his coffee again, Gibbs looked over the mug to ask, "Who is this guy?"

"I actually don't know who he is. He's a hacker I've had contact with for about ten years. The only fact I know about him is he's located in Mexico City."

"How do you know that?"

JR smiled. "I needed his assistance on a project a few years ago."

Gibbs smiled and nodded.

Knoll sat his coffee mug down. "JR, could this guy have moved since then?"

"Sandy, I'm not even sure it's a guy. I've always assumed he was. The hacker community is gender neutral and faceless. But the point is, he's still in Mexico City."

"Okay, how do you propose we find him?"

"I make contact and ask for help again."

Raising his eyebrows, Gibbs said, "Again?"

Knoll frowned. "You probably need to tell Jimmie what he did for you seven years ago."

Nodding slowly, JR said, "He's the individual who arranged for a body, identified as Plymel, to be found in Mexico City?"

Knoll grinned.

"So, what actually happened to Plymel?" Gibbs asked.

"He never left Missouri. His body is at the bottom of the deepest part of Stockton Lake."

"How'd that happen?"

JR just smiled.

"Oh..." Gibbs grinned. "So, this Plymel guy was really a Russian named Kozlov?"

"Yes."

"You think Orlov knew him?"

"That's the current working theory."

"The what?"

"Sean was able to determine the truth and discovered Plymel was really Kozlov, a former KGB sleeper agent. Orlov's job with the KGB, before the fall of the Soviet Union, was overseeing the department responsible for those types of agents. The thinking is Orlov knew about Kozlov and when he disappeared, started making inquiries."

Taking another sip of his coffee, Gibbs was quiet for a few moments. "So, you think this hacker in Mexico sold you out?"

"Kind of a harsh way to put it, but yeah."

"How dangerous was this Kozlov person?"

"He hired someone to look for me and when he did, Mia was kidnapped." He paused and took a deep breath. "She almost died. Once again, without the help of Sean and Sandy, she wouldn't have made it. After that, Kozlov went on a killing spree. That's when he shot Sandy and Mike at my old building."

"We lost a good man that day." Knoll crossed his arms over this massive chest, his gaze on a distant spot out the sliding glass door of Joseph's house.

JR continued, "I made a deal with Kozlov: I would return his money if he left us all alone. He agreed, although I knew he had no intention of keeping his end of the bargain. So, I didn't either."

Knoll broke out of his funk to pick up the story.

"A year later I got curious and visited the spot where you shot Kozlov." He turned to Gibbs. "Eight hundred yards from the loft of a rickety, falling-down barn. How many shots did it take, JR? Two?"

"I don't remember," JR shrugged. "Just that the first one missed."

"JR hadn't made a long range shot in over ten years and nails it with two shots."

Gibbs stared at JR with new-found respect. "Huh."

JR returned to his narrative. "The bottom line is I had to get rid of the body and make it look like he had escaped. Kozlov's passport and twenty thousand dollars ended up in Mexico City. The hacker arranged for an unrecognizable body to be found with the passport."

"Got it," Gibbs said. "So, how do we find this guy in Mexico?"

"I'm going to ask him to help me disappear. Again."

Knoll's eyebrows shot up. Gibbs just laughed.

———

ALEXIA MONTREAL SCROLLED through various postings in a computer chat room she frequented. The suicide of the American vice president and then, two weeks later, the fatal aneurism suffered by the president, had caused the hacker world to hyperventilate. Conspiracy theories were sprouting like mushrooms in a forest after a rain. They fluctuated from an alien invasion from another galaxy to a secret cabal of Washington operatives staging a coup.

If her suspicions were correct, the US President died of natural causes. Granted, both the VP and president dying within a short period of time of each other was bound to raise the possibilities of a conspiracy. But she knew the real reason the VP committed suicide. It had to do with a long-term connection with the old KGB and now the FSB. A relationship generated in Pittman's youth, a fact known by only a few residents within the confines of the Dark Web. She sat back as she stared at her computer.

Knowledge of this connection was dangerous. Several well-known hackers with knowledge of the connection had gone silent in recent days. She felt comfortable with her safety. Everyone within the community thought she was a man.

She guarded the myth of being male with the utmost security. Standing five feet nine, Alexia was tall by Western European standards. Born in Spain, both of her parents were stanch supporters of Catalonia, harboring a deep distrust of the government in Madrid. After completing her studies at the University of Barcelona, she worked for an ISP provider as a security analyst until she discovered a more lucrative career. Hacking.

During the early years of her hacking, she became a member of an invisible group of revolutionaries working toward the demise of the Madrid government. At the time, she called the Latin Quarter of Paris home. She liked the bohemian atmosphere and was able to blend into the culture with ease. However, greed got to her one night, drawing the unwanted attention of the French General Directorate for Internal Security, the DGSI. After a hastily arranged midnight flight out of Charles de Gaulle International airport to Mexico City, she settled in the La Condesa district.

She was pencil thin and when in public, wore loose fitting clothes. She did not consider herself unattractive, but most people, if they noticed her at all in a crowd, would consider her plain, a perception she fostered with no make-up, oversized glasses and short tousled black hair. She lived alone, no cats or dogs. Too much trouble if she had to disappear suddenly.

She was staring at her computer screen when an encrypted message arrived in one of her older email addresses.

Five seconds later, a message appeared in a newer address with the key to the encrypted note.

She sat back, frowned and tried to decide if she should unencrypt the file. After several moments of indecision, she did.

The message was short: *Seven years ago, you helped with a problem. New problem has arisen. Need to disappear with new ID. Will you assist? Zardoz.*

It was a name from her early days in Mexico City. She assumed he was dead as he had disappeared from the hacker chat rooms years ago. The reappearance of Zardoz offered numerous possibilities.

The first was the opportunity to add finances to her slowly depleting bank account. Zardoz paid well and promptly.

Another possibility, someone was setting a trap for her. The appearance of a message from him on the same day she was trying to determine why several members of a select group of hackers disappeared, gave her pause.

The third possibility she would have to think about. It might be the solution to the larger problem she faced.

She stared at the message for several minutes. Finally, her need for income was more critical than being paranoid.

She composed an encrypted message and hit the send key.

Chapter Sixteen

"HE HASN'T BEEN SEEN since he walked out of his office yesterday, Sean."

Ryan Clark pressed the cell phone to his ear as he stood in the lobby of the Rothenburg and Sandifer law firm. Additional FBI agents were questioning the various members of the company as Clark spoke to Kruger.

"Did he say where he was going when he left, Ryan?"

"No. His admin said after the large man left, Sandifer kept his door closed for about forty-five minutes, then rushed out without saying a word or closing his office door. She said he only leaves the door open if he's going to return in a few minutes. If he's leaving for an extended period of time or for the day, the door is closed and locked."

"Does he normally tell her where he's going?"

"Yeah, but not this time."

"Do we have any other sightings of Volkov and Popov?"

"None. The surveillance video is the only time they've been seen."

"What about Sandifer's house?"

"No one's home. Neighbors say the wife left around three in the afternoon the same day and hasn't returned."

Kruger frowned, his frustration growing.

"What about his sons?" he asked.

"Both are grown and married. Oldest is an attorney in Chicago and the youngest is a doctor living in Dallas. Neither have heard from their parents in a week. Which, by the way, both tell me is not unusual."

"Okay, if he's still alive, we need to find him, Ryan. Check all the airports to see if they flew somewhere."

"JR could do it faster."

"Yes, but we have to do this one by the book. We have, uh...complications that have to be addressed."

Clark did not comment immediately. "Care to explain?"

"I can't right now. I will as soon as we understand more."

Kruger could not see his expression, but Clark smiled.

"Okay, got it. I'll let you know what we find at the airports."

"Thanks, Ryan. Sorry to be so vague, I just can't explain right now."

"No problem, talk to you soon."

The call ended and Kruger put his phone down on Joseph's kitchen table. He placed his elbows on the table straddling the phone and pressed the palms of his hands against his eyes.

JR sipped his coffee, then asked, "Why don't you let me look for Sandifer?"

Shaking his head, Kruger looked at JR. "Until we know how Orlov found you, you need to go dark."

Gibbs gave a low whistle and looked at Kruger. "You think it's that bad, Sean?"

"Too many incidents converging at the same time: Jolene Sander's murder with a Russian nerve agent, Pittman's suicide, the president's death, Boris Volkov suddenly appearing at Kyle

Sandifer's office and his vanishing act immediately after the visit. Are they all related? My guess is they are. But how JR fits into this is something I can't wrap my head around."

———

DMITRI ORLOV FROWNED as he listened to his assistant standing in front of his desk. When the man finished, Orlov took a deep breath and let it out slowly.

"So, they do not know where he is?"

Uri Yanovich shook his head. "No."

"Unfortunate."

Yanovich did not reply.

Orlov stood and turned to face the window behind his desk.

"Where are Volkov and Popov now?' he asked, his eyes tracking pedestrians on the sidewalk.

"Buffalo, New York, waiting on instructions."

"Tell them to go on to Toronto and then have Popov fly to Mexico City. We have too many loose ends right now. We need to tie up a few."

"Yes, sir. What about Sandifer?"

"He is a minor player, but will need to be dealt with at the proper time. The hacker in Mexico City worries me."

"Why?"

"He knows too much."

Yanovich remained quiet.

"Anyone who would provide the information he gave us, just for money, would also be willing to sell it to the Americans. We cannot allow that to happen."

"Remember, he did not contact you specifically, Dmitri."

"No, you are correct, he did not. But he knew enough to get this information to the right person. We have to deal with it. In addition, a certain individual in Moscow feels this person in Mexico is a potential problem we don't want or need at the moment. It is now my problem to resolve."

"What about the FBI agent?"

"Kruger?"

Yanovich nodded.

"Plans are in place. The individual assigned to the task is just waiting for me to give him the go-ahead."

"When will that be?"

"Soon, my dear Uri, soon."

Chapter Seventeen

IN ADDITION TO JIMMIE GIBBS' accomplishments in swimming, he had a natural talent for languages. The melting pot of different cultures in Southern California helped stimulate Jimmie's love of language. By the time he joined the military, Jimmie could pass for a resident of multiple Mexican communities utilizing the proper dialect and accent.

The Navy recognized his talent and before sending him to Seal training, immersed him in multiple language schools. Now in his late thirties, Jimmie was fluent in Spanish, Catalonian, French, German, working toward fluency in Arabic and Farsi and conversational Russian.

Sitting in a small café in the Condesa section of Mexico City, it reminded him of the bistros in the Latin Quarter of Paris. Except for the local flora, the art deco architecture felt like sitting in the 5th or 6th arrondissement of Paris. Jimmie was in this particular establishment, not because it reminded him of Paris, but because JR identified it as one of the locations the Mexico City hacker accessed the internet.

With Jimmie's ability to speak with a local accent, the team utilized him as their point man. On the fourth day of his observation, he received a text message from JR indicating the hacker was at his location and accessing the web.

Jimmie discreetly scanned the small room and observed only one person using a computer. A female. He calmly stood, threw a 200 peso note on the table and walked out of the café. Now across the street, with the front of the bistro still in sight, he pulled out his cell phone and called JR. His call was answered on the second ring.

"JR, the only person in the café on a computer was a woman."

"Huh…"

"What does that mean?"

"It means she has perpetuated the illusion of being male for over ten years."

"So, he is a she."

"It would appear so. Did you see where she came from?"

"No, I saw her come in but was looking for a guy. I didn't pay too much attention to her. She doesn't dress like your typical Mexican thirty-something female."

"What do you mean?"

"Loose pants, cotton long-sleeved pullover, floppy hat. The way she moves is male, but I heard her order her meal. Definitely female."

JR remained silent for a few moments. "Is Sandy close?"

"He can be. Why?"

"You two need to follow her and see where she lives. If I know the location, I can determine her name."

"Most of the residences around here are apartments, JR."

"Well, that makes it more challenging, but it can be done."

"Okay, we'll make it happen."

Jimmie ended the call and sent a text message to Knoll. Five minutes later, he saw the big man a block from his location. He sent another text telling him their target was a tall woman with short black hair, glasses, tan hat. He observed

Knoll consult his phone and nod once. Keeping his eyes on the front door of the restaurant, Gibbs walked into a small bookstore across from the café and started to browse.

Fifteen minutes later, the woman exited the café with a backpack on her shoulder and turned left. Gibbs casually walked out of the bookstore and followed her from the opposite side of the street. He passed Knoll, neither acknowledging the other's presence.

After walking several blocks, the woman stopped to look into the window of a clothing store. Gibbs recognized the move. She was trying to determine if anyone might be following her. He kept on walking on the opposite side of the street until he was past her. He turned a corner and waited for Sandy to let him know what direction she had taken.

Jimmie wore his standard dress: cargo shorts, open linen shirt with a tan t-shirt underneath and sandals. With a need to be flexible in his appearance, he had tucked his hair under a baseball cap. If spotted, he could let Knoll keep track of the woman as he took his linen shirt off and let his hair down. From a distance, he would be a different person.

The woman made one more stop, after which Jimmie took over the surveillance. Three blocks later, she walked into a two-story apartment building.

With the apartment building's GPS coordinates sent to JR, they settled in to keep tabs on the building, Knoll in the back, Jimmie out front.

———

JR LOOKED up from his laptop and watched Kruger pace. They were still at the Mexico City Marriott Reforma Hotel. It was the team's headquarters and the location JR used to set up his computers.

"I've found her."

Kruger stopped pacing and turned toward JR.

"Who is she?"

"Alexia Montreal. She's a Spanish ex-pat with an impressive resume, both academic and French DGSI."

"Why the French DGSI?"

"Not sure, but they have the equivalent of a Be-On-The-Look-Out issued for her through INTERPOL."

Kruger frowned. "Mexico is part of INTERPOL, so why would she keep her real name."

"Twenty-one million individuals in and around the Greater Mexico City area. She's hiding in plain sight."

"Huh..." Kruger pursed his lips and crossed his arms over his chest. "Shall we go meet your Mexico City hacker?"

JR nodded as he placed his laptops into a backpack.

"HER APARTMENT IS the last one on the left side of the hallway. I used a snake camera under the door about ten minutes ago. She's staring at a laptop on a small breakfast bar in the kitchen area. The place is small, looks French." Jimmie Gibbs briefed Kruger and JR at the top of the staircase leading to the second floor of the apartment building. "Knoll's got the back of the building covered."

Kruger nodded. He turned to JR, "Do you want to knock on the door, or have Jimmie and I breach it?"

"She'll have an escape plan in place if we knock on the door. I would."

Jimmie smiled. "I'll call Sandy."

Ten minutes later, Knoll, Gibbs and Kruger were stationed outside of Alexia's apartment door. Jimmie placed small breaching charges on the outside of each door hinge. With Knoll, Kruger and himself prepared, he touched an icon on his cell phone and the charges detonated with a muffled thump. As the charges took out the hinges, Knoll shouldered his way into the apartment, followed by Gibbs and Kruger, each with weapons drawn.

A surprised Alexia Montreal sat wide-eyed as the three men rushed into her apartment and restrained her. JR followed and took control of her computer. He turned to her and said, "Sorry, Alexia, we need answers to a few questions."

She stared at JR as Knoll placed flexi-cuffs on her wrists and Gibbs positioned a strip of light-colored surgical tape over her mouth before she could cry for help. JR secured her laptop in his backpack and looked around the room. Seeing what he needed, he disconnected the modem from the wall, placed it in his backpack and followed the three men escorting their detainee toward the staircase at the end of the hall.

As they headed down, he heard numerous doors open and close swiftly. He grinned. Curiosity in Mexico was still a dangerous habit.

———

THE FBI GULFSTREAM G550 lifted off from Mexico City International Airport two hours later with one additional passenger aboard for the return to the United States. JR sat across from Alexia and asked, "Why did you suddenly let down your protocol for masking your location?"

Alexia shrugged, looking at the floor of the aircraft. Her restraints had been removed and she sat in a chair toward the rear of the plane. She was offered water and something to eat, but declined both.

"You basically let me find you."

She nodded.

"Why?"

She looked up at JR. "I am in trouble and need your help."

JR tilted his head to the side and stared at Alexia. "Really? What kind of trouble?"

"I did something stupid a few years ago and now it could get me killed."

"What did you do?" Kruger asked.

She shook her head and stared at the floor again. "When I got your message, I thought you might help me if you found me. You found me."

"Why didn't you just ask me?"

Smiling slightly, she looked up at JR, "You would have thought it a trap."

JR chuckled. "Yeah, you're probably right." He looked over at Kruger. "Do you have any questions?"

Kruger sat in the chair in front of Alexia. He smiled slightly. "I'm sorry for the way this was handled, but we needed you out of Mexico City."

"I know," she nodded.

"Alexia, I'm with the FBI. We need to know about your involvement with Dmitri Orlov."

"I have never heard of this person."

With a slight smile, Kruger changed the question.

"We need to know about your involvement with the Russian FSB."

"They paid for information. I needed money."

Gibbs was sitting a few seats away and laughed out loud. The woman glared at him, but kept silent.

With a paternal smile, Kruger asked, "What type of information?"

"All kinds."

Nodding slightly, Kruger changed tactics.

"Who is John Zachara?" he asked.

With a grim smile, Alexia pointed toward JR.

JR stared at her for several moments, but said nothing.

Kruger watched his friend to make sure he was okay and

then turned his attention back to Alexia. "How did you know?"

"I've always known who he was. Even after he changed his name to JR Diminski and posed as Zardoz in chat rooms. Why do you think I let you guys find me?"

Shaking his head, JR took a deep breath and let it out slowly. "How?"

"You have a singularly unique way of writing code that I have always admired."

JR's eyes were now wide. "You've kept track of me?"

She nodded.

"Did you sell my real name to the Russians?"

She studied the carpet below her seat and shrugged.

Kruger frowned. "We'll take that as a yes."

"I needed money. It was when they were frantically trying to confirm a body found in Mexico City was Alexi Kozlov."

Gibbs was not smiling anymore. "Seven years ago?"

She nodded.

"How did you know they were trying to confirm it?" Kruger asked.

"It was all over the Russian Dark Web chat rooms."

"Was the name Abel Plymel ever used?"

"Constantly. When he dropped out of sight, the chat rooms went hysterical. When a body without a face was found in Mexico City with Kozlov's identification on it, a reward for information was offered."

"How much were they offering?" Kruger was now kneeling in the aisle, eyeball to eyeball with the woman.

She glanced at him and then returned her attention to the floor. "I didn't tell them anything until the reward reached half-a-million Euros."

Closing his eyes briefly, Kruger took a deep breath. "What information did you sell them?"

Tears welled in her eyes as she blinked rapidly and turned

to stare out the window next to her seat. She didn't answer the question.

"Alexia, I need an answer."

She shook her head as tears flowed down her cheek. Finally, after a minute, she answered, "I told them the body found in Mexico was not Kozlov."

"Did you tell them where the body was?"

Shaking her head, she spoke in a whisper. "I did not know where Kozlov's body was." She took a breath and more tears rolled down her cheek. "I told them a man named John Zachara did."

"Did you tell them where he was?"

She snapped her head up and stared Kruger in the eyes. "No."

"Did you tell them Zachara was JR Diminski?"

She shook her head.

"Did they pay you the reward?"

Taking a deep breath, she let it out slowly as tears flowed. "No."

"Then how did they know JR is Zachara?"

Alexia moaned and closed her eyes. "I told them a week ago after they offered a million euros."

Kruger stood and looked at JR. He was staring at Alexia wide-eyed, his face as pale as the interior walls of the Gulfstream.

Chapter Eighteen

JR RETREATED to the back of the plane and buried himself in his laptop. Further questioning of the woman stopped as the team determined their next steps. His silence continued until they walked into Joseph's home four hours later. JR took Mia's hand and they both retreated to the second-floor room she and Joey were sharing.

An hour after arriving, Jimmie Gibbs poured a cup of coffee for Alexia Montreal. She was sitting at the breakfast bar of the rural home, staring out the sliding glass door in the kitchen. She had just taken a sip of the brew and made a face.

In her native Catalonian, she asked, "How can Americans drink this shit?"

Gibbs smiled, then answered her question in the same language with an accent heard on the streets of Barcelona. "It's an acquired taste."

Her eyes widened and she stared at Gibbs. "I have not heard my language spoken like that in a long time. Are you from Barcelona?"

He shook his head. "Southern California, but I've spent some time there."

She smiled grimly and returned to staring out the door. After a moment she looked back at him. "Am I a prisoner here?"

Gibbs returned to English. "No, you're free to come and go as you please."

She chuckled and answered in accented English, "Go where? I do not know where I am?"

"Central United States."

"Well, that narrows it down."

Gibbs smiled. "You look different."

Alexia shrugged. She had taken a shower and now wore black leggings with a beige pull-over peasant blouse with black piping. Her hair was styled and she had on a hint of make-up. Gibbs was amazed at the transition. She was pretty.

"The woman who owns this house is the same size. The FBI agent told me I could borrow some of her clothes." Her smile disappeared as she glared at Gibbs. "It seems I was brought here without any of my own."

"It was deemed wise to get you out of Mexico as fast as possible."

She nodded and returned to staring out the glass door.

Gibbs returned to Catalonian. "Alexia, why did you sell JR's name to the Russians?"

Tears welled up in her eyes as she blinked rapidly. Wiping the back of her hand against them, she shook her head. After a minute, she said. "I really don't know. It seemed like a good idea at the time, but when they did not put funds into the bank account I gave them—well…"

"So, they reneged on the deal."

Closing her eyes, she nodded slightly. "Again. A week and a half ago, I saw a man I had never seen before in the neighborhood paying too much attention to the café across from my apartment. I followed him when he left. He walked about a half a kilometer from the café and got in a black Mercedes."

"Did you ever see him again?"

"The next day. He watched the café again but not the next. Different man watched for a few days and then the slender one returned four days ago. I did not see anyone yesterday or today. That is why I was able to get to the place where you found me."

Gibbs leaned his back against the breakfast bar. "Can you describe them?"

"First man was tall, slender with black hair combed back. Second man more heavy set with bushy eyebrows and mustache."

Gibbs pursed his lips and opened the picture gallery on his cell phone. He found the picture he sought and showed it to her. "Is this one of the guys?"

Alexia stared at the picture.

"Yes, first man. How did you know?"

"His name is Yuri Popov."

She looked at the picture and then again at Gibbs. "How do you know of this man?"

He gave her a slight smile. "He's part of a tag team with a man named Boris Volkov." He changed the picture on his cell phone and showed a picture of Volkov taken in Paris. "Recognize him?"

She shook her head. "He is not the second man. Who is he?"

"That's Boris Volkov."

"What is tag team? I have never heard of this term."

"They work together and do, uh, favors for Dmitri Orlov."

Nodding, she sipped her coffee. "Then I was lucky JR found me first."

"Yes." He paused. "You are." Sipping his coffee, he did not take his eyes off of her. "Alexia, how did they find you?"

Another shrug. "Probably something I told them."

"What?"

"I told them about the café near where I lived."

"You're kidding?"

"No."

"Why?"

Another shrug.

"Alexia, we can't help you if you don't tell us the truth."

She slammed the coffee mug on the table and glared at Gibbs.

"I DO NOT KNOW." She took a deep breath and let it out slowly. "Maybe I am tired of hiding, maybe I unconsciously want my exile to end." She paused and looked at him, tears welling in her eyes. "I have been alone for more than ten years. No family, no friends, no lovers, no pets, nothing. I don't even remember what it feels like to be held by someone. The only companions I have had are words on a computer screen, written by individuals I never see. People who do not tell me their real names. I am tired of it."

Gibbs said nothing as he contemplated his own self-imposed exile after the death of his sister and parents. "I understand."

She glared at him again. "Do you? Do you really understand, or are you just saying it?"

He nodded. "Yes, I understand. It's not the same, but I have not allowed myself to get close to anyone since everyone I cared about died."

Nodding, she returned to staring at the coffee mug. Finally, after several silent moments she looked at him and asked, "Who were they?"

Jimmie Gibbs gave the woman a sad smile and just sipped his coffee.

———

LEAVING THE AIRPORT, Kruger drove immediately to his house. Entering the neighborhood, he looked for cars he didn't recognize parked along the street. When they first moved in, he had committed to memory which cars belonged to which house and who parked on the street. The practice had paid off before. Today he did not see anything unusual as he approached his home, except the Greene County sheriff's car parked in front of it. A smile appeared for the first time since learning the hacker revealed JR's name to Dmitri Orlov.

Joseph had called the local sheriff and requested the car and escort for Kruger and his family. As he pulled into the garage, he saw Stephanie exit the house with Mikey in her arms and Kristin following. Her first words were laced with concern.

"Sean, what did Joseph mean when he said we needed to stay at his house for a few days?"

Kruger took Mikey and opened the back-passenger door of Stephanie's Jeep. As he strapped the toddler into the car seat, he answered.

"We found the hacker."

She looked at him as she situated Kristin in her booster seat. "And why does that mean we have to disrupt our lives for a few days?"

"For precaution."

"That doesn't answer my question, Mr. Kruger." It was her way of telling him he needed to be more truthful with her.

He finished with Mikey and looked over at her. "When I left for Mexico City, I told you there was a possibility JR, Mia and Joey were in danger. It seems that could extend to us as well."

"Why?"

Taking a deep breath, he let it out slowly. "I'll explain as we drive to Joseph's. I need to talk to the deputy first."

She nodded and finished buckling Kristin into her booster seat.

When Kruger returned and got behind the steering wheel, he backed the Jeep out of the garage and headed up the street. The sheriff's car followed at a discreet distance. Still searching for cars that did not belong in the neighborhood, he glanced at Stephanie.

"We found the hacker."

"You told me that."

"Did I mention that he was a she?"

Stephanie turned her attention to her husband and shook her head. "No, you didn't."

"How many individuals know who JR really is?"

She frowned. "Not that many. Just you, me, Joseph, Mary and Mia. That's all I'm aware of."

"You forgot a former president who pardoned that individual a few years back."

"Yes, I did forget."

"As far as we knew, those are the only individuals with knowledge of JR's birth name. Until we talked to the hacker."

"Uh oh."

"Yeah, she knew exactly who he was, his background, why he was on the run and what happened to Alexi Kozlov."

Stephanie was quiet as she stared out the front windshield.

"Now, because of some reason she won't discuss, Dmitri Orlov knows. And he knows were JR lives. I will assume he knows we live across from him."

"What did she do?"

"She sold the information to Orlov."

"Why would she do that?"

"Good question. Hopefully, someone is talking to her right now trying to figure it out."

"Where is she?"

"Joseph's."

Stephanie turned in her seat and stared at her husband. "Did you kidnap her, Sean?"

"Kinda, but I had help."

"Doesn't matter. Why?"

"To protect her, mainly. There are too many working pieces to this puzzle and I need more information from her before we start fitting them together.

"Okay, I'm not angry about spending time at Joseph's anymore."

"I'm not happy about it, but at this point, it's the only way to keep you and the kids safe until we figure this out."

She looked at her husband and just nodded.

Chapter Nineteen

WITH A CELL PHONE pressed to his ears, Dmitri Orlov listened to the caller. Silence dominated his side of the conversation as he stared out the window behind his desk. His guest sat quietly in front as he watched Orlov.

Finally, Orlov said. "You found the hacker's apartment?" More silence. "I see. No clue to where she might have gone?"

The man listened.

"Very well. I need you in Dallas, Texas. Let me know when you arrive."

Orlov set the cell phone down on his desk and looked at Uri Yanovich. "It appears our hacker is not a man."

"Oh?"

Nodding, Orlov rubbed his chin. "Popov found her apartment. The door was breached and she was gone."

"Did he find her laptop?"

"No, but he found all of her clothes. That was when he discovered he was a she. He found only women's undergarments and tampons in the bathroom."

"Who do you think found her first?"

"I would be guessing" Orlov shook his head. "But it was

someone with military training. She protected her identity and location very closely until just recently. Why, I do not know."

"Did Popov question any of the neighbors?"

"No, I told him to be discreet. We don't need questions being asked about a Russian taking interest in this person. Besides, everyone in Mexico is reluctant to get involved. Bad for your health."

"What are your instructions?"

"As you heard, I told Popov to fly to Dallas. We need to send a message to Mr. Sandifer. He is not cooperating at the moment."

———

"YOU NEED to leave for the airport now."

"Kyle, I cannot just drop everything and leave right now. Besides, Richard doesn't know I'm coming."

"I've already called him and explained the reason. He is looking forward to our visit."

"Our?"

"Yes, I will be joining you in a few days."

"Why a few days?"

"I'm going to drive."

"What on earth for?"

"I need to speak to someone on the way."

"Just fly to where this someone is and then fly on into Dallas. You don't need to drive, Kyle."

"Yes, I do, Virginia. Please, listen to me. It is very important for you to leave this afternoon. You have a first-class ticket waiting for you at the American Airline ticket counter at Reagan."

"When did you plan this trip out, Kyle?"

"During the noon hour. Virginia, I will explain everything

when I get there. Just leave the house and go to Reagan National Airport. Please."

"Ever since you sold the firm, you've been acting weird. Very well, I'll pack a few things and leave. When will I see you?"

"I'll call you from the road."

Having called his wife from a suite at the Pentagon City Ritz-Carlton, Sandifer spent the first twenty-four hours raiding the mini-bar and trying to determine how to get to Dallas without leaving a trail the FBI or the Russian could follow. Only using room service, he spent the next five days sleeping fitfully and planning his escape from Washington, D.C. He determined the route he would take, where he would meet the individual he needed to talk to and what kind of vehicle he would drive. When he was done planning he took an Ambien, slept for twenty four hours and checked out of his room.

"MR. SANDIFER, there is a substantial financial penalty for early termination of the lease on your Mercedes. Especially since it's an AMG E63S. Are you sure that's what you want to do?"

"Mr. Bowman, how many years have we been doing business with each other?"

Jefferey Bowman, the owner of the Mercedes-Benz dealership in Arlington, sighed. Sandifer would only do business with him, nobody else. Today, the lawyer was cashing in on this long-term relationship.

"You were my first customer, Mr. Sandifer and we've been in business for twenty years."

"Exactly. And how many times have I asked for any extra consideration?"

Bowman hesitated. Every time Sandifer dealt with

Bowman, he brought up the how-long-have-we-been-doing-business-together line.

"Only on rare occasions, Mr. Sandifer."

"Exactly. That's why I would appreciate your consideration to terminate my lease early."

Taking a deep breath, Bowman nodded slightly. "May I ask why?"

"My wife and I have decided to retire early and do a little traveling. We will be driving to places where a Mercedes will raise eyebrows and invite curiosity we don't want."

"I see. Are you wanting to buy a car?"

"That's my plan."

"From me?"

Sandifer pointed at a black Jeep Grand Cherokee in the used car area. "I want to buy that Jeep."

"I believe we can come to an agreement," Bowman smiled. "Why don't you join me in my office, Mr. Sandifer?"

AT ELEVEN MINUTES AFTER MIDNIGHT, Kyle Sandifer pulled into the driveway of his home in the Woodmont subdivision of Arlington. He closed the door to the garage before stepping out of his new vehicle. He did not turn on any lights, using only a flashlight to navigate the house he and his wife had occupied for thirty years.

Forty minutes later, having removed the light bulb from the garage door opener, he backed out of his driveway in darkness. Suddenly, a thought crossed his mind. This could be the last time he would ever see his beloved home. He hoped not, but survival was more important. During the forty minutes spent throwing clothes and toiletries into a suitcase, he also retrieved from a gun safe his Dan Wesson Valor 1911 .45 caliber pistol and fifty thousand dollars in cash.

The cash was a gift from a client he successfully defended him on a drug charge. A day after the man was found not guilty, he showed up at Sandifer's office and handed him an attaché case. Without a word, he left his office, disappeared and was never heard from again. Inside the case were stacks of tens, twenties and one-hundred-dollar bills. Closing the door to his office, he counted the money. Apparently, this was a bonus since the client was current on his legal bills. Sandifer never declared the money to the IRS or the firm. He simply put it in his gun safe for a rainy day. Now five years later, it was pouring and he was glad he made the decision to keep it.

At a 24-hour Walmart Supercenter in Woodstock, Virginia he purchased a HP Chrome laptop, a Samsung prepaid no-contract cell phone, sunglasses, two pairs of Wrangler jeans, two hooded sweatshirts and a Washington Nationals baseball cap. Back on I-81, he retrieved the business card taken from his desk and glanced at the time. He would have to wait to make the call.

Six hours and five cups of coffee later, he pulled into a rest stop near Knoxville, Tennessee, and placed the call to the number on the business card.

"Kruger."

"Agent Kruger, this is Kyle Sandifer."

"Mr. Sandifer, thank you for calling. You have a lot of individuals worried at your office and at the FBI. Where are you?"

Smiling, Sandifer answered, "Not in Washington, D.C."

"We gathered that. Care to tell me?"

"Agent, I'm not sure my location is of importance at the moment. I do, however, need to speak to you privately without curious eavesdroppers listening to our conversation."

"That might be difficult since you won't tell me where you are."

"Are you at the address on your business card?"

"Not at the moment. I can be. Why?"

"There is an art gallery located in Northwest Arkansas created by a client I did work for several years ago. I will meet you there."

"When?"

"I will text you the information tomorrow. Since you are only two hours from this location, there should be no problems in meeting me."

"Okay. Are you in trouble, Mr. Sandifer?"

"Myself and our country, Agent Kruger. We will discuss it further when we meet."

Sandifer pressed the end call icon. He turned the phone off, placed it in one of the Jeep's front cup holders and started looking for an out-of-the-way motel where cash would be welcomed.

———

JOSEPH WATCHED Kruger as the call ended. He was back at his Christian County home to attend to a few matters and to check on everyone.

"He wouldn't tell you were he was, would he?"

Shaking his head, Kruger returned the cell phone to his jean pocket. "When did you start getting cell phone reception out here?"

"About a month ago."

Kruger stared out over the property at the tree line behind the house. "Has JR emerged from their room yet?"

"No."

Taking a deep breath, Kruger let it out slowly. "Time to get him out of his funk."

After the third knock on the bedroom door, it opened. JR stared at Kruger.

"Yeah?"

"You done sulking?"

137

"Not what I'm doing."

"Sure, it is. This was eventually going to happen. Now it's time to do damage control and make sure it doesn't disrupt your life. Besides, I need you to find someone."

JR stood silently as he blinked several times.

Mia appeared behind him and put her arms around his waist. "Sean's right, JR, time to go back to doing what you do best. We can stay here until we figure it out."

Glancing back at Mia and then Kruger, he nodded his head once. "I'll get my laptop."

———

JR POINTED to a map displayed on his laptop. "The call originated from a cell phone tower near Knoxville, Tennessee. A Walmart in Woodstock, Virginia, located just off I-81, sold the phone. It was purchased with cash and a thousand minutes of time."

"Kyle's handled enough criminal defense cases, he could probably teach a course on how to disappear." Pausing for a moment, Kruger rubbed his chin. "Is the phone still on?"

Shaking his head, JR pointed to the map again. "It's last contact with a cell phone tower was in Knoxville."

"He's heading west." Kruger paused to think. "Probably Dallas. He has a son there. I'd bet that's where the wife is."

JR looked up at Kruger. "Any way to check?"

"Yeah, I'll have the Dallas field office contact them."

Joseph was looking over JR's shoulder at the map. "I-81 becomes I-40 near Knoxville. If he stays on it, that will take him to Fort Smith, Arkansas," he pointed. "If he's meeting you at Crystal Bridges, it's less than a hundred miles from Fort Smith."

Kruger glanced at Joseph. "You think it's Crystal Bridges?"

Nodding, the older man straightened and crossed his arms

over his chest. "A Walmart heiress developed it. Lots of walking trails meandering through the wooded area surrounding the facility. It makes sense he'd want to meet there."

"When do you have to be back in Washington, Joseph?"

Glancing at Kruger, Joseph pursed his lips. "Jimmie wants to establish residency in Christian County. We're getting an official rental agreement finalized, so it will take a few days. Why?"

"Want to take a walk in the woods?"

Joseph smiled.

Chapter Twenty

WEATHER IN THE OZARKS, especially during late September and early October, can fluctuate wildly, particularly after the Autumnal Equinox. A day can start out hot and dry and by afternoon be cool and misty. It was one of those transitional days. A twenty-mile-an-hour wind out of the northwest swept a cold front across the plains of Kansas into the region. Dark, moisture-laden clouds scurried across the sky delivering a fine swirling mist and leaving damp surfaces everywhere.

Ignoring the weather, Kruger stood on the sidewalk leading to the Crystal Bridges art museum entrance, his focus on the parking lot. With hands tucked into pockets of the same leather jacket worn during a meeting in Paris not quite ten months ago, he stood waiting. Jeans, hiking boots, a black crew neck sweater over a blue oxford shirt and his Glock 19 in a holster strapped to his belt completed his attire. Dark aviator style Ray-Bans, while unneeded with the cloudy sky, kept anyone from knowing the direction of his focus.

A tall gentleman dressed similarly to Kruger and resembling the actor Morgan Freeman, walked up to him and said in a low voice, "He just pulled into the parking area. Black Jeep Grand Cherokee, Virginia plates. Jimmie has eyeballs on him."

"Good. Sandy's in the security office watching on the security monitors. Don't go too far. I want him to know you're here."

"Got it." Joseph Kincaid turned and faced the same direction as Kruger but backed up several paces to his left.

Within a few minutes, a tall man dressed in jeans, black hooded sweatshirt and a baseball cap, its brim pulled low over the eyes, approached the two. Kyle Sandifer stopped in front of Kruger and offered his hand. The two men stared at each other as they shook.

Sandifer frowned and glanced at Joseph, "Who's he?"

"Old family friend."

"Thought we were meeting alone."

"You didn't specify any conditions when we spoke. Besides, he's the new president's National Security Adviser. I borrowed him for a few days."

Even though Sandifer could not see Kruger's eyes, he was searching behind the man to make sure no one followed.

"I didn't know you were so well connected."

Kruger shrugged.

Sandifer's eyes didn't leave Joseph for several moments. "Yes, now I recognize him. Will he be reporting this meeting to the president?"

"Depends."

"What does that mean?"

"It depends on what you tell us."

Hesitation was Sandifer's first reaction. Then Kruger saw his shoulders slump and the stern look subside. He returned his attention to the FBI agent. "Let's walk."

The two men followed the sidewalk toward the walking trail entrance on the east side of the complex. It was several minutes before Sandifer spoke again.

"Are you going to arrest me, Agent Kruger?"

"Should I?"

"I would prefer you not."

"Have you committed a federal crime?"

Shaking his head, Sandifer lapsed into silence again as they entered a canopy of trees. This early in the fall season, leaves still clung securely to their hosts.

Once they were under the tree cover, the attorney said in a whisper, "If being greedy and stupid is a federal crime, maybe you should."

Kruger smiled slightly at the comment but did not acknowledge it.

"You mentioned, when you called, you were in trouble and needed to talk."

A nod.

"So, talk, Kyle."

"In our haste to sell the firm, my partner and I may have inadvertently made a huge mistake."

"Oh? What would that be, Kyle?"

Sandifer looked up at the trees above him as he walked. "Who we sold it to."

"Dmitri Orlov?"

The reaction from Sandifer was expected. He stopped walking and glared at Kruger. "You already know?"

Nodding, Kruger stopped, looked at the man and tilted his head to the side. "What did Boris Volkov say to you? And why are you driving across the country instead of flying?"

"You know more than I do. He never introduced himself, just said that he had a message from Orlov."

"Volkov can be that way. So, what was the message?"

"He told me they knew I was the attorney of record for a number of U.S. senators and more than a few Cabinet members."

"Public knowledge."

"Yes, but…"

"But what, Kyle?"

"The public doesn't threaten my family if I refuse to violate the confidentiality rights of my clients."

"Your family is safe, Kyle. I have FBI agents in Dallas and Chicago watching over them."

Sandifer's expression relaxed noticeably, but it was temporary. A few moments passed before he responded. "Thank you."

Kruger nodded.

"He did not state why they want my files, but to me, it sounded like they want to find high-level government officials they can blackmail."

After several moments of silence, Kruger lifted his gaze from the sidewalk to Sandifer. "They do. Did you ever meet Robert Burns Sr., the former senator?"

Sandifer shook his head.

"They owned him. From what we found out, after the son was murdered, most of the father's wealth was based on funds secured from the Russians. While he was a senator, Senior helped introduce banking laws in the early 2000s that indirectly caused the financial collapse in 2008. Orlov was the one who suggested Burns introduce those bills, some later became regulations. The original goal was to help his banks make more money. They didn't anticipate the consequences but were overjoyed with the results. The Russians are now searching for individuals that will help them create more government dysfunction."

With his hands buried in the pockets of his hooded sweat shirt, Sandifer studied the sidewalk as they traveled deeper into the wooded landscape. He remained quiet for a long while.

Finally, he said. "Can't you arrest them?"

"For what? We can't prove anything. Orlov stays in Paris most of the time and the gentleman who visited you is on a watch list and being investigated. How he got into the country is anybody's guess. Plus, they have contacts all over the country we know nothing about."

Sandifer looked back at Joseph, who was only a few steps behind them. "Is that why he's here?"

"Yes. We need the president to know more about your meeting with the Russian."

"How many people know I'm here talking to you?"

"A few."

Nodding his head, Sandifer took a deep breath. "Can we find someplace that's not so damn wet and cold?"

————

THE COFFEE WAS hot and good. Kruger displayed a small grin after tasting it. Most of the tables were empty at this time of day. In a corner booth, one man munched on a club sandwich while his three companions only drank coffee. Kruger sat to Sandifer's right and watched him eat. Joseph was to his left and Sandy Knoll next to Joseph. Jimmie Gibbs and a local Northwest Arkansas FBI agent sat at a table next to the booth, watching the restaurant and keeping others from sitting too close.

Sandifer's appearance was not that of a successful Washington, D.C., attorney. His hair was noticeably grayer and disheveled, white whiskers sprouted from his face and he ate the sandwich with the gusto of someone who had been deprived of food for a while.

Kruger took a sip of coffee. "If you're still hungry, they have good pie."

Glancing at Kruger, Sandifer put the sandwich down. "You eat here often?"

"No, never been in this one, but it's a chain. They have one where I live."

Nodding, the attorney returned to his sandwich. "I like chocolate."

Kruger motioned for their waitress and asked, "Can we have a slice of French Silk for this gentleman?" She nodded and hustled away to get it.

When she sat the plate down in front of Sandifer, he stared at it and smiled. With his sandwich finished, he attacked the pie. After consuming the last bite, he sat back. "That was good."

Joseph sipped his coffee and stared at Sandifer. "Want to tell us more about your meeting with Volkov?"

Nodding, the attorney wiped his lips with a napkin. "Gentlemen, I don't scare easily. Too many years of dealing with individuals who feel their own self-worth is far more important than anyone else on the planet. The Russian scared me."

"Why?" Kruger asked.

"Don't know, but he did."

Knoll chuckled. "Volkov can be an arrogant prick when he wants to be."

"You know him?" Sandifer stared at the big man.

Shaking his head, Knoll replied, "Let's just say I've had to deal with him in the past."

"Kyle," it was Kruger's turn to ask the question, "tell me more about your meeting. Exactly what did he want?"

Taking a deep breath, Sandifer let it out slowly. "Files. He wanted copies of my client files."

No one spoke, waiting for the attorney to continue.

"Apparently, Orlov bought the firm not for the revenue stream, but for two other reasons: our client files and the lobbying department." He paused and took a sip of his coffee. "Over the past few decades, we have represented a lot of politicians. Most of the time it was for mundane, boring reasons. But not always. Without going into detail, we've kept their embarrassing misbehavior quiet and out of the media.

Behavior, which if publicly known, would end the career and family life of many of our clients."

"Are those politicians still in office?" This came from Joseph.

Nodding, Sandifer sipped his coffee again. "A few have retired and some are dead. But the majority are still active in some aspect of our government. Mostly senators and a few House members who have graduated into leadership roles. Several have returned to their state and serve as governors."

Kruger held his coffee cup with both hands as he watched Sandifer talk, waiting for the attorney to finish his thought. "How many are you referring to, Kyle?"

With a grim smile, Sandifer turned to Kruger. "Without counting, probably close to sixty."

"Did you give him any files?"

"No."

"Was that when he threatened your family?"

"He asked if I had heard about the death of Jolene Sanders. I told him I had. He then paused and looked at the pictures of my family. He gave me a weird smile and mentioned how proud I must be of them. He then told me where they lived and what they did. The message was very clear."

"What did you tell him?"

"I ignored the comment about my family and told him I would be violating attorney client privileges and several United States laws, if those files were turned over to him. He laughed and told me I did not own the firm anymore and those files were the property of the owner."

"Why do you think they killed Jolene, Kyle?"

The attorney shook his head. "I wish I knew."

"We think she had information on Vice President Pittman. Is that possible?"

Sandier studied his coffee cup as he turned it clockwise. Taking a deep breath, he nodded.

No one at the table spoke.

Finally, after a half minute of awkward silence, he continued. "I represented Donald Pittman for years. Most of my work with him occurred during his tenure as the governor of Virginia."

"Go on."

After taking a sip of coffee, Sandifer closed his eyes. "I'm not proud of it, but I helped hide a very key part of Pittman's past from the media." He paused. "I'm violating so many ethical principals in telling you this."

"The man is dead, Kyle," Kruger said.

"I know, but, still…"

"If it will help us solve the murder of Jolene Sanders, we need to know."

"Donald Pittman was caught in a honey trap by the Russians."

Joseph nodded. "I figured it was something like that. When did this occur, Kyle?"

"His first year as governor. He attended a conference in Paris to represent the tobacco farmers of Virginia. After a few too many drinks, a young woman accompanied him back to his hotel room. Afterward, she threatened to tell his wife about the tryst. I intervened and we reached, what I thought was, an agreement with the woman."

"That happens all the time," Knoll chuckled. "Why would he commit suicide over it?"

Sandifer looked at him with sad eyes. "Because neither Pittman nor myself knew the woman was sent there by the Russians to trap him. After that incident, they owned Donald Pittman. They contributed heavily to his campaign and brought pressure on other compromised politicians who forced Bryant to take him as his running mate."

Nodding slowly, Joseph said, "A modern-day Manchurian Candidate."

Sandifer nodded.

Joseph continued, "He was so far in, he had no way out but to cooperate with them or lose everything."

Again, Sandifer nodded.

"What was your role?" Kruger looked at the attorney with suspicion.

"My role was benign at first. I was the attorney handling the pay-off of the woman. I didn't know about the Russian connection until Volkov told me all about it during his visit. He thought the media would love to hear about my part in the cover-up."

Kruger pursed his lips and studied his coffee cup. "You mentioned they also wanted the lobbying department. Why?"

Sandifer chuckled slightly. "When you think about it, it was a brilliant decision considering their goal."

"I don't like the direction this is taking, Kyle," Joseph frowned. "Are you saying they would use information from your lobbying department files to point out Congressmen who are susceptible to being influenced by money?"

"The Russian didn't say it, but I got the impression that was exactly what they would do."

Kruger sat back in his seat and frowned. "They're looking for more targets, aren't they?"

Nodding, Sandifer studied the crumbs on his plate left from the consumed pie. "He didn't say it that way, but that was my assumption."

Taking a deep breath, Joseph stared at Sandifer. "With the constant need to raise funds for their re-election campaigns, no telling how many congressmen would be susceptible to accepting their money."

"Particularly if they already have something in their background that could jeopardize their career." Everyone looked at

Kruger, who had taken a sip of coffee after making the comment.

Sandifer nodded. "That's why they want my client files. To identify those individuals."

Kruger turned his attention back to Sandifer. "Most lobbying firms have clients that supply the money for this type of activity. Who's paying for the lobbying?"

"Banks and financial institutions with foreign ownership. The public has no idea how many of these institutions are not owned by American interests."

Knoll let out a slow whistle. Joseph frowned and Kruger said, "Kyle, does Volkov know how many files you have?"

The man shook his head. "Not yet. I was told new management would be in place soon and my services would no longer be needed."

Kruger turned to Joseph, "I believe you'd better tell the President about this."

With a grim expression, Joseph nodded.

Chapter Twenty-One

THE RENTED white Chevrolet Cruze drove past the house on Southgate Drive in Plano, Texas.

In this particular neighborhood, on this particular street, a Chevy Cruse was more conspicuous than the driver intended. The cheapest home within the subdivision sold for north of three quarters of a million dollars. Few, if any, cars in the neighborhood were Chevrolets, unless they were tricked out Suburbans or Silverado pickups. Even new sixteen-year-old drivers drove nothing less than a BMW. This car stood out like a business suit in a biker bar.

But then, Yuri Popov did not know this. His interest lay in a house located near the center of the subdivision, a house owned by Dr. Richard Sandifer, Kyle's son. As he passed the residence, he noticed a black Suburban with US government plates parked in the circle drive. A man in a gray suit with dark wrap-around sunglasses stood next to the SUV and followed his passing. Popov realized, too late, the FBI knew someone had interest in the younger Sandifer.

Popov did not see the FBI agent raise his hand to his

mouth and he did not realize the jogger he passed thirty seconds later took his picture with a cell phone.

Decisions made in the field can and do have consequences. Popov made the decision, without consulting Volkov or Orlov, to abort his directive to give a message to Kyle Sandifer through the son. With the FBI already protecting him, there would be no way to deliver it.

Forty-five minutes later, Popov pulled into the Hertz car return, stepped out and opened the trunk to retrieve his small carry-on travel bag. As he reached in to extract the bag, two men dressed as Hertz employees, grabbed him by the arms and hustled him into a newly arrived Ford transit van directly behind the Chevy Cruze. With a Hertz logo on the side, the van drew zero attention as it exited the return area. A third man closed the car's trunk with the bag still in it and sat in the driver's seat. With the keys still in the ignition, he started the car and followed the van out of the Hertz facility. All of these events occurred within the span of twenty seconds.

Once inside the transit van, Popov looked at the two men who still held him by the arms and started to protest.

The larger of the two men put his finger to his lips and said in English-accented Russian, "zat KNEESS!"

Suddenly understanding his situation, Popov complied and shut up.

———

TWENTY-FOUR HOURS LATER, FBI agents Sean Kruger and Jimmie Gibbs stood in the FBI field office at the Dallas-Fort Worth airport examining the contents of the carry-on bag previously in the possession of Yuri Popov. At the same time Popov, occupying one of the facility's interrogation rooms, demanded to see a lawyer.

One of the arresting agents pointed to a passport and said,

"We found that one on him." He pointed to another one. "That one was hidden in the lining of his suitcase."

Kruger picked up the one Popov carried and opened it. "George Alexander. Interesting." Flipping through the pages, he stopped at the one in the back. "Our Mr. Alexander has been a busy traveler. It appears he flew in from Mexico City a few days before he drove past the Sandifer home in Plano."

Gibbs looked up and asked, "How long was he in Mexico?"

"Looks like he was there for four days, flew to Montreal, then flew back to Mexico City from Regan National."

"That would explain his absence watching the café for a few days."

Kruger nodded. "And it explains his presence in front of Kyle Sandifer's law firm. Let's have a chat with Mr. Alexander."

Gibbs smiled.

Kruger opened the door to the interrogation room and sat down across from Popov. Gibbs leaned against the wall.

"Remember me, Yuri?" Kruger asked.

The Russian stared at Kruger and slowly shook his head. "You have me confused with someone else."

His English contained only a slight Eastern European accent.

Gibbs spoke to him in Russian.

Popov's eyes widened slightly, but he returned his glare to Kruger. "I want a lawyer."

"Can't have one."

"I am familiar with your laws in the United States. It is my right to have an attorney."

"In your case, not really."

"Why?"

Kruger placed the George Alexander passport on the table and smiled. "Entering the United States under a false or forged passport is a violation of US Code Title 18, Section 1543. That offense carries a penalty of up to twenty-five years in a federal prison. Plus, since you're not really a citizen of the United States, we are forced to believe you have entered the country to commit a terrorist act. Therefore, you are being declared an enemy combatant and not entitled to an attorney."

"I am not an enemy combatant."

"How do we know that?"

"Call my embassy. They will tell you I am a businessman."

"What embassy? Your passport identifies you as an American citizen, which we know is false. How do we determine your real nationality? You leave us no choice but to hold you on a John Doe warrant."

"You know who I am. Both of you do."

"How would I know who you are?" He turned to Gibbs. "Jimmie, do you know who this man is?"

Gibbs displayed a slight grin, tilted his head to the side as he studied Popov for a few moments. "Nope, can't say that I do."

Kruger turned back to Popov and narrowed his eyes as he spoke. "See, neither one of us knows who you are. Now, why did you enter the country under a false ID? And why did you drive by a house owned by the son of Kyle Sandifer?"

Extracting two pictures from inside his suit coat, Kruger laid them down on the table. One picture showed Popov looking back at traffic outside the offices of Rothenburg and Sandifer in Washington, D.C. The other showed him driving the Chevy Cruse close to Richard Sandifer's house.

Popov glared at Kruger and then at Gibbs. "So, I am driving car. There is no crime in driving a car. Everyone in this country does."

"True, but not everyone enters the country using a false passport."

No response came from Popov.

"I'm going to give you a chance to save yourself. Tell me why your buddy, Boris Volkov, met with Kyle Sandifer and what they discussed."

Popov shrugged. "I do not know what you are talking about."

Kruger tapped the picture of Popov in Washington, D.C. "You picked him up after their meeting. I would assume you knew the topic of their conversation."

"I am finished answering questions." He folded his arms over his chest and sat back in the chair.

With a smile and a grating metallic screech, Kruger scooted his chair back and stood. He turned to leave. Just before Gibbs opened the door, Kruger paused and returned his attention to Popov. "Two things I forgot to mention. First, we haven't decided on where to send you. I mentioned ADX Florence, others have suggested Camp Delta at Guantanamo Bay. At ADX, you'll never see the sun again and at Camp Delta, well…" He paused, "Let's put it this way, no one will hear you scream."

Popov glared at Kruger, but remained quiet.

"Since you will be held as a John Doe, if anyone from your country makes inquiries about you, the system can honestly say we don't have you in custody. You will, for all practical purposes, disappear. Second, we sent your iPhone to our labs for examination."

He saw Popov display a sly smile.

"Oh, don't worry, they cracked your security code in a couple of hours. Apparently, your fingerprints on the screen gave them a clue to the code. After that it was just a matter of trying different combinations. Isn't technology great?"

The smile disappeared.

"I'm told everyone is giddy over all the information they're getting out of it."

Kruger's cell phone vibrated. After looking at the screen and reading the message, he smiled. "One last item, we just learned from one of your emails that you have a wife and two daughters."

Popov's eyes narrowed as he continued to glare.

"That's too bad. Do you know why it's too bad?"

Popov did not answer.

"You'll never see them again."

Kruger's face displayed a hard smile as he stared at Popov. He turned, Gibbs opened the door and Kruger walked out followed by the ex-Navy Seal. Before exiting, Gibbs turned, gave Popov a big smile and an exaggerated good-bye wave. "Say goodbye, Yuri."

As they walked down the hall away from the room, Gibbs turned to Kruger. "Think it will work?"

"Don't know. What do you think?"

"He's well trained and, at one time, a member of an elite Special Forces team in Russia."

Kruger glanced at Gibbs. "Would you give it up?"

"No, but I don't have a wife and two daughters."

"If you did, would you then?"

Gibbs ignored the question. "He's in a tough spot. If he tells us anything, he can't go back. If he doesn't tell us, we won't let him go back."

"I know. Time for him to contemplate his predicament for a few days. Then we can offer him an alternative."

Chapter Twenty-Two

AT 11:03 A.M., Dmitri Orlov placed the cell phone on his desk. He stood, turned with his back to the desk and stared out the window of his office. Across the Seine, sightseers crowded the grounds of Notre-Dame. Below his office, traffic snarled the Quai de Montebello, where street merchants peddled their old books, paintings, drawings and other wares to the tourists who flocked to Paris each fall. Aromas from the restaurant below his office always permeated the air at this time of day.

Orlov perceived none of this. His thoughts dwelled on a new problem, or was it a true crisis? He did not know at this point.

He turned at a knock on his office door.

"Da."

The door opened and his assistant in Paris, Grigori Pushkin, stepped in and closed the door. Pushkin possessed a thin face, pale blue eyes and sandy hair cut short. A hawk-shaped nose supported wire-rimmed glasses.

"Did you need to see me, sir?"

"Grigori, we may have a problem."

Pushkin stood ramrod straight, a habit learned during his time as a GRU agent. "How can I help?"

"When did we last hear from Popov?"

Blinking several times, Pushkin relaxed noticeably and said, "Three days ago. He called after arriving in Dallas."

"Nothing since?"

"No, sir."

Orlov nodded. "Calls to his phone go straight to voicemail."

The assistant did not respond.

"I just talked to Volkov and he has not heard from him either. Why do you think that is, Grigori?"

"If I had to guess?"

"Yes, if you had to guess."

"He is either under surveillance, or worse, the FBI has him in custody."

"My guess would be he is in custody. Is there a way you can make quiet inquiries?"

"What about our embassy?"

Orlov shook his head. "He is traveling using an American passport."

"That will make it difficult, but I will see what I can find out."

"Keep me informed."

Pushkin nodded and left the office.

Turning to look out his window again, Orlov surveyed the street below. The disappearance of Kyle Sandifer and Yuri Popov could not be a coincidence. He sat back down at his desk, pulled out a drawer on the bottom right side and extracted an iPhone. This was a phone only a few individuals knew about. He dialed a number and waited for the call to be answered.

———

PETER YANOVICH MAINTAINED a quiet life as a divorced Arlington, Virginia attorney. His practice consisted of negotiating real estate transactions and mergers and acquisition contracts. Now in his late forties, he made a decent living performing these activities. His real money came from being Dmitri Orlov's lawyer in the United States. Born in Fox River, Alaska, to Russian immigrants, Yanovich fled the state after he graduated from high school. With a law degree from Georgetown Law School, Yanovich met Orlov at a banking seminar five years after opening his one-man shop.

Yanovich's loyalties were to neither family, country, nor political philosophy. His loyalty was simply to money. Dmitri Orlov made Peter Yanovich a rich man, more so than his small law practice ever would and therefore he was loyal to Orlov.

Growing up in Alaska, Yanovich enjoyed the outdoors more than his legal practice. He maintained a lean body by biking to work each morning and constant hiking excursions on weekends. Of average height and average looks, he could blend into any crowd and never be remembered. This was the one trait Orlov found invaluable about Yanovich. He was forgettable.

His cell phone announced a call at 6:15 a.m. Having just stepped out of the shower, Yanovich thought about not answering until he saw the number and quickly accepted the call.

"Good morning, Dmitri."

"I know it is early there, Peter, but something has come up and I need you to jump on it immediately."

"Very well. What can I do for you?"

"Remember I asked you, sometime ago, to look into the background of an FBI agent named Sean Kruger?"

"I remember. You asked me to wait until I heard back from you."

"Well, it is time to start."

"How deep do you want me to go?"

"I want to know everything about him. Family, residence, education, wants, desires, you name it, I want to know about it."

"Very well. How soon?"

"Yesterday."

"Then I had better get busy."

———

DESPITE HIS FORGETTABLE LOOKS, Yanovich's profession and money allowed him to indulge his preference for having a variety of women in his life. He'd learned to never let them spend the night. It became too difficult to get them to leave.

One of the women Yanovich dated off-and-on worked for the Washington Post as a researcher, not a journalist. Brenda Kozlow slaved over a computer confirming backgrounds and sources for stories the paper intended to publish. They met for drinks after work later that evening.

"Thanks for meeting me on such short notice," Peter began as they sat down at a bistro table in one corner of the restaurant's bar area.

"I always enjoy meeting you, Peter." Brenda took a sip from her glass of Merlot. While not fashion-model pretty, she possessed a face most men considered pleasant. Her hazel eyes and long brown hair added to the attraction Peter felt for her. "You mentioned you wanted to ask me something?"

Yanovich smiled. "I need some advice."

She took another sip of wine. "Okay, about what?"

"Uh…" He paused as he sipped his glass of Cabernet. "Do you remember the terrorist attack in Fayetteville, Arkansas, a few years back?"

"Sure, who doesn't."

"I've always been fascinated about how it was prevented. I'm thinking about writing a book about it."

"Really. Have you ever written a book?"

"No," he shook his head. "That's what I wanted to ask you. You're a researcher—how do you do it?"

She smiled. "I could help and show you how."

"That would be nice. When?"

"How about tonight, your place?"

"Would we get any work done?"

"Maybe, but I doubt it."

He chuckled. "I was thinking about starting with the FBI agent who is credited with stopping it. How would I find more about him?"

"Oh, that's easy. I did an extensive work-up on him. Unfortunately, the paper didn't use any of the material."

"Why?"

"I was never told for sure, but I heard a wild rumor the president asked the publisher not to print the story."

"Really?"

She nodded as she sipped her wine again.

"Could I look at it?"

"I don't see why not. I can access the file from my laptop. Will I get credit in your book?"

"I'll definitely give you credit when it's published."

———

BRENDA WAS CORRECT. They got very little work done after returning to Yanovich's apartment. The nude woman lay next to him, gently snoring. He quietly slipped out of bed and put on a pair of jogging pants. When he was in the kitchen, he took the flash drive she had saved the file to and inserted it in his own laptop.

The information on the FBI agent was extensive and followed Kruger's career as he rose in stature within the Bureau. It outlined his personal status as married and living in Kansas City, Missouri.

After he finished reading the file, he did a Google search on FBI Agent Sean Kruger. The information provided was disappointing. He found very little information from the search more recent than five years ago. His curiosity for the evening satisfied, he returned to his bed, stripped off his jogging pants and curled up next to the sleeping woman.

He decided violating his rule concerning women spending the night was in order. They needed to get some work done in the morning.

———

THE TIME APPROACHED 11 p.m. in the room shared by JR and Mia at Joseph's home. Joey lay sound asleep on a folding bed in the same room. Mia sat up in bed as she waited for JR to join her. As he lay down, his cell phone chirped with a series of sharp tones. They both frowned.

"What is it, JR?"

Shaking his head, he picked up his phone and read the message.

"I warned Larry Page about this when he was developing Google," JR murmured.

Mia blinked several times, her eyes wide. "You know Larry Page?"

"Not really, I was at MIT when he was at Princeton. We knew of each other through various projects we worked on. He had a problem and posted a question online to our department. I got in touch with him and offered a suggestion on how to solve the issue. It did."

"JR, are you telling me you helped develop Google?"

"No, all I did was solve an algorithm problem that helped with the search engine."

"Oh? You never told me about it."

"Nothing to tell," he shrugged. "He never acknowledged the suggestion fixed it. I do remember telling him, when we spoke on the phone, his project would lead to privacy violations. He laughed and our conversation ended. It was the only time we ever spoke to each other. I am sure he forgot about me. So, a few years ago, I hacked into their system found the algorithm and modified it, uh…" He paused and gave her a mischievous grin. "Just a bit."

She chuckled. "What did you do, JR?"

"Well, let's just say I know how to protect you and me, Sean and Stephanie, Brian and Michelle, Joseph and Mary, plus everyone on our team from being searched by Google. Plus, I'm warned if anyone tries to search for any of us."

Mia frowned. "Was that the warning just now? Was it about you?"

JR shook his head. "Someone is trying to determine where Sean lives."

Chapter Twenty-Three

IT WAS noon before Brenda Kozlow dressed and, with a promise to use Washington Post resources to find more information about FBI Special Agent Kruger, left the apartment. After her departure, Yanovich inserted the flash drive and read, in more detail, the information given to him by the researcher.

The FBI agent did not have a presence on Facebook or Twitter, nor did his wife or son. After a quick search for Kruger's ex-wife and the son's mother, Yanovich discovered the woman was deceased. With this dead-end staring him in the face, he chose a different route.

The information provided by Kozlow identified Kruger's residence as Kansas City. Using tricks learned as a real estate attorney, he found the property, a condo on the western side of the Plaza. Unfortunately, ownership of the property changed hands four years earlier. Further search of the surrounding counties proved fruitless in his search for the agent's new residence. Knowing full well the FBI would not tell him where Kruger lived, he searched the data on the flash drive until he found the maiden name of Kruger's wife. A quick Google search found little about the woman except a reference to an old LinkedIn posting made before she was married. Most of it he already knew. The one piece of new information referred to a sister in Overland Park, Kansas.

A quick search of the Johnson County, Kansas, property tax files gave him an address and a phone number.

His phone call was answered on the fourth ring.

———

LINDA BENTON RESEMBLED Stephanie Kruger in numerous ways. Both inherited their mother's naturally curly brown hair and both were petite. Linda, being the younger of the two sisters, possessed hazel eyes compared to her older sibling's blue eyes. Both earned college degrees, but Linda's interests changed after graduation. Where Stephanie went on to graduate school and later a corporate career path, Linda followed her parents into the medical field by becoming a Registered Nurse. Now twenty years later, with additional training, she held the title Nurse Practitioner.

Childless, she and her husband, David, led a hectic life both socially and career wise. Currently the administrator for the hospital system employing Linda, demands on David's time were considerable.

The caller ID on her cell phone displayed the number and a location of the call, Washington, D.C. Curiosity overcame caution, so she answered the call.

"Hello?"

"Is this Linda Benton?"

Remembering a recent staff meeting with a discussion of phone scams, she did not answer with yes, but instead, "Who's calling?"

Yanovich recognized the ploy.

"My name is Oscar Malkovich. I'm an attorney in Washington, D.C. and I'm trying to get in touch with Linda Benton."

"What's this concerning?"

"Ms. Benton, I can assure you there is nothing sinister about this call. I am merely trying to locate your sister, Stephanie."

"I see. Well, Mr. Malkovich, I don't know you or if you are actually an attorney, so I'm hesitant to continue this conversation."

"I understand your concern. Let me explain the reason we need to contact Stephanie Kruger."

"Please."

"During her time with Hallmark, Inc. several lawsuits were filed against the company for discrimination. Ms. Kruger was named in these suits. I wanted to let her know those cases have been dismissed by an appellate court in Washington."

Linda smiled. Now she knew the call was bogus.

"I see. I'm not comfortable giving you any contact information, Mr. Malkovich. I would prefer you give me your number and I will have her call you."

The call ended without any additional comment from the attorney. Smiling, Linda Benton dialed her sister's cell phone number.

———

STEPHANIE KRUGER SMILED when she glanced at the caller ID. A call from her sister was always a welcome reprieve from her day-to-day activities.

"Hi, sis."

"Steph, where are you?"

Frowning, Stephanie hesitated for just a few moments.

"On my way to pick up Mikey at daycare. Why?"

"Have you had any strange calls recently?"

"No, why?"

"I just got a weird one. Someone in Washington is trying to contact you."

"What did they want?"

"Your contact information. When I offered to give you his phone number, he hung up."

"Huh."

"You sound like Sean."

"He can rub off on you. Tell me more about the call."

"He mentioned the lawsuit you were in years ago and told me he needed to tell you it was dismissed in an appeals court in Washington."

Stephanie frowned again. "That was settled—like seven years ago. Do you think it was a scam?"

"I would say so. Kind of worries me how he found me."

"Let me talk to Sean and I'll call you back later. Okay?"

"That would make me feel better."

———

KRUGER LISTENED on the speaker of Stephanie's cell phone as Linda Benton summarized the phone call from Washington. He remained quiet until she completed her narrative.

"First, thank you for not responding to his questions, Linda. It was a fishing expedition. Someone is trying to locate us."

He heard a gasp, then silence for a few moments. "Why?" Linda asked.

Ignoring the question, Kruger said, "Call the security company you and David use and alert them about the call."

"You're scaring me, Sean. Should we be worried?"

"Maybe. Give me the phone number from your caller ID. I have a friend who can trace it."

She did and afterward asked, "What should we do now, Sean?"

"At this point, nothing. Let me see what I can find out. I'm sure it was nothing but I want to make sure. Okay?"

"Okay. I called David. He wants to talk to you when he gets home."

"Just have him call."

"Okay, thanks, Sean."

The call ended and Kruger took a deep breath. Stephanie stared at him with her arms crossed over her chest. "I've seen that look before. You're worried."

With a half-smile, he nodded. "Too many related incidents for them to be a coincidence. I need to get that phone number to JR and let him do his magic. Let's hope I'm being paranoid."

She only nodded.

"IT'S a cell phone belonging to a D.C. attorney named Peter Yanovich. His website indicates he specializes in real estate law and merger and acquisitions negotiation."

"Huh."

"Born in Alaska, he moved to D.C. after getting his law degree and has been there ever since."

"His name sounds Russian."

"It is. His parents immigrated back in the early sixties during all the Cuban missile crisis nonsense. They settled in Alaska and became citizens in 1975. The son was born a year later."

"JR, can you tie him to Orlov in anyway?"

The computer hacker grinned and nodded. "He's the M&A attorney for one of Orlov's banks."

"Damn." Kruger paused and rubbed his chin. "How could he have found Steph's sister?"

"Don't know, but I would guess something on social media. Plus, as an attorney doing real estate, I'm sure he knows how to search county property tax data."

"Then he can find Steph and me."

"He would have to know where to look first. Lots of counties to search, Sean."

"I'm not going to assume he isn't looking."

"Wise."

They were both sitting in the conference room on the second floor of JR's building. Kruger stood and started pacing. After several silent laps, Kruger stopped, tilted his head to the side and asked, "How much more information can you find on Yanovich?"

"First pass was cursory. Social media, Better Business Reports, his website, American Bar Association, etc. I'm sure there's more out there."

"Find it. Then I'm going to have a few FBI agents pay him a visit."

TRACY ADKINS LOOKED up from her computer. Brenda Kozlow stood at the entrance to her cubicle with a vanilla-colored file folder in her hands. Tracy smiled and greeted her, "Good afternoon, Brenda."

"Hi, Tracy. I have the background you wanted." She handed the folder to Adkins.

"Thank you." She placed the folder on her desk and directed her attention back to the story she needed to finish before deadline.

Brenda remained standing, trying to regain Tracy's attention. Finally, Adkins looked up again. "Is there something else,

Brenda? I'm on deadline."

"I know, I'm sorry to bother you, but would you have a few moments after you're done?"

"Sure, come back after five, I'll be here."

The afternoon passed slowly, but Brenda appeared at Tracy's cubicle promptly at 5.

"What can I help you with, Brenda?"

The researcher smiled and sat in the lone chair on the opposite side of Tracy's desk. "You know FBI Agent Sean Kruger, don't you?"

Adkins nodded.

"A friend of mine is working on a book about the terrorist attack on the Bud Walton Arena four years ago."

"Really, how interesting."

"Yes, it is. He wants to pursue it from the perspective of the FBI. So, he's interested in interviewing Agent Kruger, but can't seem to find any current information about him. Do you know how to contact him?"

Adkins raised an eyebrow. "What's his name?"

"His name is Peter Yanovich; he's an attorney. We've been seeing each other for about a year now. It's kind of exciting, our relationship has progressed to the point he told me about his interest in writing a book. I'd like to help him if I can. Do you think Agent Kruger would grant him an interview?"

Blinking several times, Adkins did not respond immediately. "I don't know, Brenda. He's a very private individual and, as far as I know, never granted an interview about the incident. Trust me, I've tried. But I can ask him."

Brenda Kozlov stood, a big smile on her face. "Thank you, Tracy. I really appreciate it."

Adkins pulled up Google and performed several searches on her computer after the young woman left. Frowning at what she read, she waited almost ten minutes before shutting off her computer. She gathered her things and left the cubicle. Once in her car, she scrolled through her contact list on her cell phone, found the number she was looking for and pressed send. The call was answered immediately.

"Kruger."

"Sean, it's Tracy. How many Russians have you pissed off recently?"

"Depends, why do you ask?"

"Ever hear of an attorney named Peter Yanovich?"

The call went silent.

"I will take your silence as a yes."

"What about him?"

"He's supposedly writing a book about the incident in Fayetteville and wants to interview you."

"Interesting. How did you come to know this bit of information, Tracy?"

"Apparently, one of our researchers is dating him and he's using her to get information about you. Did you know he has a business connection to Dmitri Orlov?"

"You're just full of good news today, Tracy."

"What do you want me to do?"

"Don't know. Let me think about it."

"Do you want me to tell Ryan?"

"Yeah. Maybe Ryan needs to have a little chat with Mr. Yanovich. Tell him I'll call him tonight."

Chapter Twenty-Four

NOW IN HIS third week as President of the United States, Roy Griffin stepped off the treadmill in the White House gym and used a towel to wipe the sweat running down his face. Running five miles inside was unlike running five miles outside.

Outside you could smell nature, see small creatures scurry out of your way, wipe rain out of your eyes, watch the sunrise, the list was endless. Inside all he could do was monitor the various news feeds on the TV monitor placed in the gym, or read briefing papers. Boring. Unlike Bill Clinton, the Secret Service would not allow him to run on the streets anymore. Too many crazies with an agenda only they knew about.

As he walked toward the door leading to the resident's quarters, a familiar figure joined him as he walked.

"Good morning, Joseph."

"Good morning, Mr. President."

"You're here awfully early."

"First day back in Washington, sir. I wanted to get an early start."

Grinning, Griffin glanced at his new National Security

Advisor. "Bullshit, Joseph. Don't start lying to me this early in your tenure."

Joseph Kincaid laughed. "What I really wanted to do was to talk to you before it got too hectic around here. I have an update on what Sean Kruger has learned about the problem you asked him to check out."

Both men stopped walking. Griffin frowned, "Is it bad?"

Nodding, Joseph said in a voice barely above a whisper, "I wouldn't use the word bad, but it's not good either."

"Let's go to my private study and we can discuss it there."

———

IMMEDIATELY OFF THE Oval Office is a short hallway containing the president's private lavatory and kitchenette. Across from those two rooms is a small room sometimes used as the president's personal study. Griffin jumped at the opportunity to have a smaller, more intimate place to read and prepare for the day. It also provided a location for private discussions with his staff.

The room had changed very little since the Blair administration. Griffin was told the previous occupant of the Oval Office distained the room due to its size and lack of splendor. Griffin held the opposite opinion; the room was perfect. He sat in the leather office chair situated in front of a small writing desk and turned to look at Joseph, who sat in one of the two cushioned chairs in the room.

"Okay, what did Sean find out?"

"He met with Kyle Sandifer in Arkansas."

Griffin raised an eyebrow. "Really?"

Joseph nodded. "Apparently the visit from Boris Volkov shook him up enough that he left Washington, D.C. and drove across the country."

"He drove?"

Another nod. "From what Sandifer told Sean, Orlov bought the firm for two reasons. First, he wanted the firm's legal files to learn which government figures had legal issues, personal or financial. Second, and this is the part that disturbed Sean the most, they were going to use those files and the premise of the lobbying function of the law firm to basically blackmail those individuals. How they planned to do it, Sandifer was not told."

The new president pursed his lips and stared out one of the two windows in the room. Finally, after several moments, Griffin said, "Is Mr. Sandifer safe?"

"Yes, he's in Dallas now with his family. Sandifer has a lot of connections with security firms and they are being watched around the clock."

"Good."

"Sean has one of Orlov's assistants in custody."

Returning his attention to Joseph, Griffin smiled. "Does Orlov know this?"

"We don't think so. Sean has him detained on a John Doe warrant. If Orlov has someone make an inquiry, the State Department will not have a record of anyone by that name being held."

Griffin's eyes danced with merriment. "Sean continues to surprise me with his unique approach."

"Yes, he is resourceful." Joseph kept his expression neutral, but felt pride in his recruitment of Kruger over two decades ago. "There's another complication, sir."

The president sighed. "Tell me."

"One of Orlov's attorneys here in the states is trying to locate Sean. Why, we can only guess, but so far, we think he hasn't been successful."

"Joseph, I don't like where this is going. Who is it?"

"An American citizen with Russian parents. He does

mergers and acquisitions for two of Orlov's banks here in the states."

Griffin smiled. "Has he done any lobbying for those banks?"

Joseph paused. Realizing what Griffin was thinking, he too smiled. "Don't know. But it would be interesting to find out."

"Yes, very interesting."

"I do want to caution you about one thing."

"What's that, Joseph?"

"As I mentioned earlier, Sean has one of Orlov's associates detained. If we detain another one, the man might lash out like a trapped animal."

Another smile graced Griffin's lips. "And do what?"

Joseph shook his head. "Not sure. Russians can be unpredictable...at least the ones I've dealt with over the years were. Add that to the fact Orlov and the Russian president are very close."

The smile disappeared as Griffin's eyes grew narrow. "How close?"

"They were both KGB foreign intelligence officers and rose to the rank of Lieutenant Colonel. Both resigned in 1991. One went into politics and Orlov into banking. The NSA believes they speak regularly to each other."

Griffin was quiet as he looked over Joseph's shoulder through one of the windows. "I've only spoken to the man once. Should I discuss this with him?"

"No, not yet, sir. We need Sean to gather more evidence about who's pulling Orlov's strings. If we find evidence the Kremlin is behind it, you will have the facts to back you up."

"When did Russians believe facts?"

A wry smile appeared on Joseph's face. "As a rule, never."

———

RYAN CLARK PRESSED his cell phone to his ear after accepting the call.

"Yeah, I just got off the phone with Sean. He's flying in this afternoon."

Joseph sat at his new desk in his new office in the West Wing of the White House. The atmosphere of his position and surroundings would intimidate most men, but Joseph took it in stride. Having survived some of the world's most dangerous hot spots during his CIA career, this was a walk in the park.

"The DOJ is preparing a warrant for the arrest of Peter Yanovich and they want you to serve it."

Chuckling, Clark said. "That was fast. What's he done?"

"He's doing work for a couple of banks Dmitri Orlov owns and is not registered as a foreign agent."

"Joseph, that isn't a crime if he's working as an attorney."

"No, but he did lobby a few members of congress to get several M&A deals approved for the banks."

"Whoops."

"Yes, our Mr. Yanovich may not realize he has violated the Foreign Agents Registration Act of 1938." Joseph paused briefly. "There's another concern."

"Which is?"

"We need to know if Yanovich was involved in the deaths of Jolene Sanders and Keira Pennington."

"Give me the details and I'll serve the warrant."

———

THE GRAY CHEVROLET MALIBU parked in an empty slot twenty feet from the entrance to Peter Yanovich's office. Ryan Clark and FBI Special Agent Samantha Warren exited the car and walked purposely toward the office door. The one-story building containing the attorney's office occupied the north side of the multi-use complex. Utilizing a spartan motif, each building provided low-cost office space for businesses ranging from dentists and lawyers to insurance agents.

Clark held the door as Warren walked in. A reception desk occupied the space immediately in front of the door where a young woman, barely out of her teens, sat. She looked up from the computer screen in front of her and asked, "Good afternoon, how can we help you?"

Smiling, Clark held his FBI credentials so the receptionist could see. "I'm Special Agent Ryan Clark and this," he nodded toward his partner, "is Special Agent Samantha Warren. We need to speak to Peter Yanovich immediately."

"Do you have an appointment?"

"No."

The receptionist blinked several times, sighed, reached for a phone and muttered, "Great, I was just starting to like this job."

She punched in two numbers and waited.

"Peter, there are two FBI agents here to see you." She was silent. "No, they didn't say." More silence. "Okay, I'll tell them."

After replacing the phone handle in its receptacle, she looked up. "He'll be right out."

One minute later, a slender man of average height opened the door behind the receptionist. He wore a white oxford shirt, open at the collar, with its sleeves rolled up to his elbows and a loosened tie. His dark brown hair appeared professionally styled and black frame glasses sat on a prominent nose in front of dark eyes that glared at the two FBI agents.

"What's this about?"

"Peter Yanovich?" Clark held his credentials so the attorney could see them.

"Yes."

"I am Special Agent Clark and this is Special Agent

Warren. We need to ask you a few questions. Is there somewhere private we can talk?"

Yanovich blinked several times, glanced at the receptionist and then back at Clark. He nodded and motioned for them to follow him.

Once they were in his office and the door closed, Clark said, "Mr. Yanovich, are you aware you are in violation of the Foreign Agent Registration Act?"

A frown was Yanovich's only reaction. Finally, after several moments of silence, he smiled. "You're kidding me, right?"

"No, sir," Warren said. "We're not kidding, this is very serious."

The attorney lost his smile and looked at Warren, then at Clark. "I'm a real estate attorney. How can that violate the Foreign Agent Registration law?"

Clark tilted his head slightly. "Are you denying you do Merger and Acquisition work for PC National and United Mutual Banks here in D.C.?"

Yanovich was silent.

Reading from the warrant she held in her hand, Warren said, "On October 13 of last year, did you meet with five senators serving on the Senate Subcommittee on Antitrust, Competition Policy and Consumer Rights?"

Without thinking, Yanovich nodded, "Yes."

Warren continued, "In this meeting, did you offer to contribute to each senator's PAC if they approved the merger of Graystone Pharmaceutical and Pharma Pro? A merger being financed by PC National."

Suddenly realizing the direction her questioning was headed, Yanovich did not respond.

"Answer the question, Peter." Clark stood next to Warren, his arms crossed over his chest.

"I want my attorney present before I answer any additional questions."

Clark smiled. "That is your right, Mr. Yanovich." He paused for a moment. "In addition to the violation of the Foreign Agents Act, you are a person of interest in the deaths of Jolene Sanders and Keira Pennington."

The attorney's eyes grew wide and he started to stammer, "A person of interest? Where the hell did that come from?"

Clark narrowed his eyes. "Since you have requested an attorney, you can discuss that charge with him." He turned to his fellow agent to say, "Agent Warren, please read Mr. Yanovich his rights and place him under arrest."

Chapter Twenty-Five

THE GLASS of house burgundy sat forgotten in front of Dmitri Orlov as he held his cell phone to his ear. Seated at his regular table in the bistro on the ground floor of his office building, a plate of bruschetta with tomatoes sat untouched as he listened to the caller. With every revelation from the person on the other end of the call, the tint of crimson on Orlov's face deepened.

Finally, the caller ceased talking. Orlov remained silent, aware of the public nature of his surroundings. After several moments, he replied in his native Russian, his voice barely controlled. "I see."

Taking a few more moments to squelch his anger, he took a deep breath. "Has he posted bail?"

Again, silence as he listened. "Please arrange for his release as soon as possible. Have him call me at his first opportunity."

The call ended and Orlov stared at his untouched wine. Without thinking, he raised it to his lips and emptied the glass. Standing, he reached into his pocket and withdrew his wallet. He placed a ten and a twenty Euro note on the table and walked back to the entrance to his third-floor office suite.

Sergey Brutka witnessed the entire episode from a table in the center of the bistro. Far enough away to remain unseen by Orlov, but close enough to hear the Russian's responses to the phone call. Utilizing his understanding of the Russian language, he assumed his American colleagues arrested one of Orlov's flunkies in the States.

Earlier when Orlov accepted the phone call, unbeknownst to him, Brutka sent a text message to a phone number given to him by Joseph Kincaid. The message was short: *O on phone C.* The message notified a specific individual in the enormous NSA complex to concentrate on a recently discovered phone number owned by the Russian.

After receiving the text message, the technician typed rapidly on a keyboard, setting in motion a complex series of events designed to pluck Dmitri Orlov's phone call out of the ether and preserve it for eternity within the NSA's massive Utah Data Center.

Speech-to-text software converted, in real-time, the conversation into bits and bytes then to Cyrillic symbols on a computer screen. When the conversation was complete, the young lady entered the file into a Russian-to-English translation program. Once this was done, she checked the original Russian against the translation. Being fluent in both languages, she made a few editorial notes to clarify the translation and saved the file. The English version of the conversation then traveled, via encrypted email, to a computer on the National Security Advisor's desk at the White House. The individual currently assigned to this position by the new President opened the email and read the transcribed conversation. When he finished, a small smile appeared.

All of this occurred before Orlov could sit down at his desk on the third floor.

———

YANOVICH SAT in a chair in the interrogation room, his orange jumpsuit ill-fitting and his hands restrained. As Kruger watched on the observation monitor, he noticed a trickle of sweat roll down the prisoner's forehead.

With a slight grin, he turned to the man standing next to him. "Have them turn up the thermostat a few more degrees."

Ryan Clark nodded and left Kruger's side to accomplish his assignment. Fifteen minutes later, they both entered the room. The odor of male sweat assaulted their nostrils. Kruger waved the air.

"Whew, it's kind of hot in here, Peter."

Yanovich stared at him, his forehead bathed in streams of water rolling toward his eyes. He stopped his constant blinking to stare at Kruger. "Who are you?"

"The man you've been wanting to interview for a so-called book you never intend to write."

"I want my lawyer."

"He'll be here shortly." Kruger paused and sat down across the table. "But not right now."

"I'm not answering any questions."

"That's a wise decision. However, I won't be asking any. I'm here more as a courtesy."

Yanovich blinked several times and shook his head. The sweat sprayed in all directions. He returned his stare to Kruger. "How considerate."

"Yes, I think so. We've filed several complaints against you in federal court. First, a violation of the Foreign Agents Registration Act and secondly, as a person of interest in the deaths of Keira Pennington and Jolene Sanders."

His blinking ceased as he stared at Kruger. "You're kidding me."

"No, I'm not. We have several witnesses that identify you as the man who walked up to the park bench and removed Ms. Pennington's purse."

The attorney started to say something, but caught himself. Instead, he smiled. "Nice try, Agent. I was in court that day."

"Yes, you were," Kruger nodded. "But not when the murder occurred. Two men approached the bench. The first one pointed an object at the two women and walked off. You've been identified as the second man."

Yanovich shook his head.

"Because of this identification, we were able to get a search warrant for your office and apartment."

The prisoner sat straighter in his chair and bit his lower lip. He narrowed his eyes, "There was nothing to find, Agent. I wasn't there."

A small smile appeared on Kruger's lips. "Right."

He stood and walked toward the door. Clark opened it and walked out first, but Kruger turned just before exiting.

"We've turned the air-conditioning up, so it will be nice and cool in here before your attorney arrives. He'll be curious about why you're sweating. He'll probably ask me and I'll tell him."

"Tell him what? You put me in a sauna?"

"No," Kruger smiled. "You must be nervous about something."

With this comment, he left the room and closed the door.

WHEN KRUGER CAUGHT up with Clark in the hallway, he saw a report in his hand.

"What's that?"

With a smile, Clark handed the file to his mentor. "Third paragraph. Chemical analysis of a pair of shoes found in Yanovich's closet. Both soles had residue left over from decomposed A-232."

Kruger read the paragraph, smiled and handed the papers

back. "Apparently our Mr. Yanovich isn't as smart as I first thought. He should have thrown the shoes away. Was that the only article with residue?"

Clark nodded.

"Okay, let's do this by the book. Charge him as an accessory in the deaths of Jolene Sanders and Keira Pennington."

"A good defense attorney will have a hundred reasons why that's possible."

Putting his hand on Clarks shoulder, Kruger smiled and nodded. "I'm counting on it. Yanovich isn't the fish I want. I want Orlov. This connects Orlov, however slim, to the deaths of the two women. All we have to do is to make that connection stronger. Once Yanovich is released on bail, I don't want him to be able to sneeze without us knowing it."

"How're we going to do that?"

"Your team and one of mine. JR."

A sly smile appeared on Clark's lips.

———

SERGEY BRUTKA REMAINED at his seat in the small bistro after Orlov's sudden departure. He sipped on his espresso, keeping an occasional eye on a young female on the opposite side of the restaurant. Brutka's age and self-awareness gave him the ability to know his allure to the opposite sex faded years ago, especially to younger women. Now this particular woman kept an unconcealed nonchalant attempt to hide her interest in his presence. He suspected her duties included watching for anyone paying too much attention to Orlov.

Using the ruse of a phone call, Brutka snapped a picture of the woman and sent it to a colleague at the headquarters of Interpol in Lyon, France. It would be interesting to see who she was. Now it became a waiting game to see who would leave the bistro first.

Forty-five minutes into his vigil, a text message arrived on his cell phone identifying his watcher. With a calm demeanor, he rose from his seat and strolled toward the restroom area of the bistro. Encountering his waiter on the way, he stopped him and said in his Ukrainian accented French, "Monsieur, thank you for your service today." He handed the man a fifty Euro note for a fifteen-Euro meal and continued. "A woman whom I do not wish to converse with, if you know what I mean, has just arrived. Is there a back entrance I can leave by?"

The waiter looked at the money, smiled and whispered. "Of course, monsieur. Just go through the kitchen; there is a loading dock you can use."

"Merci."

A few minutes later, Brutka was in a position to observe the front of the bistro without being seen. He could see the woman checking her phone occasionally and looking around the restaurant. She made a call, listened for a few moments, dropped money on the table, stood and left the establishment. Brutka was pleased to see his suspicions were correct as she headed straight for the door on the sidewalk leading to Orlov's offices.

He extracted his cell phone.

"THE OFFICE IS CLOSED?" Sean Kruger looked up from the report in front of him.

Clark nodded. "All calls go to a voicemail message announcing the office was closed until further notice."

"Are any of the associates talking?"

"No. The ones we've interviewed were as surprised as we were at the sudden closing. No one seems to have been notified."

"When did it close?" Kruger took his reading glasses off

and looked around the conference table. "Please don't tell me last Friday."

Another nod from Clark. "When everyone left last Friday, it was business as usual. Monday, the locks had been changed, the lights are out and nobody's home."

"Did anybody check with the utility company?"

FBI agent Samantha Warren nodded. She was a seasoned agent with over twenty years of experience and Ryan Clark's current partner. In her mid-forties, short hair, stocky build and a no-nonsense attitude, Kruger knew her as an exemplary member of the FBI.

"Utility company did not receive a discontinuation of service notice," she said. "As far as they know, nothing changed from Friday to Monday. I spoke to the baristas at the Starbucks across the street. Several of them saw a U-Haul there early Saturday morning and a lock company arrived after the truck left. Most didn't really pay much attention."

"Did any of them remember the name of the locksmith?"

Warren shook her head. "Wish we could've been that lucky."

"Alright," Kruger frowned, "we will assume the files are gone."

Chapter Twenty-Six

U.S. HOUSE OF REPRESENTATIVE member Anthony "Tony" Holt served at the discretion of the voters in the 5th District of Tennessee. Born and raised in Nashville, as a teenager, he envisioned a career as a session guitarist in the various recording studios around the city. Unfortunately, talent played a major part in the pursuit of such an occupation. Holt's musical talents were mediocre, at best, so this career path never materialized.

But he did have the talent to make people like him and believe in his honesty and integrity.

He possessed neither.

First elected to Congress in 2006, following the death of the previous representative, Holt maintained a high profile in Congress. Using his talent to make people believe in him, he successfully maneuvered the halls of Congress, making deals for his district and making sure key donors in his home district kept the money flowing into his campaign coffers. His ambitions were higher than just being in the House of Representatives.

Standing six foot, he kept a lean body by exercising daily in the House gym. With a head of dark brown hair, a bright smile, an ex-cheerleader wife and two athletic boys in high school, he presented himself as the all-American candidate. The voters rewarded him by returning him to Congress every two years. With twelve years in Congress and a growing seniority, he now chaired the House Permanent Select Committee on Intelligence, a high-profile position he relished and would use for national exposure.

Unknown to his colleagues, wife and voters back home, Holt kept a rather embarrassing episode of his life well hidden. One night, during his second campaign for re-election, he consumed more beers than he could remember. As the crowd thinned, one of his young female volunteers caught his eye. After offering to buy her a late dinner, he raped her in the back of his car. With the help of Kyle Sandifer, the young woman agreed to keep quiet, take the money offered and move to Fayetteville, Arkansas, where her tuition at the University of Arkansas would be paid in full.

So far, the episode remained hidden from the public eye.

Holt returned to his office in the Cannon House Office Building to find a large man waiting in the reception area. His assistant was nowhere to be seen. Startled and somewhat annoyed he looked at the man and asked, "Can I help you?"

The man smiled, held up an iPad for Holt to see and said, "We need to talk in private."

The accent was European, but Holt could not identify the country. "Do you have an appointment?"

Another smile and the stranger pointed to the iPad again. "What is on here gives me the appointment. Your office?"

Frowning and wishing to keep attention away from the encounter, Holt walked toward the door and followed him inside. Once the office door was closed, he turned to the man and demanded, "Now, care to tell me what this is all about?"

The large man activated the iPad and handed it to Holt.

As he read the screen, his eyes grew wider. After two pages, he stopped and glared at his guest. "Where the hell did you get this?"

"Kyle Sandifer was gracious enough to share his files with us. We need a little help."

Not fully understanding the meaning, Holt shook his head. "I'm not following you. What kind of help?"

"We need to know where FBI Agent Sean Kruger lives."

"Now how and why would I know that?"

"You are chairman of the committee that oversees the FBI, correct?"

Nodding his head, Holt narrowed his eyes.

"That doesn't mean I know where the agents live."

"No, but you have the power to find out. Find out."

"And why would I do that?"

Boris Volkov proceeded to explain.

Chapter Twenty-Seven

THE ASSASSIN EXITED the American Airline jet and walked through the terminal of the Springfield-Branson National Airport, pulling a small wheeled carry-on bag through the terminal. Dressed similarly to other male passengers on the flight, he was as invisible as all the other travelers in the airport. He did not speak to anyone on his trek toward the rental car kiosks, and when he arrived, he spoke with a non-descript American accent. No one paid attention to his presence and no one would remember he passed through the facility.

Two hours later, after checking into a hotel on the south side of town under a false name, the assassin drove down a sleepy neighborhood street containing the house owned by Sean and Stephanie Kruger. He noticed a few cars parked on the street, lawn services attending to yards, stay-at-home moms' power-walking strollers containing small infants, and squirrels dashing across the street in front of his car.

One house in particular drew his attention. It sat on the north side of the street with a large oak tree in front of a window on the west side. According to his source, this was the

FBI agent's residence. He parked the car in front and looked at the structure. He saw no signs of any being home. He watched an elderly couple approaching his vehicle on the sidewalk. He stepped out as they grew near and waved. "Hi," he said cheerfully.

The man nodded and the woman smiled. Neither spoke.

"Can you tell me if this is the home of Sean Kruger?"

The couple stopped walking and the man tilted his head to the side. "Maybe, do you know him?"

"I used to work with him. Thought I would say hello."

"They aren't home."

"I see. Are you sure?"

"We have a neighborhood watch website. When one of us is out of town, we alert the neighbors about it. You know, keeping an extra eye on things. Can't be too careful nowadays."

"No, you can't. I appreciate the information. I'll have to catch him later."

The assassin sat back down in the car before the couple could ask any more questions.

As he pulled the car away from the curb, he said to himself, "No, you can't be too careful. Thanks for the info, old man."

The car accelerated through the neighborhood as the driver thought over several options for completing his assigned task.

———

STEPHANIE KRUGER PULLED her Jeep Cherokee into the driveway of her house. Mia Diminski turned to her and said, "I'll just be a moment. I have a few things to get and I'll be right back."

"I won't be long, either. Hope Sean and JR don't find out we snuck back to the houses for a few moments."

Mia chuckled. "How would they find out if neither of us say anything?"

Both women smiled and proceeded inside their respective homes.

———

ON THE THIRD day of watching Kruger's home from inside a large pickup truck parked two houses west, the assassin's patience paid off. Through binoculars, he identified Stephanie Kruger as she walked into the now-open garage. His plan had worked better than he imagined. After appropriating a large F-250 pickup from a temporarily closed plumbing company, the assassin was able to park in the neighborhood without attracting too much attention.

When the Jeep Cherokee backed out of the driveway, the assassin started the vehicle and slowly pulled away from the curb.

———

MIA WATCHED the highway ahead as Stephanie drove back toward the turnoff to Joseph's property in Christian County. She took a deep breath and sighed.

"We've been at Joseph's place a week, now. How much longer do we have to stay?"

"I don't know. While I love the view and the solitude, I really need to get back to the house. Driving to and from the university from this far out is getting old."

"I know. JR won't even let me go into the office until he thinks it's safer. We've had a few harsh words about it, but his logic makes sense."

"Yes, I hate it when they're right."

Both women chuckled.

Mia turned to look at Stephanie as she said, "I haven't told you this yet, but JR and I are expecting another child."

Stephanie smiled and shot a quick glance at her friend before returning her eyes to the highway. "That's wonderful. When?"

"Sometime in July. The doctor thinks about the third week."

Stephanie was about to look at her friend again when she noticed something in her rearview mirror.

"Uh-oh," she murmured.

Mia frowned. "What?"

"Truck coming up behind us extremely fast. He's about to pass, but it's going to be close. Hang on, Mia, this is…"

As the truck flashed past, it appeared to be less than a yard from Stephanie's door. Stephanie slammed on the brakes just as the truck inched toward them. The Jeep slowed enough that instead of a full broadside collision, the large pick-up clipped the front quarter panel of the SUV. As the Jeep went into a spin, the rear end collided with the beginning section of a guardrail on the right side of the highway.

KRUGER GLANCED at the caller ID on his phone. With a slight smile, he accepted the call. His oldest son rarely called unless he needed something.

"Hey, Brian. How are you?"

"Dad, Mom's been in an accident. She's alive, but she's hurt. How fast can you get home?"

Kruger blinked rapidly for several quiet moments. He pushed his worst fears down and took a deep breath.

"How bad is she, Brian?"

"The doctor told me she has several broken ribs, a punctured lung, some internal injuries and possibly a concussion.

Nothing life threatening, but she's in intensive care. And, Dad..."

"Yeah."

"Mia was with her in the car."

"Oh dear God, please tell me she's okay."

"Wish I could. She's hurt worse than Mom."

"Is JR there?"

"Yes, he was here when Michelle and I arrived."

"Have you seen your mom?"

"Briefly."

"Which hospital?"

"Mercy."

"Okay." Kruger paused as he collected his thoughts. "I'll see if I can catch the first flight out of Reagan. What happened? Do you know?"

"That's the scary part, Dad. She was run off the road by a hit-and-run driver."

Closing his eyes, Kruger brought his free hand up to cover them. After a deep breath, he let it out slowly. "Where were they?"

"Southbound on 65."

Kruger immediately knew what that meant—they were heading back to Joseph's.

"Do you know any other details?"

"Not really. All I know is what drivers behind them told the Highway Patrol. A large pickup truck clipped Mom's Jeep in the front and spun it around. Cops and EMTs were there within five minutes. The EMT I spoke to told me if the Jeep had hit the end of the guardrail head on, Mom and Mia probably would not have survived."

Silence was Kruger's response. Finally, after a few moments he said, "Brian, I want you to listen to me. Do not, under any circumstance, leave the hospital until I get there."

"Okay, but why?"

"That was not a hit-and-run. It was done on purpose. Someone tried to kill Stephanie. I'll be home as quickly as I can find a flight. I'll call you when I know more."

His next call was to Joseph.

———

JOSEPH WAS good on his word to find Kruger a flight home. An hour after taking the call from his son, Kruger sat in the passenger seat of a Gulfstream G280 on the tarmac of Reagan National Airport. The private jet, owned by a personal friend of Joseph Kincaid, would have him on the ground in Springfield in under two hours. As the plane taxied toward the runway, he made another call on his cell phone.

"Knoll."

"Sandy, it's Sean."

"I just heard. What can I do to help?"

"Where are you?"

"Heading toward the hospital."

"Where's Jimmie?"

"Babysitting. He's not happy about it, but he drew the short straw."

"Good," Kruger smiled." Someone is here, Sandy. Somehow they found out where I live."

Knoll was quiet for a few moments. "How?"

"I don't know. Where are your boys?"

"Pete's stationed at Bragg and Bobby's in the middle of Seal training."

"Good, they're safe. What about your wife?"

"I just spoke to her. She's fine."

"Brian and Michelle are at the hospital. I've told them to stay put until I get there," he glanced at this watch, "which should be about two and a half hours from now."

"I'll see you there."

KRUGER HELD his wife's hand as he surveyed the various tubes and wires attached to her body. Her closed eyes worried him. Turning his attention to the heart and respiration monitor, both measures appeared normal. He glanced at her blood pressure. A little low, but considering the medication in the IV, understandable.

Having been at her bedside for forty-five minutes, he watched as her swollen eyes fluttered and slowly opened. As she focused on him, she smiled. "Heck of a way to get you home, huh?"

Leaning over, he kissed her forehead. "Sorry I wasn't here for you."

She shook her head slowly as she whispered, "Nothing you could have done."

"What happened?"

"I don't remember much, just a large truck speeding up behind us."

"You're lucky it wasn't worse."

"No, I'm lucky to have a husband who continues to pound into my head, all the time, to be suspicious of anything unusual. I was ready when he came around. I slammed on the brakes..." Her eyes widened. "Oh, my gawd, how's Mia?"

"She's still in intensive care. She has a broken pelvis and some internal injuries. But I spoke to JR and she will recover."

"Sean, she's pregnant."

A grim smile crossed Kruger lips. He closed his eyes and shook his head slowly.

Stephanie shut her eyes as moisture leaked from the corners. He watched as her body convulsed with a sob. She shook her head slowly and muttered, "Oh—no."

He held her hand until she calmed. "Steph, I'm going to

send in Brian and Michelle. I need to speak to Sandy for a few moments."

She nodded, but did not speak. Releasing her hand, he left the room.

———

THE MALE NURSE pushed the gurney past Stephanie Kruger's room. He watched out of the corner of his eye as the subject of his task exited the room and started talking to a large man standing at parade rest outside. He continued his trek down the hall until he reached the elevator. Looking back down the hall, he smiled. His plan had worked. Simple, really. Put the wife in danger and the husband would show up.

He pushed the gurney into the elevator and continued to watch his quarry as the doors closed.

———

KRUGER NOTICED the male nurse passing the room as he walked up to Sandy Knoll, the moment not registering as important.

"What've you learned, Sandy?"

Sandy Knoll tracked the same nurse with his eyes as the gurney was pushed down the hall. As soon as the man was out of ear-shot, he responded.

"I just spoke to a Greene County deputy who had an update. A truck registered to AAA Plumbing was found abandoned in the parking lot of a Walmart on the southeast side of town. Right rear quarter panel showed evidence of a collision with a vehicle with black paint. They took samples and will let me know if it matches Stephanie's Jeep."

Kruger nodded.

Knoll continued, "The truck was reported stolen by the owner about midday today."

Frowning, Kruger pursed his lips. "The accident occurred this morning."

"Yeah, the owner told deputies he parked the truck behind his shop on Saturday and didn't need it until today. That's when he discovered it missing."

"That's over five days ago. What the hell does that mean?"

"The owner was, uh, indisposed for a few days."

"Drunk?"

With a nod, Knoll answered, "Yeah, DUI and a guest in the Greene County jail."

The FBI agent stared down the hall. "He checks to see who's been arrested, then determines who'd have an appropriate vehicle to use. Pretty smart." He returned his attention to Knoll. "We're dealing with someone who's done this before."

He looked back at the door to Stephanie's room. "He's still here somewhere. This isn't over."

"I would agree."

"Okay, it's time to get Brian, Michelle and the kids to somewhere they can't be found."

"I have somewhere," Knoll smiled.

"Oh, where?"

"We have a place at the Lake of the Ozarks."

Shaking his head, Kruger returned Knoll's smile.

"You are full of surprises sometimes."

The large man shrugged and said, "My wife volunteered to help. She's flying into Springfield and offered to take everyone there."

"That puts her in danger, too, Sandy."

Knoll laughed out loud as he put his hand on Kruger's shoulder. "Sean, she's a retired Marine. She's tougher than I am."

———

KRUGER FOUND his son and daughter-in-law sitting in Stephanie's room. He noticed his wife's eyes appeared closed so he turned to his son, "Is your mom asleep?"

Stephanie answered without opening them, "No, the light was bothering my eyes. I'm awake."

"Good, you need to hear this." He turned to look at his grown son.

Brian Kruger was the spitting image of his father: just over six feet tall, slender and muscled like a swimmer. Currently working as a computer programmer with a local tech company, he wore his dark brown hair longer than current fashion. Where Kruger had crystal blue eyes, Brian's were hazel and changed shades with the prevailing light. The father and son looked more like twins, except for the age difference. Kruger's hair was short, which allowed a growing amount of gray to show at his temples. He also possessed worry lines on his forehead and around his eyes.

Michelle stood five inches shorter than Brian, with a slender body, now featuring the effects of being four months pregnant with their first child. Her long brunette hair and emerald green eyes enhanced her oval face. She was pretty in a subtle way, an honest beauty, not enhanced with make-up. Her smile lit up any room she occupied, displaying a natural confidence in herself.

With as stern a voice as he could muster, Kruger said, "Brian, it's not safe here for you and Michelle. Your first priority is to protect yourselves and your unborn child. Plus, I have to ask a favor."

"Sure, Dad, what?"

"I need you to take your sister and brother plus JR's son, Joey, to a place at the Lake of the Ozarks. Sandy has a condo there, plus his wife is on her way and will help with the kids."

Brian blinked several times, as Michelle held his hand. He looked at her for several moments and returned his attention to his father. "Is it that bad?"

"Yes, I believe it is."

The couple did not respond immediately, but eventually both nodded in agreement.

"I have to find JR and let him know what we have planned. Sandy will be arranging transportation." Smiling and placing a hand on each of their shoulders, he said in a relatively calm voice. "Don't worry. Spend a few days at the lake and try to relax."

"Sure, Dad. Fat chance."

The FBI agent turned and left the room.

Kruger found JR sitting in the waiting room next to the intensive care unit. With his head leaned back in a cushioned chair, he looked asleep, but Kruger knew he wasn't.

"How is she?"

"Improving," JR answered. "They're running some tests right now and told me to wait out here."

Kruger sat in a chair next to him. "We've arranged for the children to spend some time away from here under the careful supervision of an ex-Marine."

A small smile came to JR's lips, but he did not open his eyes. "Sandy's wife?"

"How'd you know?"

"I've known about her for a long time. Looked up her military record once."

"And?"

"Let's put it this way, she probably runs the house with Sandy standing at attention and shouting, 'Yes, ma'am' a lot."

Kruger chuckled, glad for a brief amount of humor.

JR opened his eyes, lifted his head and stared at his friend. "This is now personal, Sean."

Leaning his head back in his chair, Kruger closed his eyes

and nodded. "Yes, it is. But I have to blame myself at this point."

"Why?"

"I didn't anticipate Orlov lashing out this way."

"How'd you think he'd react?"

Taking a deep breath, the FBI agent slowly shook his head. "That's the problem, JR, I didn't think it through. Whoever did this isn't finished. He's still out there, waiting for me to make a mistake."

"Then don't make a mistake."

Smiling, Kruger opened his eyes and focused them on JR. "That's the plan."

Chapter Twenty-Eight

KRUGER ARRANGED with the local police department to be spirited away from the hospital in the back of an ambulance, his Ford Mustang left in plain sight in the hospital parking lot. The ambulance deposited him on the third level of a parking garage in the south side of town next to two identical dark gray GMC Denalis. After thanking the ambulance driver, he exited the vehicle and rushed into the front passenger seat of the closest SUV.

As the ambulance pulled away, Kruger turned to the driver. "Thanks for doing this, Sandy." He turned in his seat and looked at the woman sitting behind him. "I assume you are Linda Knoll?"

She offered her hand and Kruger shook it. Linda Knoll was nothing like Kruger imagined. Brown hair, showing streaks of gray here and there, average height and build, she possessed a round face, tanned like her husband's and eyes betraying innate wisdom and knowledge.

She smiled with a disarming grin, nodded and with a slight Texas drawl, replied, "I am. It's a pleasure to finally meet you, Agent Kruger."

"Please, call me Sean."

Another grin. "Very well, what kind of trouble have you gotten my husband into this time, Sean?"

Feeling a momentary spasm of guilt and concern, he took a quick glance at Sandy Knoll sitting in the driver's seat. The large man displayed a wide grin and a sparkle in his eye. Realizing the situation, he turned his attention back to Linda, relaxed and said, "Oh, nothing too complicated. Just trying to save our country from the grips of suppression and political corruption."

Knoll laughed out loud and his wife chuckled.

"Sandy said you had a good sense of humor when you chose to show it." Her smile disappeared. "Seriously, how can I help?"

Kruger explained.

———

JIMMIE GIBBS WATCHED from the front porch as two GMC Denalis parked, one behind the other, in the circle drive of Joseph Kincaid's Christian County home. The dark tinted windows hid from outside observation any passengers inside.

Alexia Montreal stood next to him, her hand on his back displaying, in full view, the growing affection each felt for the other. A woman Gibbs immediately recognized stepped out of the driver's side of the rear Denali and waved to him. He smiled and waved back. Turning to Alexia, he said, "That's Sandy's wife, Linda. She's an amazing woman. I've spent a lot of time at their house over the past few years. She's kind of turned into a substitute mom to me."

He paused as he realized what he had said.

Alexia placed her head on his shoulder. "You're lucky. Those are hard to find."

Gibbs nodded and briefly wondered if their growing feelings for each other would lead anywhere. Those thoughts did not last long as Sandy Knoll and Sean Kruger exited the front Denali. With a grim smile, he said, "Babysitting's over. Time to go to work."

Linda entered the house, followed by Sandy and Kruger.

Kristin Kruger ran to her father and he scooped her up in a big hug. "Where's your brother, Kristin?"

She pointed toward the back of the house. "Playing with Joey. I was babysitting."

Kruger gave her a smile. "You're neglecting your duties, aren't you?"

She frowned and shook her head. "No, I'm with you." He squeezed her tighter. She laughed and buried her head on his shoulder. She looked up and frowned, "Where's Mommy?"

Not sure how to explain what happened to a five-year-old, he chose not to lie. "Kristin, Mommy's been hurt and has to stay in a hospital for a few days."

Tears welled up in the little girl's eyes. "Can I see her?"

Shaking his head slowly, he looked at his daughter with a sad smile.

"Not right now. You're going to spend a few days with Brian and Michelle until Mommy feels better. Okay?"

Her sad look disappeared and she nodded her head rapidly. He returned his daughter to the floor. "Now, go back and make sure your brother and Joey aren't getting into trouble."

She ran off to the back of the house to find her brother.

While Knoll showed his wife around the massive home, Alexia said, "I'd better go check on the kids."

Once out of earshot, Kruger turned to Gibbs, "Can I speak to you on the back deck?"

The retired Seal nodded and followed Kruger out the sliding glass door in the kitchen.

Gibbs spoke first when they were on the deck. "How're Stephanie and Mia?"

Kruger could see his friend seemed afraid of the answer. "They'll both be okay, but Steph is doing better than Mia."

Gibbs visibly relaxed and took a deep breath, letting it out slowly. "Will Mia be okay?"

Kruger nodded, not taking his eyes off Jimmie. "How's Alexia doing?"

"Pretty good. I think she's been starved for human contact. She hasn't stopped playing with the kids since Sandy left."

Hesitating to ask his next question, Kruger said, "Uh…" He paused for a heartbeat. "How are you and Alexia getting along?"

"You noticed?"

He nodded.

"She's a remarkable woman, Sean."

Kruger gave him a half-smile but remained quiet.

"I don't think she realized how isolated and alone she was until we brought her here."

"Kind of like yourself?"

Gibbs stared at his friend and then slowly nodded, "Yeah, kind of like myself."

"Jimmie, can I offer some advice?"

Gibbs just looked at the FBI agent.

"Be careful. Situational relationships can be… situational."

"I know."

Placing his hand on Gibbs' shoulder, he responded. "Jimmie, just remember, she's been hiding from the world for over a decade."

He nodded, but did not respond.

Kruger blinked several times, his smile gone. "There's someone here who may be working for the Russians. I believe he's the one who ran Stephanie and Mia off the road and he may not be done yet."

"Why?

"He's here for me."

Remaining quiet, Gibbs turned to stare out toward the tree line.

"We're going to send the children to a safer place and then lure him here. I need you to do what you do best."

A half-smile came to the ex-Seal's mouth as he turned toward the FBI agent. "I'll need some equipment."

"Sandy anticipated you would. He ordered them yesterday."

Gibbs smiled and returned his attention to the tree line. "I hate being predictable."

"You're not," Kruger chuckled. "Just professional. There's something else."

Turning, Gibbs lost his smile. "What?"

"As long as Mia is in intensive care, JR won't leave her side. We won't have his assistance for a few days. Do you think Alexia could help us?"

Jimmie Gibbs surprised Kruger with an expression he could only describe as pride.

"I'm sure she would be happy to."

The FBI agent nodded and explained the plan.

THE ASSASSIN FOUND a room in a hotel room across from the hospital parking lot. The eastern window allowed a clear and unobstructed view of the Ford Mustang owned by Sean Kruger. Instead of keeping the car under surveillance in a parked car, which would eventually draw unwanted attention, the hotel room provided an excellent alternative. The one problem the location presented was the time consumed getting to his car to following the Mustang. The solution was a small GPS tracker unit, now hidden in the rear passenger wheel well. This would give him an advantage of following at a distance.

Twenty-four hours after he located the car, the FBI agent remained inside the hospital. The assassin, after several two- and three-hour naps, maintained his vigil on the parked Ford. So far, no one approached it and no one tried to move it.

He settled in for more waiting.

———

GIBBS' pace, as they moved through the tree line behind Joseph's house, reminded Alexia of a casual stroll in a Paris park rather than a purposeful walk. He would stop every ten or fifteen feet and look at the back of the house. Every third or fourth stop, he knelt down and stared for several minutes. Then he would walk further into the thicket, then reemerge.

"What are you doing, Jimmie?"

"Looking for spots that offer the best tactical position for a sniper."

She blinked several times and stared at Gibbs, her mouth open. "You're kidding?"

"No."

"A sniper?"

He nodded. "Sean believes Orlov sent someone to silence him." He looked at her. "The car wreck was not an accident."

"Does he know about this place?"

"We don't see how he could. The plan is to lead him here."

Her eyes grew wide and she covered her mouth with one hand. "Is that not dangerous? What if he is not a sniper? What if he plants bomb?"

Gibbs chuckled. "Rifles are easy to get, bomb material, not so much. Besides, a sniper shot is his best bet for a clean escape."

"What if he does not use the spot you pick?"

"I'm looking for more than one. When I find them, we'll put a 4G Trail Cam with night vision and motion detection near the locations to monitor any movement. We'll also place one at the entrance to the property to watch anyone who drives by. This place is so isolated, any strange vehicles will be suspect."

She was quiet. "How are you going to monitor them?"

"JR is out of commission until Mia gets out of intensive care. We were hoping you could help set it up so all of the cameras can be monitored from one computer screen."

She smiled. "I would love to. How many cameras?"

"After Sandy drops Sean off at the hospital, he'll pick up ten he arranged to be delivered to a FedEx store. My job is to determine where to place them."

"What if you do not pick the right spots?"

Gibbs shrugged. "I've got a little practice finding hides."

Pursing her lips, she tilted her head. "What if you make mistake?"

"Let's hope I don't."

She fell quiet as they continued his search for locations to place the cameras. After ten minutes of watching him, she asked, "How long will you be staying here?"

Without taking his eyes away from his quest, he answered, "About a year. I'm watching the place for Joseph and Mary."

"I know. What then?"

Gibbs smiled and looked at her. "I really like this part of the country. It's not as crowded as California and the cost of living is a lot cheaper. I have some money my father left me. Plus, I get to live here practically rent-free while they're gone so I can save a few more bucks. There are a lot of lakes in this area. I like the water, so I was thinking about finding a place like this, only smaller and closer to a lake. What about you?"

"I have no home at the moment. I do not know where I can go to be safe."

"You can stay here with me until you decide."

Tears filled her eyes as she wiped them with the back of her hand. She stepped closer to him and pinned him against a tree. Their embrace lasted until she stopped sobbing.

Chapter Twenty-Nine

"ARE WE BEING PARANOID, SANDY?"

Knoll kept his eyes on the road as he maneuvered the big SUV through Springfield traffic.

"No, I don't think we are. Too many variables. The pickup that ran Stephanie and Mia off the road was stolen. Stolen from a man in jail at the time. Kind of hard to report a stolen vehicle if you don't know it's missing."

"True."

"Then the truck is abandoned in a crowded parking lot right after the accident."

"Did anyone bother to view the parking lot security camera tapes?"

"SPD did. One of the detectives told me whoever it was knew where the camera blind spots were. There isn't a clear picture of him after he exits the truck."

"I kind of remember someone telling me that when I first got to the hospital after the accident. I just didn't pay much attention to him."

"Well, you had something else on your mind."

"Yeah, I did."

Sandy made a left turn into the north parking lot of the massive Mercy Hospital complex and drove into the circle drive in front of the hospital entrance.

"Your car is on the opposite side of the building. I doubt he has the resources to watch this side and the south side."

"I would agree."

The big man handed him a small object resembling an old cell phone.

Kruger looked at it and asked, "What's this? I've got a phone."

"If someone placed an active GPS tracking unit on your car, that," he pointed at the device, "will tell you. Just turn it on when you start your car. Once you start driving, you'll get a tone every time any kind of tracking unit transmits your position. No tone, no device. My guess is you'll get a tone."

Kruger nodded and opened the door. Before getting out, he turned to Sandy. "How long do you two need to set up?"

"Couple of hours. Jimmie already knows where he wants the cameras."

Kruger nodded. "I'll call you when I head back."

"Got it."

———

WHEN KRUGER RETURNED to his car in the south parking lot, the dimming light in the western sky indicated dusk would soon be night. He sat in the car and stared at the brightly lit hospital in front of him. He took a deep breath and let it out slowly. Moisture welled in his eyes and he wiped it away with the back of his hand. His job had placed Stephanie in danger twice since their marriage.

The first time involved a man hired by a serial killer he was pursuing. She and Kristin were taken from her sister's house in Kansas City, where he thought they would be safe. JR tracked the kidnapper's cell phone when he called to tell Kruger how to get them back. The first incident only scared her, but this time, she was physically hurt. When he started the Mustang and backed out of the parking slot, he muttered under his breath, "You're going to pay for this, Orlov."

Just before exiting the parking lot, he remembered to turn on the small unit given to him by Knoll. As he turned left and merged into traffic heading south, the little unit emitted a low-pitch tone. Kruger smiled, reached for his cell phone and made a call as he drove toward Joseph's place in the country.

Knoll answered. "You heading this way?"

"Yeah, I got a tone."

"Kind of thought you would. We're ready. Things might get interesting tonight."

ALEXIA USED a 40-inch flat screen TV found in one of the upstairs bedrooms as a monitor. She connected it to a laptop Knoll purchased on his way back from the FedEx location. While Gibbs placed the 4G Trail Cams in the locations he picked out, she downloaded the software needed to set up the monitoring system. When Kruger walked into the house, everything was ready.

Knoll pointed to the kitchen table Alexia used as her workstation and said to Kruger, "Everything is in place and all the cameras are online."

"Good."

Gibbs was at the breakfast bar cleaning parts of a Weatherby Mark V CarbonMark rifle with an Armasight Gen 2+ scope attached.

Kruger stared at the rifle. "Whose gun?"

Gibbs smiled and looked up from his task. "Mine."

Knoll chimed in, "Joseph told Jimmie, when he asked him

to stay here, there were tons of deer on his property. Didn't know we would have a predator on it as well."

Alexia looked up from the computer and announced, "A car just drove past the camera located at the entrance."

Kruger walked over and stood behind her.

"Did it stop?" he asked.

"Yes, for a moment, then drove off."

Three minutes later, he watched the car slowly drive past the camera again going the opposite direction. This time the driver side was exposed to the camera. Kruger could see the fuzzy image of a male driver.

"Can you enhance the picture?"

"Not much. Pixel count on these cameras won't allow too much detail, particularly with night vision."

He nodded.

———

THE ASSASSIN DROVE SLOWLY down the dark country lane called Fairview Road, the vehicle's headlights the only illumination. The signal from the tracking device no longer moved and appeared to be about a quarter of a mile to his west. He slowed the car and stopped briefly in front of a narrow turnoff on his right. Without knowing more information about his surroundings, he decided to see where the current road took him. Five hundred yards later, it ended. Doing a K-turn, he retraced his route and slowed to look at the only exit located on this end of the lane.

He remembered passing an exit with numerous restaurants on the highway about ten miles north. It was time to do a little research about the area. Then and only then, he would decide his next move.

Twenty minutes later, sitting in a back booth with his back to the rear wall, he ordered dinner and opened his laptop. The diner offered free WIFI so he pulled up Google Earth and explored the area.

The last path off Fairview Road led to a parcel of land five miles south of Sparta. Once found, he noted it ran to a large house occupying the center of a grassy area surrounded by woods. A circle drive could be observed in front of the home with parked vehicles present at the time the satellite image was taken. Using the distance measuring function of the website, he found the house to be right at fourteen hundred feet from Fairview Road. Exactly where the GPS tracking device indicated the Mustang should be.

He sat back in his seat and studied the area. The land appeared clear for about a hundred feet behind and to the sides of the house. From this point on, trees dominated the western side of the property. A stream labeled Fork Bull Creek lay a hundred yards north. To the south lay more open land until dense trees appeared. Measuring the distance on the website, they lay over five hundred yards away. Not knowing the property lines did not really matter to him. Knowing the topography did. With this information, a plan started to form.

SANDY KNOLL NOTICED a change in Alexia. She smiled more. She wore her hair more stylish, she seemed more conscious of her looks and she even wore a touch of makeup. Her clothes no longer hid her gender and the dark circles under her eyes were gone. As he watched her interact with Jimmie, his original concerns started to dissipate as he saw a change in Jimmie. Not as drastic as Alexia, his changes were subtler. His normally biting sarcasm seemed to have lost some of its edge. And he smiled more.

One characteristic of Jimmie remained unchanged: his intensity about completing an assigned task.

Now, Gibbs looked up from reassembling his rifle. "Sandy, I don't think anything is going to happen until closer to dawn, if then."

Knoll nodded and Jimmie continued, "I'm going to get a few hours' sleep, then be in position around three. Can you watch the camera feeds until then?"

"No problem. Good plan, Jimmie."

Gibbs and Alexia walked toward the back of the house where the stairs to the second-floor bedrooms were located. Kruger had watched the exchange from the kitchen while he finished making a pot of coffee. "What do you think, Sandy?"

"Not sure. Part of me is happy for Jimmie, the other half is scratching my head and worried."

With a half-smile, Kruger nodded.

"I spoke to him about it earlier."

Tilting his head slightly, Knoll's eyebrows shot up. "And?"

"He's aware of our concerns. He doesn't share them, but he's aware of them."

"Good."

Kruger chuckled. "Our Mr. Gibbs is a bright and intelligent individual, Sandy. Like Alexia, he's had a few demons he's had to exorcise over the years."

Remaining quiet, Knoll kept his gaze on Kruger.

"Did you know Jimmie's younger sister was kidnapped and murdered when he was sixteen?"

Knoll's eyes widened and he shook his head.

"I didn't either until Joseph told me. I spoke to him about it a few days ago."

"Didn't know he had a sister. What happened?"

Kruger nodded. "He showed me a picture of her. Beautiful young girl. She had just turned fourteen when she disappeared. Jimmie told me she was a better swimmer than he was at that age."

Knoll's eyebrows rose again. "Damn, Jimmie's still classified as the best swimmer the Seals ever produced."

"Yeah, well, according to him, she was better. His parents were told by all of her swimming coaches she was bound for the Olympics, He told me who some of them were, they were best coaches of that era."

"Huh."

"After she was abducted and later found murdered, it tore his mom and dad apart. The mother died of cancer two years later and his father suffered from severe depression. He later committed suicide. All of this before Jimmie joined the military."

"Did Jimmie tell you how it made him feel?"

Kruger shook his head. "Individuals like Jimmie don't realize how a life-changing event effects them. They bury it deep inside. I don't know this for a fact, but I bet the death of his sister drove him to set all those swimming records with the Seals."

Looking down the hallway toward the stairs, Knoll remained quiet. Finally, he returned his attention to Kruger and asked, "Should I quit worrying about his attraction for Alexia?"

"Yes, Dad, you should."

Knoll chuckled. "Yeah, I do think of him that way, sometimes."

"Don't stop caring about him. Let him explore a relationship. He's never allowed himself to have one until now."

"I thought…"

With a slight smile, Kruger shook his head. "Jimmie told me he hasn't dated much over the years. He concentrated on his military career."

Returning his gaze to the stairs, Knoll just smiled.

Chapter Thirty

BY 3:10 A.M., Jimmie Gibbs occupied his sniper hide on the south side of the house. He faced the western tree line nestled in a tall patch of decorative fountain grass. Dressed in his prized Ghillie Suit, he would be basically invisible once the sun came up. A wireless communication system occupied the left side of his face with an ear-piece and a microphone in front of his lips for communicating with Alexia. She now manned the computer with the camera feeds. The scope attached to his Weatherby possessed night-vision capabilities, allowing him to scan the tree line.

"I'm all set, Alexia. Anything on the cameras?"

"Nothing at this time. Do you think he will show up, Jimmie?"

"Don't know. All we can do is wait."

Knoll and Kruger stood behind her. Kruger stifled a yawn before he said, "How long do we wait in the morning before we pull Jimmie out of there?"

"That's his call. Back when I was recruiting him for Joseph's team, I was told by one of his commanding officers

that during his final series of sniper tests, Gibbs waited three days before taking his shot. Needless to say, he aced the test."

Alexia looked up at Knoll, her eyes filled with worry. "Three days?"

A nod was her answer.

Five minutes later after staring out the back door, Kruger turned to Knoll. "I have an idea. Sandy, come with me. I think I saw something upstairs we might need."

At fifteen minutes after 4 in the morning, Alexia caught a fleeting glimpse of movement in the northern-most camera.

"Jimmie."

"Yeah."

"Movement on camera one."

Moving his night scope in that direction, only trees and brush were visible.

"Nothing on my end. Keep watching."

Five minutes later, a shadowy image appeared briefly in the lens of camera three. Knoll pointed to the image. "There, looks like a man."

Kruger nodded and bent over to examine the video feed. "Possibly."

"Jimmie, something just passed camera three." Alexia enlarged the picture, but the pixel count became compromised.

"Okay." He moved his scope toward the area the camera covered. "I don't see... Wait one." An image in his scope appeared briefly in an area between cameras three and four. The shadowy figure stared toward the house, then disappeared back into the cover of the tree line.

"Alexia, I just saw someone between three and four. Enhance the images on cameras four and five."

"Okay, Jimmie."

Ten minutes elapsed without another glimpse of the figure.

Then it became twenty minutes. Knoll said, "He may have chosen a spot not covered by the cameras."

Kruger nodded, "But we know he's out there."

"Yeah."

Alexia suddenly enlarged the image on camera six. "There."

Kruger watched as the outer limits of the camera's perspective showed a figure moving further out of range. "Tell Jimmie he's between five and six."

She relayed the message.

———

ACCESS to the property came via a dirt path, straddling a fence and wading Fork Bull Creek, a slow-moving stream of water ranging between six and ten inches deep. With a waxing crescent moon in the east and wispy intermittent clouds, he navigated with the aid of night-vision goggles. Wearing camo pants, boots, shirt, watch cap and gloves purchased at a Walmart near the diner, he blended into his surroundings. Carrying his SR-25 rifle, he made his way westward toward the tree line behind the house. Lights were still on in the lower levels on the side facing the trees.

He watched for several minutes, but did not see any movement within the house. As he entered the tree line, he stopped and took stock of the task ahead. The angle where he stood did not offer a straight-in shot. He needed to be more perpendicular to the back of the house.

Several times, he approached the edge of the tree line to check his position. It was not until he found a location allowing him to see a sliding glass door and the interior of the home that he stopped and studied the back of the structure. Satisfied he was where he needed to be, he moved back north to seek a position where he could be further back in the tree line and still have a straight shot into the house. Laying prone, he took his gloves off, unfolded the bi-pod stand on the front side of the rifle's barrel and sighted in on the sliding glass door.

GIBBS GLANCED at his wrist watch as the eastern sky brightened. A crescent moon appeared to be forty-five degrees above the eastern horizon as the first sign of dawn marked a new day. The motion-detecting cameras showed no movement in the tree line except for several deer seen by camera ten on the far south side of the property.

He whispered into his mic, "Any sign of him?"

"Not for thirty minutes," Alexia answered. "We still think he's between five and six."

"Okay."

Concentrating his scope on the indicated area, he switched off the night vision function and surveyed the scene in true light. Taking his time, he looked for straight horizontal lines in a world where none should exist.

THE ASSASSIN LAY STILL, his eye against the rifle scope, his body still as he lay in the leaf-littered floor beneath the tree canopy above him. Images could be seen moving behind the sliding door of the house. They were indistinguishable in the gloom and distorted by the glass.

His breathing was smooth and unhurried, his heartbeat slow and regular. His finger held a slight pressure on the rifle's trigger as he waited. Minutes passed. He did not count them, he merely experienced them. Time meant nothing to him at this stage of the operation. The thrill of the hunt behind him, his quarry cornered, he merely waited for the right moment to finish the job.

An image appeared in the glass door, a tall, slender male with dark hair holding a cup of coffee. Pressure grew on the rifle trigger until it broke and sent a 7.62×51mm NATO round toward the target at 2,733 feet per second. The bullet arrived milliseconds before the sound. Immediately returning his sight to the target, he saw broken glass and no one standing.

———

THE MUZZLE FLASH appeared on the right side of his scope image. Jimmie adjusted his aim and fired twice. The silence of the morning was now broken by three reverberating rifle shots and the sound of birds scattering from the sudden noise. Not unusual during deer season, but very unusual this time of year.

Jimmie waited. He felt his heart pound in his chest like it would soon explode. In reality, his heart rate remained the same. Another rifle shot and the earth exploded ten feet to his left. As the sun peeked over the eastern horizon, a brief reflection from a man-made object appeared in his scope. He fired again and sent another round exactly were the reflection occurred.

The quiet and tranquility of early morning once again returned to the property five miles south of Sparta.

———

WHEN THE GLASS door disintegrated from the rifle shot, Alexia was secure in a room in the back portion of the house, monitoring the cameras. She jumped to her feet and ran toward the kitchen. She heard more rifle shots and screamed, "Jimmie!"

Chapter Thirty-One

THE SECRETARY of Education began to summarize her presentation as President Roy Griffin sat quietly. As with the other speakers during this meeting, he said little, unless requesting the speaker to clarify a statement or thanking them at the conclusion of their presentations. At his first full Cabinet meeting since taking the oath of office, he listened to each individual. Each was selected by the prior president. Several Cabinet members, prior to the start, offered their resignations again. But Griffin declined for the second time to accept them. Changes would come later.

Joseph Kincaid sat behind him, listening to each member and making notes for the conversation he would have with the president later.

When the meeting concluded, Griffin stood, thanked the group and left the room. Joseph followed. Neither spoke as they made their way to the Oval Office. They passed into the small office across from the president's private restroom. When both were seated and the door closed, Griffin sat in the desk chair he was beginning to feel was his. Joseph sat in a cushioned chair next to the window.

"What'd you think?"

His adviser smiled. "It's not really about what I think. What were your impressions?"

Returning the smile, the president hesitated for a moment. "I believe a few know what they're doing and have the nation's interest at heart."

"But…"

"Several have their own self-interest in mind and are totally incompetent."

Joseph just nodded.

With a slight shake of his head, Griffin leaned forward in his chair and put his elbows on his knees.

"You're my National Security Adviser, so… advise."

"Do you want to know what needs to be done, or what is practical to do?"

"Both."

"You need to fire all of them. But that would be impractical at this time."

"Agreed. Who should go?"

"First, the Secretary of Education."

"Why?"

Tilting his head to the side, Joseph grinned and observed, "You know why. You just want someone else to say it."

"Indulge me."

"She lacks a background in teaching or educational administration. Her presentation today was a disjointed series of random thoughts. Why was she appointed and how was she confirmed?"

Roy Griffin sat up straight in his chair. "You'd have to ask the senators who slept through her confirmation hearings. Okay, who else?"

Joseph evaded the question. "Have you decided on a Chief of Staff?"

Griffin shook his head. "I'm thinking about asking Bob Short to take the position."

"I think he would be an excellent choice, Mr. President. He served President Blair well."

"I've also been in contact with President Blair and he agrees with you about the Cabinet. Although he cautioned me about putting members of his administration into those positions. He indicated it would have bad optics."

"Good advice, Mr. President."

"He did give me some names." Griffin turned back to his desk, opened the top drawer and removed a sheet of paper with the president's handwritten notes on it. He handed the sheet to Joseph. "Those are his suggestions."

Studying the page, Joseph nodded and handed it back. "Good list."

Griffin nodded and placed the sheet back in the drawer.

Joseph cleared his throat, "Uh, Mr. President."

"Yes?"

"We had a serious development the other day. I just found out about it before your Cabinet meeting and did not have an opportunity to discuss it with you."

Frowning, Griffin pursed his lips. "What happened, Joseph?"

"Someone tried to kill Stephanie Kruger and Mia Diminski."

Sitting back in his chair, the president took a deep breath. "Good God. You said tried, I hope they're okay."

Joseph explained about the accident, their injuries and which hospital they occupied. "Sean believes forces are trying to intimidate him into dropping his investigation of Dmitri Orlov."

"I would tend to agree with him."

"One other thing."

"Yes."

"Sean has gone to great lengths to hide where he lives. JR has been instrumental in keeping this information out of the public domain. Both of them believe there is a leak here in Washington and I tend to agree with them."

"Who would have this information outside of the FBI and the Department of Justice?"

"Actually, the DOJ does not have the personnel records; the FBI maintains them. But Director Stumpf assures me the information is unknown to anyone but a few individuals at the Bureau. He did mention a possibility."

Griffin did not respond, but kept his gaze on Joseph and waited for him to finish the thought.

Pausing for a moment, Joseph continued, "Paul believes there are a few members of the House Permanent Select Committee on Intelligence who might know where Kruger lives. If not the exact address, at least the city."

"Why would anyone on that committee know?"

"Because they conducted an inquiry into the terrorist attack on Bud Walton Arena. The inquiries did not start until Sean and Stephanie moved to Springfield. He was subpoenaed as a witness. To issue it, the committee would have needed his current address."

"If I remember correctly, those were closed sessions. No public information was ever released."

"True, but the members of the committee would remember."

"Do you think one of them could be the source?"

"Paul thinks so and so do I."

The President placed his elbow on the small desk and rested his chin on his palm, one finger covering his lips. It was the same pose he struck during the Cabinet meeting earlier. He was quiet for several minutes.

"How do we find this individual without revealing we know?"

"Let me handle it."

The President nodded.

———

AFTER DECADES WORKING for the CIA, Joseph Kincaid knew more "spooks" than most people in Washington. The correct title within the agency remained "operations officer." Currently, the former CIA employee he was meeting earned his living as a consultant: a fancy way of saying he charged a lot of money for information other people needed.

The time approached 10 p.m. as Joseph sat at a table in a small bistro he and Mary frequented. The individual approached the table and smiled as he pulled out a chair.

Extending his hand, he said, "It's been awhile, Joseph. Congratulations on joining the ruling class."

William Fischer, better known as Will to his friends, did not possess the looks of the stereotypical Hollywood spy. On the contrary, Fischer displayed unruly dark rusty brown hair, bushy eyebrows he refused to trim, a round face accented by a broad nose and a red walrus mustache. Dark green eyes looked at Joseph through smudged lenses of his black horn-rimmed glasses. His dress could best be described as thrift shop chic: rumpled corduroy sport coat, khaki pants two inches too long, scuffed loafers and a wrinkled white oxford shirt.

"It's a temp job, Will. Helping the new president get his feet on the ground."

"Right." He looked around the sparsely-populated café. "What's with the clandestine meeting this far off the D.C. circuit?"

"I like the place."

"Whatever. I need a beer." He looked around and waved at a waiter.

"Relax, Will, I have one coming. I ordered it when I saw you enter."

The larger man tilted his head slightly. "Guinness?"

"Of course—what other kind of beer is there?"

"None." Fischer smiled. "You know how to get me in a compliant mood."

When the beer arrived in front of Fischer, he took a long pull, wiped his lips with the back of a hand and looked over the top of his glasses at Joseph. "What do you need this time?"

"Information."

"What kind?"

"Info on members of the House Permanent Select Committee on Intelligence."

"Which one?"

"Don't know. We think someone on the committee is selling information or could be compromised by a foreign agent."

Fischer chuckled. "Half the guys on the committee fit that description. You'll have to be more specific."

"That's all I can give you."

"Huh. Let me think about it." He took another long pull of his beer. "You're gonna have to order another one. My brain isn't as fast as it used to be."

The grin on his face told Joseph the man had something to say.

Joseph looked around, spotted his waitress and pointed at Fischer's beer. The young college student nodded and went to get another.

After setting down his now-empty glass, Fischer took off his glasses and started wiping the lenses with his cloth napkin. "Ever hear of a law firm called Rothenburg and Sandifer?"

Joseph sipped on his own beer ordered earlier. "They were the firm who represented Robert Burns Jr."

"Exactly. It's pretty much common knowledge the two

managing partners sold out right after the unfortunate accident Junior suffered."

Joseph nodded.

"What's not commonly known in this town is who actually bought the firm."

"I heard Dmitri Orlov."

Fischer smiled and took a swig of the new beer sitting in front of him. "You heard correct, but another individual was also involved."

Raising his eyebrows, Joseph looked at his guest. "Oh?"

"Who's rumored to be the richest person in the world?"

"Last I knew it was Jeff Bezos."

"I'm not talking about what Forbes reports, I'm talking individuals who don't discuss their wealth. People who don't exactly earn their money, they just take it."

Now Joseph stared at Fischer. "He's involved?"

"According to my source. Orlov just brokered the deal and the money came from a longtime friend from his KGB days."

"Did your source tell you why they bought out the attorneys?"

Fischer shook his head. "No, but I can guess."

"I'm listening."

"Sandifer has been an attorney for decades. He's represented more than a few members of Congress in his day. You can draw your own conclusions from that statement."

"Influence?"

"That would be a logical guess."

"So, who would be vulnerable on the committee?"

"First name that comes to mind is Tony Holt."

"Why?"

"He's the chairman and quite possibly the biggest piece of shit in the entire House of Representatives."

"Do you think he's dirty?"

"He maintains a squeaky-clean image, which he perpetuates every time he gets in front of a camera lens. Deep down, he's a scumbag."

Joseph frowned. "Being a scumbag's not a crime. Why do you suspect Holt?"

"He's been represented by Sandifer for over ten years. I'm sure the new owners of Rothenburg and Sandifer know all of his secrets."

"Who else might be vulnerable?"

"I can think of about twenty off the top of my head. You need a list?"

"It would be helpful."

Chapter Thirty-Two

JIMMIE GIBBS WAITED until the reverberation from the rifle shots stopped before switching his communication device back on. What he heard brought a smile to his face. Someone was actually worried about him.

Alexia's voice was frantically calling his name.

"Jimmie, Jimmie, are you okay? Jimmie, answer me, please, please answer me, are you okay?"

"Yes, Alexia, I'm fine. How is everyone inside?"

"Everyone is fine."

"No one hurt?"

"No, just a lot of shattered glass everywhere. Your friend Sean Kruger will have seven years bad luck."

"Why?"

"Because he made that man shoot a mirror."

Gibbs chuckled to himself. "He did what?"

"He stood off to the side, with a mirror reflecting his image out the door."

Now laughing out loud, he shook his head. "Where's Sean now?"

229

"He and Sandy are going to look for the man who fired the rifle."

"Is the man still out there?"

"They do not think so, but are taking precautions. They are going to drive the big SUV out to see if they can find him."

A cold chill went up Jimmie Gibbs' spine. The adrenaline started to subside and he took stock of the situation. With full daylight now available, he trained his rifle scope on the spot where he sent his last bullet. What he saw allowed him to relax.

He keyed his mic. "Alexia, tell them not to bother. Target is down."

————

GIBBS WAS the first to arrive at the site. After shedding his Ghillie Suit at the hide, he sprinted toward the spot he identified as the last place for the sniper. What he found gave him pause as he stared at the prone unmoving body before him.

The assassin remained in the same position taken after turning his rifle toward Jimmie's location. Only now his head was unrecognizable as human. The trajectory of Jimmie's bullet pierced the front lens of the rifle scope and traveled through the man's eye and out the back of his head. There remained very little of the man's skull intact.

Having seen more men die by the weapons of war than he cared to discuss, he normally felt sympathy for his fallen brethren, but not this man. He had tried to kill three of his best friends and those types of friends were hard to find.

Knoll and Kruger parked the Denali next to the tree line. Kruger got out and walked over to where Jimmie stood.

Gibbs turned and looked at him. "A mirror? Really?"

Kruger shrugged. "Worked, didn't it?"

Gibb smiled and nodded. "Glad it did." He looked back at the body lying on the ground. "Who do you think he is?"

"No idea. We'll have the sheriff's department get fingerprints. Maybe he's in a database somewhere."

Shaking his head, Gibbs said, "Guys like this don't get fingerprinted by cops. If he has fingerprints on file, they'll be with a military unit somewhere."

"You're probably right. You need to go back to the house and let Alexia know you're okay. She didn't want Sandy or I to know it, but she's been on the verge of hysteria."

Gibbs smiled and headed toward the house.

Kruger turned to Knoll. "Now comes the hard part—determining who this guy is."

The big man pointed to an exposed part of the dead man's left arm. He knelt next to it and pushed the sleeve up a few inches.

"It may not be that hard. I recognize the tattoo. This guy was with the French special forces at one time."

———

CHRISTIAN COUNTY SHERIFF JESSIE SUMMERS offered his hand, which Kruger shook. Both men smiled at the other. Summers spoke first. "It's been, what, a year, Agent Kruger?"

"Eight months, Sheriff. How've you been?"

"Good. Thought you were retired. Guess you're back, huh?"

Kruger nodded.

"Like I told you last time we worked together, once Bureau, always Bureau."

"That you did, Sheriff. That you did. Did you find the guy's vehicle?"

"Yeah, one of my deputies found an abandoned rental car about a mile north of here. A wallet with a Florida driver's license in the name of Matt Wallace was found in the glove compartment. Photo matches the assailant. He also had a couple thousand dollars and a platinum American Express Card in the same name. No wants or warrants on him, but then, no one by the name Matt Wallace lives at the address on the driver's license."

"Figures."

"You want to tell me what happened?"

"He's the guy who ran my wife and her friend off the highway the other day. He was after me."

The sheriff looked at the shattered glass still scattered around the back door. "Who shot first?"

"He did."

A half grin appeared on the older man's face. "Good. That makes my job easier. Now it's a righteous shooting. Who shot him?"

"FBI Agent James Gibbs, retired Navy Seal."

Summers made notes in a small notebook, smiled and looked over his glasses at Kruger. "You're making my job too easy, Agent Kruger."

He glanced out of the shattered door and saw an ambulance pull up and park next to the crime scene. "Looks like the medical examiner just got here. Guess I need to add my expertise to his examination."

"Thanks, Jessie."

The sheriff put his hand on Kruger's shoulder. "Sean, if you need someone to protect that wife of yours after she's out of the hospital, let me know. We've got a bunch of deputies who would be more than happy to help you after the incident at the river last year."

"I appreciate your offer, Sheriff. I'll keep it in mind. By the way, there will be a swarm of FBI agents here this afternoon. Hope you don't mind."

Summers shook his head. "They're the ones who'll be wasting their time, not me."

He turned and walked out of the room through the broken glass door. Looking at the mirror fragments, he chuckled and shook his head as he walked toward the tree line. Kruger heard the sheriff mumble as he walked out, "A mirror. Hell of an idea. I'll have to remember that."

———

THE TIME APPROACHED noon as Kruger and Knoll sat in a diner several blocks from the funeral home containing the last remains of the assassin. It was their first meal of the day after the events of the early morning. Knoll absentmindedly ate his hamburger as he read an email on his cell phone.

"Huh… They've already identified the shooter."

Kruger munched on a french fry. "Who was he?"

"DOD sent the fingerprints to the French and they immediately knew who he was. According to this, his name was Jean-Luc Larue, a member of the French Special Operations Command. He was part of the 13th Parachute Dragoon Regiment and declared MIA during the Battle of Tora Bora on December 13, 2001." Knoll looked up from his cell phone. "Guess he had a change of heart about things." He returned his attention to the email.

"Born in Marseille, his father was a diplomat stationed in Washington, D.C., during his high school years. He spoke English without an accent, was fluent in Spanish and passable in Urdu." Knoll looked up again. "Tora Bora is in the Spin Gar Mountain Range which, for lack of a better word, separates Afghanistan from Pakistan on its southeastern border."

"I'm familiar with the area."

Knoll frowned.

Kruger took a sip of his ice tea. "Long story, go on with what you were saying."

"The conclusion of the French Special Operations Group now is that he deserted and made his way into Pakistan. They have no idea where he went after that."

Kruger put his burger down without taking a bite. "Did he have a discipline problem?"

"No, not according to the report the DOD received. French authorities are wanting details about his death and where his body is. Apparently, we stirred up a hornet's nest this morning."

Finally taking a bite of his burger, Kruger chewed and stared out the window next to their table. When he turned back to Knoll, his expression was grim. "More importantly, who hired him and was he the individual who sprayed A-232 on Jolene Sanders and the reporter?"

"Don't know, but I have a funny feeling you're going to find out."

"Damn right I'm going to find out."

Knoll grinned.

———

ALEXIA MONTREAL TOOK it upon herself to rid Joseph and Mary's home of all the flying insects and bugs that had invaded while the shattered glass door allowed access to the interior. Now covered with a blue tarp and awaiting the arrival of a glass repair company, she busied herself with swatting flies, spraying wasps and capturing elusive moths. Jimmie Gibbs swept the shards of glass and searched for the rifle slug he knew imbedded itself somewhere in the home. He finally found it buried in a hardback book situated on one of Joseph's numerous bookshelves. He smiled when he read the title: Fredrick Forsyth's *The Day of the Jackal*.

Alexia watched him. "Will not your FBI want the place left like it is?"

Gibbs shook his head. "I took the necessary pictures and can claim the glass was a safety hazard. No one's going to complain. They'll be more interested in the spot he shot from."

"What now, Jimmie? I am in this country illegally without ID or passport. Will they arrest me?"

"Not a chance. Sean spoke to Joseph before they left. You are now classified as a material witness and will be provided temporary identification and visa status." He glanced at his wristwatch. "As of ten minutes ago, you were legally in the United States. A Fed Ex package will be delivered to Sean's house tomorrow with your paperwork."

Tears welled in her eyes as she walked over and engulfed him in an embrace. He returned the hug. She whispered in his ear, "When will Sandy be back?"

"Couple of hours. He and Sean are waiting for a team of FBI forensic technicians from St. Louis to take charge of the body. Sean will go on to the hospital and Sandy will come back here."

"So, we are alone for two hours?"

"At least."

She took his hand and led him toward the stairs and her bedroom.

KRUGER PACKED Stephanie's clothes and personal items in a small duffle bag he brought from their home.

"You sure you feel up to going home?"

She nodded and smiled. "Yes, this place is driving me crazy."

"JR told me Mia is doing much better and will be released tomorrow or the next day."

"I know, a nurse took me to her room this morning. She looks pretty good, considering. Are we going to our house, Sean?"

"Yes, the individual who ran you off the road is no longer a problem. His fingerprints matched prints found in the truck he used to run you and Mia off the road." He glanced at his watch. "In fact, he's being accompanied by several FBI agents and probably halfway to St. Louis by now."

He did not lie to her; he just chose not to tell her the man was dead. He would tell her later after she had time to recover further.

JR appeared at the door of Stephanie's room. "When are you being released, Stephanie?"

She smiled. "Doctor was here a few minutes ago and signed my release form. As soon as they get the paperwork straightened out, I can leave."

He nodded. "Sean, can I speak to you in the hall?"

Kruger looked at Stephanie, who nodded slightly. He followed JR into the hall.

"What's up?"

"Did you find him?"

Kruger nodded. "Jimmie found him."

The computer hacker took a deep breath and let it out slowly. "Good, I really didn't want Mia to have to go all the way back to Joseph's."

Kruger put his hand on JR's shoulder.

"The houses will be watched twenty-four seven and I've hired a local agency who will help the girls for the next few weeks with their personal care and rehab."

JR swallowed hard, struggling to keep his composure. "I don't know what to say."

"Thank you would be a good start. But you've done so much for me, it's the least I can do."

"It gives me a chance to start digging into Dmitri Orlov's network."

"Alexia can help."

"Do you trust her?"

"At first no, but now…" Kruger nodded.

"Any particular reason?"

"You'll find out."

The two friends stared at each other for a few moments and went back into the room.

Chapter Thirty-Three

KRUGER STARED at the ruined Mr. Coffee unit on the credenza behind JR's computer cubical.

"Thought this thing had an automatic shut-off."

"It does, or I should say, it did. One of my innovative colleagues worked all night a few days ago and figured out how to bypass the shut-off timer so her coffee wouldn't get cold. Then she forgot to turn it off."

Kruger held the carafe up to the light to see how thick the solid sludge of black burnt coffee appeared. No light penetrated the solid mass on the bottom of the glass container. He frowned, threw it into a waste basket next to the credenza and turned to pick out a coffee pod for the Keurig machine.

As the water was pushed through the pod into his mug, he turned. "How's Mia?"

"Better. She's moving around on crutches now and everyone seems pleased with her progress." He turned and looked at his friend. "The service you hired is doing a remarkable job with her rehab. Her doctor is confident she'll be off the crutches in ten more weeks."

"How is she emotionally?"

"She's from Texas, Sean. Just another obstacle she has to overcome. Losing the baby affected her more than the broken pelvis."

Kruger didn't press the issue. If JR wanted to say something more, he would.

"Uh…"

"Yeah?"

"From a psychological standpoint, do you think she'll want to try again?"

"For a baby?"

JR nodded.

"Not my area of expertise."

"I know, but what do you think?"

"Have you discussed it with her?"

"Afraid to."

Kruger smiled. "Do you want another child?"

JR nodded.

"Give her some time, JR. Once her pelvis heals and the trauma of the accident fades, talk to her doctor. She will be the best resource for you two to consult."

"Thanks, Sean." He turned and pointed to one of his three computer screens. "We've figured out Orlov's org chart."

Bending over to get a better view, Kruger put on his half-readers. "How'd you find it?"

"Alexia."

"Really?"

"Yup, she's good, Sean. I offered her a job."

"Did she take it?"

"Said she had to discuss it with Jimmie." He paused. "Are those two serious about each other?"

"I thought it was White-Knight Syndrome at first, but maybe not. So, what about this organizational chart?"

"Alexia found the email server used by Orlov's internet provider in Paris. We have his emails. Some of them are encrypted, most are not. Jimmie speaks and reads Russian, so he's been instrumental in interpreting them. From what we can tell, Orlov has three banks here in the United States he controls."

"We knew that from last year."

"Yes, but we didn't know what else he owns. Or, I should say, controls. We think the money is coming directly from the Kremlin."

"Have you spoken to Joseph recently?"

"No, why?"

"You just confirmed what a source told him. The money is coming from Orlov's old KGB buddy. So, what else does he control?"

"Here's where it gets interesting."

Kruger closed his eyes and shook his head. "Just tell me, JR."

With a grin, JR said, "In addition to Rothenburg and Sandifer, they have controlling interests in several CPA firms and are pursuing additional law firms."

"Why would they want CPA firms?"

"Same reason they wanted a high-profile attorney's office. Files on legislators."

Sipping his coffee, Kruger waited a few seconds before responding. "How much money are we talking about here, JR?"

"Hundreds of millions." He paused, focusing his attention on Kruger. "One other thing."

"Yeah."

"Orlov is pouring a bunch of that money into something called Free America."

"What the hell is that?"

JR shook his head. "From what Alexia and I can determine, it appears to be a tightly closed group of foreign hacktivists."

Kruger was silent for a moment as he stared at his cup of coffee. "How closed are they?"

"Locked down tight. I tried to gain access using my Zardoz alter-ego and they didn't buy it."

"What about Alexia?"

"We decided it'd be better for her to wait a while. She might actually have a better chance. We don't think her nom de guerre has been compromised like mine." He gave Kruger a sly smile. "She was quite the revolutionary when she lived in Paris and rather well-known in the European hacker community."

"So, what do you think this Free America's purpose is?"

JR wrinkled his brow and shook his head slightly. "Don't know for sure, but I can take an educated guess."

Kruger closed his eyes. JR's persistent habit of not answering questions directly always caused him frustration. But after many of years of friendship, Kruger could now tolerate it.

"Go on."

"Like I said, I have no proof."

"Spit it out, JR."

"I think their main objective is to create enough havoc with the US election process to shatter the faith everyone has in the system."

"Some would say that's already occurred."

JR shook his head. "Not like what this group can do. These guys will make Anonymous look like kindergarteners."

Silence filled the small cubicle where the two men resided. Kruger leaned against the credenza, staring at his empty coffee cup.

His next words were directed at no one. "What is Orlov's end-game?"

JR knew Kruger was posing a rhetorical question, one the

FBI agent would answer himself after careful thought. Silence dominated once again.

Minutes ticked by. JR returned his attention to his computer screen while Kruger continued to study his coffee mug. When he looked up, a slight smile appeared. "JR."

The hacker returned his attention to Kruger.

"When Robert Burns Sr. was in the Senate and Orlov blackmailed him into introducing legislation that eventually led to the 2008 recession, what was the Russian's reaction?"

Smiling, JR realized where Kruger was going.

"Surprise at the unintended consequences."

"Right. Legislation originally designed to let his banks make more profit created the background for the 2008 recession. What if the same process is at work here? Compromise our election process as much as possible, then sit back and wait for what happens."

JR studied Kruger. "Do you think that's why he is looking for compromised politicians?"

"Yeah, find them and expose them. Then disrupt elections to make sure they get re-elected or someone worse is voted in. It would be a perfect storm."

"How do we stop them?"

"We stop Orlov."

"How do we do that?"

Kruger stood, set his coffee mug down and folded his arms over his chest. "We make his buddy in Moscow believe Orlov isn't spending his money very wisely."

"I think I'm gonna enjoy that."

———

TWO DAYS LATER, Kruger sat in JR's conference room, sipping coffee from a newly purchased Mr. Coffee unit. At the moment, he occupied the room by himself. Others would be joining him shortly. His laptop maintained his attention as he re-read one specific email from Joseph.

The reason for the upcoming meeting with his team.

A closed manilla envelope resided to the left of the laptop with his left hand resting on top. His right hand moved the mouse.

One by one, his team stopped at the coffee service and either poured themselves a cup from the Mr. Coffee or made one with the Keurig. Kruger didn't pay attention, his focus remaining on making sure he relayed the meaning of Joseph's email correctly. JR rose from his cubicle outside the conference room, entered last, shut the door, sat next to Kruger and opened his laptop.

Small talk permeated the small room, most of it directed at JR for an update on Mia's condition.

"She's doing a lot better," he told the group, smiling faintly. "She can get around on crutches. With the help of Sandy's wife Linda, and a visiting nurse, she's making progress every day. Thanks for asking."

Kruger looked up from his laptop. JR sat to his right with Sandy Knoll next to him. Jimmie Gibbs and Alexia sat across from them. He turned to JR first, saying, "Ryan Clark is waiting to join us via telephone. Can you hook him up with the speakerphone?"

JR nodded and started typing on his computer. Fifteen seconds later, Ryan Clark could be heard saying hello to the attendees.

Kruger cleared his throat and the room grew silent. "I'm sure you're all wondering why I called us together like this."

Everyone nodded.

"We have a green light to go after Dmitri Orlov in whatever manner we find necessary to stop him."

Everyone smiled and nodded their heads.

Clark's voice emanated from the speaker phone: "Any restrictions?"

"He has been classified as a financial terrorist and thus an enemy combatant. Does that answer your question?"

"Sure does. What's next, Sean?"

"The U.S. imposed sanctions on Russian state-run financial institutions after the invasion of Ukraine. These sanctions restrict those types of banks from doing business in the U.S. Orlov's banks were not involved because the Federal Reserve considered them privately held institutions. However, we have uncovered evidence that leads us to believe the money behind these banks is from personal funds belonging to a high-ranking member of the Politburo."

Knoll frowned. "You mean..?"

"Yeah, the top guy."

Gibbs gave a low whistle, but did not comment.

Kruger continued, "The 2010 Dodd-Frank Act contains an amendment to the U.S. International Banking Act of 1978, which allows the U.S. financial system to determine if a foreign-owned bank offers a risk to U.S. financial stability. If those entities are determined to cause risk, the Federal Reserve can terminate their authority to operate in the United States."

JR smiled.

Ryan Clark's voice emanated from the speaker: "So, if we can prove either scenario, the Federal Reserve can shut those banks down. Am I understanding you correctly, Sean?"

"That's exactly what I'm saying. If the banks fail a stress test, and I mean really fail it, Orlov would immediately be forced to turn to his buddy for an infusion of cash so the banks could pass the stress test. All we have to do is prove where the funds come from and the Federal Reserve would revoke their ability to do business in the U.S. because of the Ukrainian sanctions.

Gibbs spoke next. "How are the banks going to fail a stress test?"

Kruger nodded at JR's and Alexia's directions. "That's their job."

"Okay, then what? How are we going to prove who sends the funds?"

"JR follows the money trail." Turning to his friend, Kruger asked, "You can do that, right?"

Returning Kruger's stare, JR gave a slight grin. "With my eyes closed."

———

BEFORE LEAVING THE CONFERENCE ROOM, Kruger handed the manila envelope to JR, said his good-byes and left the room.

With everyone understanding their tasks, they all started to exit the room. JR asked Gibbs and Alexia to stay behind. After the door closed and just the three remained, JR slid the envelope across the table to Alexia.

She opened it and found a rental agreement signed by Joseph Kincaid, a birth certificate, Florida driver's license and Social Security card in the name of Alexia Martinez. Her eyes widened and she looked at JR. "What are these?"

"Your new identity. Martinez is the sixth most common name in Spain. If you look at where you were born, you will see it's St. Augustine, Florida. Your ancestry is Spanish-American, vs Latin-American. There's a difference."

Alexia nodded, took her gaze from JR back to the documents, not sure what to say.

JR continued, "You'll find when you take those documents to a Department of Revenue office anywhere in the state, and I strongly suggest Christian County, you will be able to receive a new Missouri driver's license. Once you have secured it,

Alexia Martinez will blend into the three-hundred plus million citizens of the United States. She will be a natural citizen with no questions asked."

She looked up and stared at JR.

"How did you…?"

He put his hand up, palm facing her. "Don't ask, but Joseph's connections within the CIA helped. I did the rest. It's better if you don't know the details."

"How do I explain my accent?"

JR shrugged. "Don't. If people persist, say you spent a lot of time as a child in Spain with your grandparents. Most people won't ask. Besides, your accent has faded since you've been here and you're starting to use contractions, so it isn't that noticeable anymore."

She looked at Jimmie Gibbs and then back at JR. "I don't know what to say?"

"Don't say anything. You're as legal as I am or Jimmie for that matter." He pointed to the documents. "You can get a credit card with those and even buy a gun, if you want. They'll pass any background check."

"Does Sean know?" Gibbs asked.

JR smiled. "It was his idea."

Chapter Thirty-Four

IN A COORDINATED EFFORT, auditors from the Federal Reserve, FDIC and the IRS descended upon three banks at 9 a.m. exactly one week after the planning meeting in JR's conference room. In addition to the auditors, two FBI agents accompanied each team. Sean Kruger and Jimmie Gibbs attended the raid on Advanced Capital Bank in Arlington, VA, while Sandy Knoll and FBI Senior Agent Fred Atkins joined the auditors at BNP North America in New York City, with agents Ryan Clark and Samantha Warren present at the visit to Bank of the Atlantic, Washington, D.C.

By noon, all three banks were found to be insolvent after a surprise stress test.

Plus, during the audit by the Federal Reserve agents, a direct connection to a state-run bank in Russia was discovered, resulting in all three banks losing their charters to operate in the United States.

By 5 p.m., The Bank of America accepted receivership of all three bank operations, thus protecting consumer deposits and other assets.

AT TEN MINUTES after 7 in the evening, Paris time, Sergey Brutka noted a change in activities at the now-closed office of Dmitri Orlov. Previously alerted by Kruger, he sat watching from a park bench across the Seine as a formally dressed Orlov arrived in his private car. It skidded to a halt in front of the office and a hurried Orlov practically ran inside. A grim-faced assistant jumped into the driver seat and drove the car away. As more frantic individuals reported back to work at Orlov's office building, Brutka smiled and dialed a number on his cell phone.

His call was answered immediately. "Kruger."

"It has started."

"How so?"

"Orlov was to be at a reception tonight for the new Russian ambassador to France. He just arrived and practically ran inside. I could hear the tires screech as the car stopped and I'm on the other side of the Seine."

"Get something to eat and keep me posted. In another five hours, he won't have three banks in the U.S."

"Awwwhhh…"

"Yeah, I know, I'm feeling bad about his situation."

"As you Americans say, you will get over it."

"You're right. I already have."

Both men chuckled as Brutka ended the call. He leaned back on the bench, crossed his arms over his chest and watched as more lights appeared in windows throughout Orlov's office building.

KRUGER STEPPED outside the Advanced Capital Bank building to accept the call from Brutka. After the brief conversation ended, he pressed the digits for a telephone number only he and one other individual knew. It was answered immediately.

"Is it working?"

"So far. I'm concerned this will blow back on you, JR."

"How many years have we been doing this, Sean?"

"Okay, just being paranoid."

"Don't be. Alexia is as good as I am. We complement each other. I'm better at some things, she is better at others. Relax. It's handled."

"Brutka just called. Orlov is going crazy in Paris."

"He should. We aren't done yet."

"Should I ask?"

"Nope. Better to be curious."

———

DMITRI ORLOV HELD one cell phone with his right hand and another in his left, alternating his attention between the two. Events at two of his banks were being relayed to him in real-time by senior vice presidents, the presidents of each bank being too involved with federal authorities to take his phone call.

Since arriving at his office, his chair was unused. He paced as he listened to the descriptions of events unfolding thirty-eight hundred miles across the Atlantic. One of his assistants opened his door and leaned in, not speaking until recognized.

Orlov turned to him and lowered the phone in his left hand. He practically shouted, "What?"

"Sir, you have a call." The young man, normally dressed in a suit and tie, wore jeans and a sweater. He pointed to Orlov's desk phone.

"Who is it?"

"Moscow."

All color drained from the older man's face. He ended the calls on the cell phones without explanation as he approached his desk. Picking up the receiver, he answered, "Da."

Not wishing to be on the receiving end of Orlov's wrath, the young assistant quietly closed the door and went back to his desk.

A one-sided conversation with Moscow proceeded to occur. The responses from the Paris side were few, only a yes or a no. When the call concluded, Orlov replaced the handset back in its cradle, sat down behind his desk, placed his elbows on his desk and supported his head with his hands.

Boris Volkov opened the office door, saw Orlov off the phone and walked silently up to the desk. His presence was not immediately acknowledged. Two dozen seconds later, without lifting his head, Orlov said, "How much do you know?"

"My plane landed two hours ago. I just got here."

"Then you have not heard?"

"No."

"The Americans, in an illegal act of financial terrorism, have forced a stress test on my banks in Washington and New York. All three have failed the test and will be formally seized later.

"How..."

"It does not matter how," Orlov snapped. "They have done it. Where is Popov?"

"I do not know."

A red-faced Orlov looked up at the large man.

"What do you mean you do not know?"

"We know the Americans must have him in custody, but we cannot locate where he is being held."

Staring at Volkov, the older man did not immediately reply. Taking a deep breath, he stood and turned toward the window behind him. With his hands behind his back he asked another question. "Where is Peter Yanovich? Has he been released yet?"

Volkov hesitated, knowing the news he brought about the attorney would further agitate the man staring out his office window.

Turning to look at Volkov, Orlov demanded, "Well, has he?" He immediately returned to staring out the window.

"Not at this time."

Bowing his head and shaking it slowly, the older man did not respond immediately. Finally, Orlov turned to stare at his Chief of Security. "Why not? Did I not arrange for bail to be paid?"

"Yes, you did. However, he was charged as an accessory to the murders of the attorney and reporter. He is being held without bail."

"How can that be. He was only supposed to take the reporter's purse."

"Yes," Volkov nodded. "But the fool did not throw away the shoes he wore. The FBI found residual traces of chemicals comprising A-232 on them when they searched his home."

Shaking his head, the older man sighed. "He needs to keep his mouth shut. Can he do that?"

"I doubt it. He is more interested in his own self-preservation."

Blinking rapidly, Orlov's nostrils flared as his cheeks grew crimson. After several deep breaths, he relaxed a little. "Have you heard from the Frenchman?"

Volkov shook his head.

"You told me he was the best."

He received a shrug as an answer.

Taking a deep breath, Orlov glared at the larger man. "I will assume he failed because the meddling FBI agent is at my bank in Arlington."

With a nod, Volkov responded. "He has not communicated

with me since he forced the two women off the road, so I would agree. But he cannot be traced back to you, sir."

"He doesn't have to be. Whether he is in custody or dead, Kruger will know I sent him." Orlov raised his eyebrows and tilted his head to the side. "Yes, it makes sense now."

"What does?"

"The closing of my banks. This is his way of telling me he knows. While I was merely protecting my business interests, the attack on his wife made it personal for him. I underestimated this FBI man. He does not scare easily. I will not make that mistake again. What about that hacker in Mexico City?"

"What about her?"

"Can she help us?"

Volkov shook his head. "She has gone silent."

Orlov turned again to stare out the window. "Back to Yanovich. Do you think he will talk?"

"Definitely."

"Can someone get to him where he is being held?"

"For the right amount of money, yes."

"See to it."

With a slight bow and a single nod, Volkov left the office.

———

BRUTKA WATCHED as the large Russian emerged from the office entrance fifteen minutes after arriving. He spoke briefly to a man the same size, who nodded and hurried toward a light-colored Peugeot parked a block down the street. Volkov raised a cell phone to his ear and kept it there for several minutes until the car stopped in front of him on the street. After disappearing inside, the French coupe sped away.

Glancing back at the office windows of Orlov building, he saw the shadow of a man in a window on the third floor. With a slight grin, he stood, turned and disappeared into the darkness of the Paris night.

———

PRESIDENT ROY GRIFFIN read the briefing notes placed in front of him by his National Security Adviser. "Should I ask how the banks failed the stress test?"

"I wouldn't." Joseph replied.

The president smiled. "Better to not know?"

"Probably."

Griffin leaned back in his desk chair and pinched the bridge of his nose with his right hand.

"Is Sean prepared for the blowback on this?"

"The team is, yes."

"How are Stephanie and Mia?"

"Stephanie is doing good and Mia will recover fully."

Nodding, Griffin returned his attention to the report. When he finished, he closed the briefing binder and handed it back to his advisor. "Joseph, we need to know who, if anyone, in this government has been compromised like Robert Burns Sr. was during the early 2000s."

"Sean and his team are working on it."

Standing, Griffin started pacing in front of the Resolute Desk. Joseph remained seated on one of the sofas in front of the desk. He did not interrupt the man's thought process. After several minutes, the president stopped and looked at his friend.

"Now that we know about Orlov, we can do something about him. What keeps me up at night is how many other individuals like Orlov are out there trying to undermine our country?"

Joseph didn't answer immediately. He stared at the president and blinked several times. "With all the activity around Orlov recently, I had not thought of that. We know the

Russians do not put..." He paused for a second. "I hate clichés, but it fits—all their eggs in one basket. They will have other operations planned or currently working."

"How do we find out?"

Joseph stood. "Don't know at the moment, but we'd better figure it out."

Chapter Thirty-Five

ROLLING OVER, Ryan Clark's hand reached over and fell on an empty side of the bed. His eyes snapped open and glanced at the digital alarm clock on Tracy's side of the bed. 1:51 a.m. Where was she? Swinging his legs over the side, he stood and listened. The apartment was eerily silent. Concern crept into the back of his mind as he walked out of the bedroom toward the second room he and Tracy used as an office. A blueish light flickered on the wall visible from the hallway.

He leaned against the doorway jam and saw his fiancée illuminated by the light from a laptop computer screen. Her back to the door, he could see she wore her normal sleepwear, a thin cotton camisole with string straps and a pair of nylon running shorts.

"What's the matter, Tracy, can't sleep?"

She shot a quick glance back at him, a wide smile on her face. "I can finally read all of Keira Pennington's notes."

She returned to staring at the laptop's screen.

His mind shifted from thoughts of removing the camisole to the ramifications of knowing what the dead reporter may have been working on. He walked up behind her and placed his hands on her shoulders. Her right hand rose to cover his left hand. Glancing at the screen he saw the Word documents from the flash drives found at Keira's home.

"What happened? How?"

"I woke at midnight with a thought. I remembered something an older reporter I worked with on my first job as a journalist showed me. It was a code for taking notes. I never used it. and quite frankly, forgot about it. But something jogged my memory this morning."

She removed her hand from his and pointed at the screen. "These notes indicate she had all the evidence she needed to start writing. Jolene Sanders would be providing documents independently collaborating her story. She would have published in the next day or so."

"Did her editor know what she was working on?"

"Apparently, but he wouldn't allow her to publish without a second source. Jolene was the secondary source."

"Should I talk to the editor?"

She shook her head. "He won't tell you anything."

"Why?"

Tracy turned and stared at Clark. "Trust me, he just won't."

Clark nodded, realizing his mistake. "What was the premise of her story?"

"Apparently, she was able to identify three members of the Bryant administration who were compromised by Dmitri Orlov."

"Who?"

"Vice President Pittman, Jane Friedman, Secretary of Education and…" She hesitated, "Carl Wood, President Bryant's Chief of Staff."

Clark gave a low whistle as Tracy scrolled through the document currently on the screen. He leaned against the desk and stared at a spot on the opposite wall. "Were all three represented by Rothenburg and Sandifer at one time?"

Looking up at him, Tracy shook her head. "Don't know. It would make sense, considering Jolene was supplying Keira with documents backing up her investigation."

"Tracy, do a Google search on Freidman. We need to know who recommended her to President Bryant."

Atkins' fingers flew over the keyboard and half a minute later, she looked up. "She and Pittman went to the same university and graduated in the same class. It's not conclusive, but I know how you and Sean feel about a coincidence."

"There is no such thing as a coincidence, only connections. My bet is he suggested her to Bryant. What about Carl Wood?"

Several silent minutes passed before she said, "Nothing shows up with a cursory search, but I can look into it if you want."

"Hmmmm…" He studied the spot on the wall again. "At least it's a start." Smiling, he took her hand. "Let's get back to bed. Tomorrow might be a long day."

As they returned to their bedroom, thoughts of removing her camisole made him smile.

———

"MR. PRESIDENT." Kruger found it strange addressing Roy Griffin in this manner, but he could not bring himself to call him Roy. "We have been able to identify three individuals, one deceased, whom we believe are compromised by Dmitri Orlov."

Griffin sat at the small desk in his private office located off the Oval Office. Kruger leaned forward on the edge of one of the cushioned arm chairs as he handed the president an iPad.

Gibbs occupied an identical chair next to Kruger. Joseph leaned against the closed door.

Scanning the list, Griffin looked up at Kruger. "Pittman, we suspected. I'm a little surprised about Jane Freidman's name." He paused, frowned and looked up at Kruger. "Carl Wood? How do you know?"

"We don't. All we have are Keira Pennington's notes."

"I thought they were in an unreadable shorthand."

"Ryan Clark's fiancée figured it out."

The president smiled. "I always liked Tracy Adkins." He stopped and frowned. "She's not going to write about this is she?"

Kruger shook his head. "Not until you give her the okay, then she'll expose the entire plot using the Washington Post."

"Thought she worked for the New York Times?"

Grinning, Kruger shook his head. "Not since she and Clark became engaged."

"Ahh." He nodded slowly, an index finger on his lips. "What about Jane Friedman?"

"Clark was able to establish she and Pittman knew each other in college. After reviewing video tape of her confirmation hearings, it was confirmed Pittman suggested her to President Bryant for the position."

"What about Carl Wood?"

"I called Kyle Sandifer and asked if he ever had either Friedman or Wood as a client. He confirmed he had represented both of them. Several years ago, he helped Wood clear up an embarrassing sexual harassment charge without it leaking to the media."

"How embarrassing?"

"Career ending."

Griffin nodded and handed the tablet back to Kruger. "What should I do about them?"

"Above my pay grade, sir."

"Sean, we're old friends. There's a reason I asked you to head up this investigation. I trust your judgment."

"Pittman is no longer a problem. Jane Friedman can be isolated and kept out of the loop. Carl Wood may be another issue. He's your Chief of Staff and very involved with the day-to-day operations around here."

"I can't trust him."

"No, sir, you can't. But you can isolate him."

Griffin stared out the office window, took a deep breath and let it out slowly. "He offered his resignation after I was sworn in, but I didn't accept it."

No one spoke.

Looking up at Joseph, Griffin said, "Can you keep sensitive matters away from Carl for now?"

Joseph nodded once.

"Very well, I don't agree with it, but I will keep him on for a few more days."

Chapter Thirty-Six

"AH, MR. PRESIDENT?"

President Roy Griffin sat at the Resolute Desk reviewing his agenda for the day. The time was 7:30 a.m. and the White House was coming alive after a quiet night. He looked up. "Yes, Carl."

"Joseph gave me your agenda today. I understood that was to be my responsibility."

Griffin smiled. "Yes, it was, but I changed my mind. Joseph seems to have a better feel for the flow. Sorry, Carl. You're still in charge of personnel."

Wood gave the president a suspicious smile. "I see. Do you wish my resignation, sir?"

Griffin hesitated. He stared at the top of his desk for several moments and then looked up. "Actually, I do."

The Chief of Staff's eyes widened and a look of panic crossed his face for just a moment before returning to a neutral expression. "May I enquire as to why?"

"Dmitri Orlov."

"Beg pardon, sir?"

"Carl, please do not insult my intelligence."

"I'm sorry, I don't understand."

Griffin stood, his face turning crimson. "How dare you debase this sacred office. I know you have committed treason in your attempt to cover your indiscretion."

"Sir?"

"We know, Carl. We know."

Wood took a deep breath. "Since when?"

"It doesn't matter."

"I see." His demeanor changed, shifting from contrite to contempt. "And what do you propose I do, Mr. President? Fall on my sword for you?"

"No. You will submit to a lie-detector test."

"No."

"Want to spend the rest of your life in a federal penitentiary?"

Carl Wood stood straight and crossed his arms. "I want a lawyer."

"You will probably need more than one."

Silence filled the Oval Office as Griffin pressed a button on his desk phone. "Ms. Tillman, please send in my protection detail."

Less than two seconds later, four members of the President's protection squad stormed into the room. They surrounded the former Chief of Staff and looked to the President.

"Gentlemen, please inform Special Agent Ryan Clark his presence is needed at the White House."

The lead agent nodded and the four men escorted their charge out of the Oval Office.

Taking a deep breath, President Roy Griffin picked up the phone on his desk and said, "Ms. Tillman, please call FBI Agent Sean Kruger. Tell him I have a confession to make."

———

SEAN KRUGER'S voice emanated from the speaker phone on the Resolute Desk. "Mr. President, this may have been the better strategy."

"Sean, spare me the politically correct BS. Just tell me if I screwed up."

Kruger chuckled. "Far be it from me to tell my president something like that."

"Sean, we've been friends for over five years. I need real and truthful counsel right now."

"Very well, Mr. President."

"Please call me, Roy."

"Very well, Roy. I really believe your actions may have been the correct path. After thinking about it on the flight home last night, I may have been mistaken in my original assessment."

"Really?"

"Yes, no bullshit."

The president chuckled. "Thank you. Explain."

"We need Orlov to panic. Panic tends to produce actions hastily conceived and not properly thought through. I need Orlov to lash out like a wounded animal. Once he does that, JR and his team will be able to undermine the Kremlin's confidence in the man. The seeds have already been sown. We just need a little fertilizer to bring it to fruit and I believe you may have provided the needed manure."

Griffin chuckled. "Good." He paused, his brow furrowed suddenly. "You said team. I thought JR worked alone."

"He has a very knowledgeable recruit."

"Should I worry about this recruit?"

"Jimmie Gibbs doesn't believe so."

The President smiled and looked over at Joseph, who nodded. "Very well. I will leave this in your capable hands."

"Thank you, Mr. President."

"Uh, Sean, should I fire the Secretary of Education?"

"Once again, Mr. President, above my pay grade."

"In other words, yes."

"A good decision, sir."

The call ended and Griffin grimaced. He looked at Joseph. "Will anybody ever call me by my first name again?"

Shaking his head, Joseph smiled. "Your wife will, but no one else may for a long time, Mr. President. Not for a long time.

———

THE SPLIT SCREEN image on the wall-mounted television showed the CNN anchor on the left and two members of Congress on the right. Joseph turned up the volume to better hear the subject matter.

"...my Oversight Committee and the Select Committee on Intelligence, chaired by my colleague, Congressman Tony Holt, will be investigating the recent seizure of three large banks by the Griffin Administration."

The CNN anchor, one of the network's multitude of young attractive females, continued her questioning. "Why do you feel this needs to be investigated?"

Holt answered. "We feel the Griffin administration overstepped their authority. My committee will be investigating why a rogue FBI agent seems to be in the middle of several other recent abuses by this administration."

"Who is the agent, Congressman Holt?"

"I would prefer not to divulge his identity at the moment, as we are currently preparing subpoenas for our investigation."

"President Griffin has only been in office a short period of time. How can you claim his administration is already abusing its authority?"

"That's why we have subpoena power, to investigate if they are."

Joseph rolled his eyes as he listened. Standing with his arms crossed over his chest, he wondered where this sudden expression of defiance for the new president came from. Turning down the sound, he reached into his pocket for his cell phone and made a call.

"Kruger."

"Are you watching CNN?"

"I try not to watch those channels, Joseph."

"Did you know you are now classified as a rogue FBI Agent?"

"By whom?"

"Congressman Anthony Holt. He's chairman of the Permanent Select Committee on Intelligence. They're the committee with oversight over the FBI and DOJ."

"What's the context of his classifying me as a rogue agent?"

"The seizure of Orlov's banks."

A dozen seconds of silence passed before Joseph heard, "Really?"

"Yes, really. Are you thinking what I'm thinking?"

"Yes, I'll have JR look into it." He paused for a heartbeat. "Have Clark or Knoll talk to Yanovich. He might have some insight."

"Consider it done."

———

"WHAT DO YOU THINK, JR?"

JR's left hand covered his mouth as he stared at his computer screen. Alexia stood off to the side with her arms folded over her chest.

JR looked up at Kruger. "I think he's dirty." He pointed to his computer screen. "His history on the committee has never been anti-administration. He's always been kind of an ass-kisser for the presiding president for the past two election cycles. Political party be damned, he swings both ways."

"Orlov?"

JR nodded.

Alexia cleared her throat.

Both Kruger and JR looked at her. JR smiled and prompted, "You have an idea?"

"There's a way to check."

Kruger tilted his head and JR looked like a proud father. Kruger asked, "How?"

"I check in with my Mexico City hacker persona."

JR frowned. "How do you explain your silence?"

Alexia's eyes sparkled. "I tell them I had to relocate."

"Are you going to tell them where?"

She shook her head. "Not this time."

Both men looked at each other and grinned. JR returned his attention to Alexia. "Go for it."

———

THE PRISONER INTERROGATION room smelled of sweat and Lysol, with a lingering background of cigarette smoke from the time smoking was permitted in the room. Peter Yanovich's expression told Ryan Clark what he needed to know. The man was scared.

Sandy Knoll leaned against the interrogation room door, towering over Yanovich. Ryan Clark, sitting across from the attorney, started the questioning. "Peter, we need information."

"I need out of here."

"We can put in a good word for you with the Attorney General."

The lawyer's eyebrows rose. "The Attorney General? What's he got to do with this?"

Giving Yanovich a grim smile, Clark leaned forward in his

chair. "Your case was referred to the DOJ instead of the local District Attorney's office."

The prisoner looked at Knoll and then back to Clark. He repeated this several times before speaking, his voice now an octave higher than normal. "What the hell for?"

"They changed the charges against you from violating the Foreign Agent Registration Act to Domestic Terrorism under the USA Patriot Act to accessory to murder. Trace amounts of elements used in the manufacture of A-232 were found on a pair of shoes in your closet."

Yanovich stared wide-eyed at Clark. "You've got to be kidding me?"

A shake of the FBI agent's head was his answer.

The attorney's wide-eyed expression verged on panic.

"Plus, we caught the man who sprayed it." Clark chose not to go into detail about the Frenchman.

"How? Why? I mean, come on guys, there's no way…" He stopped, his expression changed from shock to recognition. He narrowed his eyes and smiled slightly.

"I get it. What do you want?"

Clark returned the smile. "Anthony Holt."

"What about him?"

"Is he under Dmitri Orlov's control?"

The attorney sat back in his chair, crossed his arms over his chest and smiled.

"Get me a deal. Get me out of here and I'll tell you everything I know."

"Which is?"

"More than you think I know."

"How do I know the information you have is worth it?"

"You don't, but you'll just have to trust me."

"Something I'm not inclined to do right now, Peter."

"You want to know about Holt?"

Clark nodded.

"Okay, here's a sample. Interview a woman by the name of Elizabeth Townsley. I don't know where she lives now, but she graduated from the University of Arkansas in Fayetteville in 2013 or 2014. Their alumni center might know. She can tell you a lot about Holt."

Standing, Clark nodded. "If this pans out and I get you a deal, will you tell us about Orlov's operations in the US?"

"Oh, yeah. Get me out of here first."

———

THE DRIVE to the Arkansas Alumni Association building located north of Bud Walton Arena on North Razorback Road in Fayetteville brought back unpleasant memories for Kruger. As Jimmie Gibbs drove the Range Rover past the arena, Kruger stared at it from the passenger seat. It was the first time he had returned to the site since the terrorist attack five years earlier. Gibbs slowed the SUV.

"Is this where it happened?"

Kruger nodded, lost in his own thoughts. After a dozen seconds, he said. "I first noticed the white van traveling at a high rate of speed on MLK Boulevard and then turn onto this road. I was standing there." He pointed to the west entrance of the huge arena. "Aazim Abbas drove the van off the road onto the grassy area straight at me." He looked over at Gibbs. "I'm told the explosion occurred less than thirty yards from my position. I don't know. I don't remember anything after I saw the van until I woke up in the hospital."

Gibbs smiled. "Yeah, it can happen. Glad you survived."

Chuckling, Kruger looked back at the site. "Me too. If I hadn't, Stephanie would have killed me."

Both men laughed as Gibbs pulled the black vehicle back into traffic.

After displaying their FBI credentials and explaining the

reason they needed to contact Elizabeth Townsley, the director of the center gave them her cell phone number. But not her address.

Back in the Range Rover, Kruger called the number. He heard a soft voice with a southern accent answer.

"Ms. Townsley, my name is Sean Kruger. I am a Special Agent with the FBI. I need to schedule a meeting with you."

The voice was hesitant. "A meeting? About what, Agent?"

"Congressman Anthony Holt."

"Where are you right now, Agent?"

"Fayetteville campus, we just spoke to the Alumni Center."

There was silence on the other end of the call. Finally, after a few awkward moments, he heard, "I work at the Walmart Home Office in Bentonville. I can meet you at a Starbucks located at 102 and Walton Boulevard. How soon can you be there?"

"Give us thirty minutes."

"Us?"

"Yes, there will be two of us, Ms. Townsley."

"I see."

"Will that be a problem?"

"No, I'll be waiting."

Elizabeth Townsley shook their hands after Kruger and Gibbs showed her their FBI identification. Noting her handshake was firm and her clothing professional, he assumed she worked in a managerial job for the giant retailer. Her blonde hair, which she wore in a ponytail, appeared natural. Blue eyes stared at him with apprehension and a touch of suspicion.

After receiving their coffee, the three sat in the back of the café away from the rest of the afternoon crowd. She wasted no time in starting conversation.

"What did you want to talk to me about?"

Kruger smiled. He liked getting to the point. "We need to

know about any relationship you may have had with Congressman Holt."

"Why do you think I had one?"

The question, while not unreasonable, was not the one he anticipated. "So, you did have a relationship with him?"

Townsley displayed a sly smile. "I didn't say that. I asked why you believe I had one."

"Did you?"

The smile remained. "We can dance around this until our coffee gets cold, Agent. Tell me why you want to know and I will respond to your question."

"Holt is under investigation," Gibbs answered. "That's all we can say."

The woman openly laughed, with a touch of bitterness. "Finally, somebody figured out the man is an asshole and no, I did not have a relationship with him."

Kruger spoke in a soft voice as he tilted his head. "Did he rape you, Elizabeth?"

The woman's smile vanished as she stared at her coffee. After taking a sip, she nodded slightly. "I thought with the whole 'MeToo' movement I could finally come out and accuse him of it, but after seeing how other assaulted women are treated by our so-called leaders in Washington, I decided I'd just keep my mouth shut."

"Are you married, Elizabeth?"

"Not yet. Engaged."

"Does your fiancée know?"

She nodded as she studied the coffee cup again.

"I told him about it one night when we were discussing marriage. He wanted me to speak up, but changed his mind after seeing what other women have been through." She looked up at Kruger and Gibbs, wetness welling in her eyes. "He's a good man, agents. I don't want to cause anything to come between us."

"I understand, Elizabeth. But we need to understand the severity of Holt's attack on you."

After a phone call, the woman's fiancée arrived and supported her while she told the two FBI agents her story. Over the course of the next hour, Gibbs and Kruger learned about the attack on Elizabeth Townsley.

Chapter Thirty-Seven

THE FIRST FLIGHT out of Springfield to Dallas-Fort Worth allowed Kruger to park his rental car in the driveway of Kyle Sandifer's son's home by 9:40 a.m. After showing his FBI credentials and conferring with the no-nonsense security detail still watching the house, he was escorted to the kitchen.

As he entered, Sandifer stopped pouring water into a Cuisinart coffee machine and gave him a grim smile. "I appreciate you calling ahead, but will assume this is not a social visit, Agent Kruger."

"No, sir, it is not."

Kruger watched the attorney return to preparing the coffee. His normally professionally styled hair was disheveled, displaying more pronounced streaks of gray. His usual ramrod straight posture was gone, replaced by slightly slumped shoulders. Kruger detected the beginnings of puffy dark circles under his eyes and a loss of weight.

"What has transpired, Agent?"

"Your office remains locked and closed. No one on your staff has been contacted by the new owners with any explanation."

"Dear God." Sandifer closed his eyes, slowly shook his head and stared at the caramel colored water flowing into the carafe. He remained silent until the coffee machine hummed and sputtered the last drips of water through the grinds. Reaching for two mugs in the kitchen cabinet, Sandifer looked at his guest. "Coffee?"

Kruger nodded and the two men sat at a small bistro table in a breakfast nook off the kitchen.

"Mr. Sandifer…"

"Please call me Kyle, Agent."

"Our investigation has turned up information which is, quite frankly, disturbing. Kyle, I have a few names I need to ask you about."

"I'll do my best, Agent. Who are they?"

"We know about Donald Pittman. However, the following individuals have come under scrutiny over the past few days. What can you tell me about Anthony Holt, Carl Wood and Jane Friedman?"

Sandifer let his breath out slowly and studied the liquid in his coffee mug. He was quiet for almost a minute. Kruger patiently waited.

"How much do you know?"

"I would prefer you tell me what you know."

The attorney nodded and stood. "Give me a second," he said as he turned toward the doorway.

Kruger watched as the man left the kitchen and returned twenty seconds later. He placed a black PNY flash drive in front of the FBI agent.

"When I started to suspect something amiss with the sale of our company to Orlov, I started scanning files. I didn't know the man well enough to trust him." He pointed to the small device. "That contains twelve of my most provocative files. There were more, but those individuals have left government or passed away. The files on that disk are of current high-ranking members of the Washington elite. All were my clients and all were involved in career-ending missteps I helped them —resolve."

"Twelve?"

Sandifer nodded.

"Tell me about Holt."

The attorney took a sip of his coffee and then stared at the ceiling.

"He's an ambitious little shit."

Kruger hid his grin by sipping his coffee. "Go on."

A half smile appeared at the corner of Sandifer's lip. "Did you know he is only one of three no votes during the approval process for Roy Griffin as vice president?"

"No, I don't follow Washington intrigue."

"Well, he was. The reason…" He paused and sipped his coffee. "He was thoroughly pissed he didn't get picked for the job."

"How do you know?"

"I still have a lot of friends in Congress, Agent."

Kruger nodded, no longer trying to hide his grin.

"What's he done now?" Sandifer asked.

"He's convening a hearing to investigate why the Griffin administration seized three of Dmitri Orlov's banks here in the states. Plus, he has described me as a rogue FBI agent."

Sandifer laughed out loud. "What a pompous ass."

"Kyle, I've interviewed Elizabeth Townsley. I need confirmation that Holt raped her."

"My case notes and the settlement paperwork are on that flash drive, Agent."

"What about Jane Friedman?"

"That one is a little more complicated. You would think in this age of instant news and reporters constantly seeking the next big story, someone would have discovered that she has a secret."

"Which is?"

"Her husband bought and paid for her Cabinet seat."

Hiding his surprise, Kruger sipped his coffee as he composed his next question. "How would that be possible?"

"Very simple. He asked my firm to set up a number of non-profit 501(c)(4) corporations to funnel money to the campaigns of several key senators on the Health, Education, Labor, and Pension committee. The committee approved of Friedman's nomination and sent it to the Senate floor for a vote. She was confirmed with a one-vote majority."

"I'm not sure that would be considered a federal crime."

"No, by itself it wouldn't be. Except where the money originated."

"Are you going to tell me…"

"Yes, Friedman's husband is chairman of an international investment bank based in Switzerland. He constantly indulges his wife and buys her anything she wants. She wanted a Cabinet position."

"We understand Pittman put pressure on Bryant to nominate her. Why?"

"Pittman had an affair with her before she married her current husband. She more or less told him she wanted a Cabinet position or she'd take the story to the Washington Post."

"So, Pittman was compromised in various ways?"

"Yes."

"How did you find out about the affair?"

"I was Pittman's attorney. He always dumped his mistakes in my lap. I told him to do what she wanted. It's a meaningless Cabinet position anyway. What harm could she do?"

"How's Orlov involved?"

"The husband."

"Not following you, Kyle. How?"

"The originating funds to set up the 501(c)(4)s came from

Advanced Capital Bank in Arlington, Virginia. Do you recognize the name, Agent?"

Kruger was silent for several moments. "Yes, I do. It was a bank controlled by Orlov."

"Was?"

"Federal Reserve shut it down when it failed a stress test."

Sandifer smiled, partially hiding it as he took a sip of coffee. "Interesting."

"So, you believe the money came from Orlov to pay off the senators to confirm Friedman?"

"Yes, but it wasn't Orlov's money."

"How do you know?"

"I don't. I'm speculating. If you look at all the money he's thrown around over the past few years, there has to be a bottomless pit somewhere backing him."

Silence was Kruger's response. He stared at the bistro table top for several moments. "Tell me about Carl Wood."

Sandifer dry-rubbed his face with his hands. When he was done, the attorney looked at the ceiling and took a deep breath. "One of the biggest errors I've made in chasing the almighty dollar as an attorney. I didn't see the connection until you mentioned his name earlier."

"Care to explain."

"Several years back, Wood came to me with a legal problem. He was an up-and-coming attorney with the Justice Department. His then-wife was filing for divorce, claiming physical abuse."

"Interesting."

"Yes, the charge of abuse could get him fired from the Justice Department."

"Okay, go on."

"He was technically bankrupt, but the wife just didn't know it at the time."

"Mistress?"

"No, gambling debts."

Kruger nodded.

"Our firm worked it out with the now ex-wife to drop the abuse charge and settle for a no-fault decision."

"Okay, one problem solved. How did you resolve the money issue?"

Sandifer did not answer right away. He twisted his coffee mug clockwise, then counter-clockwise. Finally, he looked up. "We shopped around for a financial institution willing to help him out of his financial hole. We found one."

Kruger tilted his head slightly as he asked, "Which one of Orlov's banks volunteered?"

"Bank of the Atlantic in Washington, D.C."

Closing his eyes, Kruger slowly shook his head.

"Let me guess, they forgave the loan."

Sandifer shook his head. "I don't know about that, but Wood's gambling debts disappeared."

"Now he's Chief of Staff for the President."

A slow nod was his answer.

Kruger stood. The attorney did not move, but just stared at the table top.

"Thank you, counselor."

———

SITTING in the gate area waiting for his flight back to Springfield, Kruger accepted a call from Ryan Clark. "Hello."

"Sean, where are you?"

"Dallas. Just finished interviewing Kyle Sandifer. Why?"

"Just received a call from the Arlington County jail."

"Uh, oh. Bad news?"

"You might say that. Peter Yanovich was stabbed while taking a shower this morning."

"How bad?"

"He was taken to the emergency room at the Virginia Hospital Center. He's still in surgery. I'm heading over there now."

"They know who did it?"

"Yeah, some guy picked up last night on a DWI. No ID, speaks very little English and all he says is 'I want lawyer'."

"Picked up last night?"

"That's what they said."

"Let me guess, he has a Russian accent?"

"Yeah, a thick one."

"He was paid to do it, Ryan. If Yanovich survives, he'll have to be put in protective custody."

"I'm told his survival is iffy."

"Okay, keep me informed."

The call ended and Kruger looked at the clock on his cell phone. Eighteen minutes until his flight boarded. Time to call Sandy Knoll.

Knoll answered the call on the third ring. "What's up, Sean?"

"Where are you?"

"Lake house. Why?"

"Someone tried to kill Yanovich this morning."

"Shit."

"Yeah, I'm flying back to Springfield from Dallas in a few minutes. Can you and Linda head back to Joseph's place?"

"No problem. What did you learn from Sandifer?"

"Orlov's been at this for a while."

"Okay, what's your plan?"

"I need to brief you and Gibbs. It's starting, Sandy. Orlov is lashing out, just like we predicted."

Chapter Thirty-Eight

THE FAINT CLICKING of a computer keyboard broke the nighttime silence on the second floor of JR's office building. At two minutes past 2 a.m., the only person in the building stopped typing and stared at the three computer monitors located in his personal cubicle next to the conference room. JR's concentration focused on the middle screen as his left arm, elbow on the desk, supported his chin with the hand covering his mouth.

The information displayed on the screen, the result of a concentrated hacking effort to trace the money trail from Moscow to banks around the globe and then to Orlov, depicted a complicated ruse. A ruse used to hide the true source of funding for Dmitri Orlov's empire.

JR's experience and knowledge of tracing international money transfers had been challenged with this exercise. As each layer of deceit was peeled away, he learned more about the tactics used by his Russian opponents. They were good, very good, but he and Alexia were as well and getting better with each layer they stripped away.

With a click of the mouse controlled by his right hand, the

computer made a call to a frequently-called cell phone number.

The call was answered by a voice, heavy with sleep. "Do you know what time it is?"

"It's time to fuck with Dmitri Orlov?"

Now totally alert, Kruger responded, "What did you find?"

"The so-called keys to the kingdom."

"Where are you? The office?"

"Yeah."

"I'll be right there."

Fifteen minutes later, a disheveled Sean Kruger in jeans and a hooded sweatshirt stood behind JR, looking at the computer screens.

"What am I looking at, JR?"

JR pointed to the left screen first, "I've created a flow chart so we can understand how money moves between Moscow and Orlov's organization." He looked up at Kruger. "Money flows both ways. From what we can see recently, more going to Moscow than out. But, sometimes more going out. Depends what they have going on, I guess."

"How much?"

A small grin appeared on the hacker's lips. "Billions."

Kruger's eyebrows rose. "Really? With a b?"

"Yeah, kind of shocked me, too. There's a computer in the Paris office controlling the flow."

"Do you have access to it?"

Nodding, JR pointed to the middle screen.

"Those are pending transfers waiting for authorization from the receiving bank."

Silence returned to the second floor. Kruger paced for a few minutes and returned to stand behind JR. "Can you divert them?"

Fingers flew over the keyboard as JR typed. "Yes."

"Did you set up an account in Orlov's name somewhere and transfer it?"

"That is not very original, Sean. Too obvious."

Crossing his arms over his chest, Kruger looked down at this friend and replied, "Sorry, I'm not a seasoned criminal like you."

"Ha ha," JR typed again. "I set up three accounts, all in the name of a fictitious company registered in Geneva. One bank is in Hong Kong, one in the Caymans and a small bank in Paris."

"Aren't there protocols for banks acknowledging transfers?"

"Yes, there are." He looked up at Kruger again. "Alexia wrote a neat little script she inserted into the controlling computer in Orlov's office. When a transfer is made, a few dollars goes to the real bank and the rest to one of the banks I just mentioned. That way, there is a receipt from both banks. Alexia's little program adds the two totals, deletes the acknowledgement from the bank they use and only displays the acknowledgement from the bank we use. No one is the wiser on the Paris end. They think the total amount was transferred to the Moscow bank. Here's the neat part. If they check the deposit at a later date, their receipt number will not match any records from their bank. They'll have no clue where the money went. It's untraceable."

Shaking his head, Kruger pursed his lips. "How long before they discover the money is missing?"

"Probably a few days. In the meantime, I'm going to move it around until it can never be traced."

"When can you start?"

"Now if you want to."

"Do it."

JR turned to face the monitors and clicked his mouse on an icon.

Kruger frowned. "That's it?"

"Yeah, sorry, no fireworks. Just a click of the mouse."

A FEW MINUTES past 6 a.m., Kruger called Joseph. "How hard would it be for the president to schedule a private meeting with Holt?"

"Not hard. Holt's telling anyone who'll listen he wants a Cabinet position."

Kruger chuckled. "Perfect. Schedule one for tomorrow. I'll fly in this afternoon and brief you on what I have."

"The president will want to be involved."

"That's even better."

"THANK you for meeting with me on such short notice, Congressman."

The president shook Anthony Holt's hand and motioned for him to sit on one of the sofas in front of the Resolute Desk.

"It's an honor, sir."

Roy Griffin raised an eyebrow and gave Holt a condescending smile. "Are you sure?"

"Beg your pardon."

"I'm afraid I have summoned you here under false pretenses, Congressman Holt."

Holt started to stand, but Griffin said in a harsh tone. "Sit down."

The congressman automatically sat, but his attitude changed to defiance. "What's this…?"

His question was interrupted by the appearance of three Secret Service agents, Joseph Kincaid and FBI Agent Sean Kruger as they entered the Oval Office. Two agents took a stance, one on either side of the president and one behind

Holt, who remained on the couch. Holt stared at Kruger and pointed, "What's he doing here? He's a danger to this country."

Kruger sat across from Holt and smiled. "As are you."

In an attempt to escape, the congressman started to stand, but was gently pushed back into his seat by the Secret Service agent standing behind him. Looking up, Holt said, "What the hell?"

Clearing his throat, Kruger placed an iPad on the coffee table and touched an icon. The voice of Elizabeth Townsley emanated from the small device and described her experience with Anthony Holt. Kruger sat on the edge of the sofa, facing the man, his elbows on his knees, hands clasped in front as he stared into the now terrified eyes of the future ex-congressman.

Holt recovered his initial shock quickly and narrowed his eyes. "I get it. Just because I'm going to investigate your illegal seizure of those banks, you're going to threaten me with this false accusation."

Smiling, Kruger placed a file folder on the coffee table. "Actually, I didn't seize them. The Federal Reserve, FDIC and the IRS did."

"At your insistence."

Kruger shook his head. "You have your facts mixed up. I was just an FBI agent there to observe the process."

Holt sat back in the sofa and crossed his arms. "This little shakedown will not prevent my moving forward with a Congressional hearing about your conduct, Agent Kruger. If all you have is a crazed woman accusing me of attacking her, then you have nothing. No one will believe her."

With a smile, Kruger opened the file folder and extracted copies of the legal agreement between Holt and Townsley prepared by the law office of Rothenburg and Sandifer and signed by a Virginia judge. He held them so the man across from him could see them.

"Recognize this?"

Holt's eyes grew wide and his mouth opened, but no words were spoken.

"This is a legal agreement, whereas, you settled financially with Ms. Townsley to hide your sexual assault on her." He removed a photograph from the back of the file and laid it so Holt could see. "Recognize the large man entering your congressional office?"

An expression of recognition and horror now appeared on the face of the congressman as he stared at the photograph. He remained quiet.

"Of course, you do. His name is Boris Volkov and he is an agent working for a Russian Oligarch named Dmitri Orlov. Orlov is under investigation by the Department of Justice for various crimes against the United States."

Kruger pointed at Holt, his voice growing colder, "We have evidence you told Volkov where I lived, a fact he did not know prior to his visit to your office. Thanks to you, there was an attempt not just on my life—but my wife's. Federal charges are being prepared against you for aiding and abetting a declared enemy of the state. I don't think the constituents in your district will be pleased."

"I only told him the city." The voice was weak, barely above a whisper.

Roy Griffin leaned against the front of his desk. "Congressman, I believe it is time for you to resign from Congress to spend more time with your family."

Gathering the paperwork and picture, Kruger returned them to the file folder and closed it. "The DOJ will not pursue legal action against you if you resign. This matter will be closed and you can go back to whatever it was you did before being in Congress."

"What if I refuse?"

"I hope you do." Kruger tapped the folder, "Then all of this will be leaked to a high-profile Washington Post reporter. Ever hear of Tracy Adkins?"

Holt only stared at Kruger.

"I've already contacted Tracy about this. She is really excited about writing the story, particularly when she would have the legal files for reference and direct access to Elizabeth Townsley."

Turning his attention to the President, Holt begged, "I don't want to resign. I'll drop the congressional hearing and enthusiastically support any and everything you want done in Congress."

Griffin chuckled. "Sorry Tony, you can't have it both ways. The only way to keep that information out of the Washington Post is to resign and..." The president paused. "And, I am very serious about the next part. Never run for elected office again. Agent Kruger has a long memory and so do I."

"I can help you."

Taking a deep breath, Griffin looked at the Secret Service agents. "Please escort Mr. Holt out. He has a resignation speech to write."

Holt was escorted out of the Oval Office by two of the Secret Service agents. When he was gone, Griffin sat behind his desk and took a deep breath. "I hope that was the best way to handle him."

Joseph spoke for the first time. "It was the only way to handle him, Mr. President. You've been in this town long enough to know how to play hardball."

"Yes, but I don't have to enjoy it."

Kruger smiled. "Roy, JR tapped into Holt's emails early this morning. He was contacting various news media outlets and raising the question of your legitimacy as president. All at the behest of Orlov."

Wide-eyed, Griffin stared at Kruger. "What were the responses?"

"Most of them blew him off as a conspiracy theorist. Some of the more radical ones were interested in talking to him, but so far no interviews confirmed."

"Do you have copies of the emails?"

Kruger nodded.

With a grim smile, Griffin closed his eyes. "I don't trust him. I have a funny feeling he'll call my bluff." He paused. "I hate this part. Leak the emails to Tracy Adkins and include the pictures and information of his meeting with a Russian agent. Make sure she has proof of Volkov's connection to Orlov. Let the American public understand the kind of Congressman he's been. Just keep the sexual assault and Elizabeth's name out of it for now."

"Good idea, sir."

285

Chapter Thirty-Nine

"WHAT DO YOU MEAN, money is missing?"

The young computer operator looked up to find Dmitri Orlov glaring at him. "It is like I said, sir. Every transfer I have made over the last seventy-two hours has not gone through. It is not in any of the banks we use. The money just vanished."

"How can that be? You have confirmation of the transfers, do you not?"

"Yes, sir. When I check with the bank where the money was sent, they tell me the confirmation numbers do not match anything they have on record. Without a valid confirmation number, they will not investigate."

Orlov's face turned crimson as he stared at the young man. Before he could say anything his assistant, Gregory Pushkin, entered the small computer room. Leaning so he could whisper in Orlov's ear, he said, "Moscow is on your private line, sir."

Wide eyed, his face still flushed with anger, Orlov stormed out of the room to listen to what he knew would be a one-sided diatribe rather than a conversation. After closing his office door, he picked up the handset. "This is Dmitri."

Those were the last words he spoke until the call ended abruptly. After replacing the handset in the phone's cradle, he sat behind his desk and buried his face in his hands. Ten minutes later, he rose from his chair and left the office.

He passed his favorite small café, continuing to walk northwest on Quai de Montebello, until he came to Rue de la Cite and turned right. Tourist traffic grew heavier as he crossed the Seine and approached the front courtyard of Notre Dame Cathedral. As he turned right, he saw one of his frequently-visited benches unoccupied. Tourists milled around taking pictures of the cathedral and the giant statue of Charlemagne on the southwest side of the church's courtyard. He sat and stared at the magnificent statue, his mind elsewhere.

Fifteen minutes later, Boris Volkov sat next to him, but did not speak. Without looking at him, Orlov said, "This FBI agent is becoming intolerable."

Volkov nodded but knew better than to say anything.

Orlov turned to the large man sitting next to him. "What would you do, if you were me?"

"How concerned is Moscow?"

"My friend is not happy. He also questions my judgement and loyalty."

"An untenable position. One that needs correcting."

"Yes." Orlov returned his gaze toward the 140-year-old statue of the 8th century so-called father of Europe. "Kruger has shown himself to be resourceful. He has assets we were unaware of."

"I would agree."

"What about this Anthony Holt? Has he started his investigation?"

"I do not have good news about him."

Frowning, Orlov kept his attention on the statue. "Tell me."

"He is no longer a member of the House of Representatives."

Orlov turned abruptly and glared. "Did you not explain our conditions for keeping silent about his past?"

"I did," Volkov nodded. "He resigned from Congress last night without giving specifics on why. We think Kruger talked to Sandifer and knew Holt's background as well. Holt had a meeting with President Griffin yesterday afternoon and then resigned that evening."

Volkov could see the older man's hands shaking as he struggled to maintain his composure.

"What about Yanovich? Is he still a problem?"

The larger man shook his head. "No."

"We are down to few assets, Boris. Are our Free America friends ready?"

"Almost. I received a communication from the hacker in Mexico City."

A calmer Orlov returned his attention to Volkov. "Oh, why has she been silent these past weeks?"

"She indicated she had to relocate."

"To where?"

"She will not tell me. She did not appreciate our sending Popov to find her."

"Have you found him yet?"

"No."

"Go on about the woman."

"She is mad at us, but more so at the Americans."

"Will she help us?"

"For the right amount of money."

"How much?"

"Two million Euros."

Orlov returned his attention to the statue. The number of tourists milling around the plaza in front of Notre Dame Cathedral grew as the minutes passed. Volkov sat quietly as his boss remained silent. Ten minutes went by before Orlov spoke again. "I don't trust her, so therefore I do not believe her."

The larger man nodded.

"Boris, I am tired of pouring money into Free America without results." Orlov stood. "Tell them it is time to show me what they can do. Otherwise, I will cease providing money. That should get their attention." He walked toward the entrance to the cathedral.

Chapter Forty

CURRENTLY THE ONLY residents staying at the house, Gibbs and Alexia wandered the tree line of Joseph's property. Hand in hand they strolled, enjoying the solitude of the morning. Sandy and Linda Knoll occasionally stopped by, but today they were at their cabin at the Lake of the Ozarks. Conversation was light, each sharing a little more of their background as they became more comfortable around each other.

Alexia turned to look at Gibbs. "Where is this property you want to buy?"

Smiling, Gibbs nodded his head toward the north. "The area is about a hundred klicks that way. I haven't really looked yet."

"What is klick?"

"Sorry, kilometer."

She nodded. "There are lakes to the south, correct?"

"Yes, but they're a lot more commercial with tons of tourists. Stockton Lake isn't as developed as Table Rock."

"What about this Lake of Ozarks? Linda talks about all the time."

"It's farther north and really crowded."

"Oh." She returned her attention to the ground as they walked. "Can I see the area sometime?"

Gibbs stopped walking and smiled at her. "Sure, when?"

"It is Sunday morning. Why not go today?."

They practically ran back to the house.

Two hours later, Gibbs turned the black Range Rover onto a dirt access road off Missouri 215. The path led to an area used at times by fishermen to launch small jon boats into the lake. Parking the SUV, they both sat and stared at the lake as it stretched out toward the north.

"This is beautiful, Jimmie. It reminds me of a place my father took us when we were little."

Gibbs smiled. "It is pretty, isn't it?" They both exited the car and walked toward the water's edge. With a sweeping gesture, Gibbs' hand created an arc in the air. "Look at that, not a boat dock or house in sight."

"It is sad."

He looked at her and raised his eyebrows. "Sad? What do you mean?"

"No one can enjoy this sight from their home."

Gibbs reached over and hugged her for a brief moment.

"That's the point, Alexia. This is a non-development area. It's done on purpose to maintain the beauty of the lake."

"Why do you want to live here, Jimmie?"

Taking a deep breath, he let it out slowly. "For most of my life, I lived in the San Francisco area of California. Very urban, very crowded. During my career in the Navy, I saw a lot of desolate locations on this planet. To me this is a compromise between over-development and desolation." He paused. "Listen. See how quiet it is?"

He stopped talking. The only sounds audible were the lapping of waves on the shore and birds chirping in the surrounding trees.

She looked around, her arms crossed tightly over her chest.

A smile slowly grew on her face and she reached for him to be closer.

"Yes, it is quiet. Not like Paris or Mexico City. But are there no people living here?"

"Lots of people live here, but not right on the lake. There's a town not too far north called Stockton. They even have a Catholic church."

She smiled and glanced at him.

"Are you Catholic?"

"Yes, but I haven't been a practicing one for years."

"I know, I have not attended mass since leaving Spain."

He brought her closer. "I'm going to ask a question, but if you are uncomfortable answering it, don't."

She looked at him, concern in her eyes. "Is this a bad question?"

"Not at all."

Smiling, she nodded. "Then you may ask."

"I saw how you interacted with Sean's and JR's kids. Do you want children of your own someday?"

She remained quiet as she stared out over the lake. Gibbs saw tears welling up in the corner of her eyes. She wiped them away.

"At one time, no. I did not live a life good for children, so I never thought about it. But now…" She grew quiet again. After a long silence, she looked at him. "Why do you ask?"

"I was curious."

"And why were you curious?"

"Oh, I don't know. My military training taught me to gather as much information as possible before making decisions."

She smiled, pulled away and punched him lightly on his bicep. "So, you are gathering information about me. Not very nice Mr. James Gibbs."

He chuckled. "I want kids someday."

She returned to his side and let him embrace her again. Then she placed her head on his shoulder and encircled his waist with her arm.

On the drive back to Joseph's property Gibbs' cell phone chirped. He answered with the Bluetooth system in the Rover.

"This is Jimmie."

"Where are you?" The voice was Kruger's, the tone matter-of-fact.

"North of Springfield, about twenty klicks, why?"

"Is Alexia with you?"

"Yeah, why?

"Get to JR's office as fast as you can."

The call ended and Gibbs looked over at Alexia. "What do you think that was all about?"

"I do not know, but I believe our lazy Sunday is over."

———

FORTY-FIVE MINUTES LATER, Gibbs and Alexia stood next to JR's cubicle and watched his hand fly across the keyboard. Without stopping, he glanced at Alexia.

"The company is experiencing a rather nasty DDoS attack. Most of the hits are probing, looking for vulnerabilities. As you know, we have protocols in place to prevent this kind of crap, but whoever is doing it is overwhelming our defenses. I need you to use our alternate ISP and trace the attack. Start with that Free America bunch."

Alexia nodded and rushed to her cubicle.

Gibbs turned to Kruger who was standing behind JR. "What the hell did he just say?"

Kruger motioned for Gibbs to follow him into the conference room. After the door was closed, Kruger turned to the younger man.

"JR and I think Orlov has a bunch of hackers attacking his

company. Just before you got here, he had it under control, but didn't have time to trace the attack. That's why he needed Alexia."

Gibbs nodded and glanced out the conference room window to watch Alexia working at her computer. "JR brought her out of her shell, Sean. She feels needed."

Kruger grinned. "She is needed. JR needs someone he can rely on to help with his growing company. Even though he is taking more of a back seat, he needs someone with the same skill set he has to do what he's always done. She's that someone."

They watched as Alexia stood up and yelled at JR, "It is them, JR."

JR nodded and yelled back, "Thought so. Remember what we discussed last week?"

"Yes."

"Do it."

Alexia smiled and sat back down.

Chapter Forty-One

MONDAY MORNING FOUND Kruger shaving in front of the mirror on his side of the vanity. Stephanie stood in front of her side, applying what little makeup she normally wore. A radio with weather alert capabilities sat on the windowsill tuned to the local NPR station for national news updates.

Kruger stopped shaving as he listened to two announcers discuss breaking news coming from Washington.

"Cynthia Stewart is at the Capital. What have you learned so far this morning, Cynthia?"

"Robert, the Speaker of the House and Senate Majority Leader, in a rare joint decision, have called an emergency meeting of Congressional leadership. Those members have been arriving for the past ten minutes and have hustled into the Senate chambers. None have spoken to reporters and all were surrounded by members of the Capital Police and escorted inside."

"Any speculation about the reason for this sudden meeting?"

"Only rumors. The meeting may have something to do

with leaked legal files, received by this reporter overnight, from the closed law firm of Rothenburg and Sandifer."

Kruger groaned. "Oh, shit." He wiped off the remaining shaving cream and reached for his cell phone laying on the bathroom countertop. He pressed an icon and waited.

"Clark."

"What the hell is going on in Washington?"

"Legal files from Rothenburg and Sandifer were leaked to the press overnight."

"Uh-boy."

"It gets worse. Sixty-two senators and members of the House of Representatives are implicated. Some of the charges are silly and frivolous, but the majority are probably career-ending. At least, that's what it looks like to me."

"Who's taken responsibility for releasing the files?"

"Guess."

Kruger closed his eyes. He hated these types of stall tactics. "Ryan, just tell me."

"It's the group being financed by Orlov, the bunch of hackers calling themselves Free America. They're claiming to be American patriots who plan to clean up government by exposing the criminal behavior of members of Congress."

"What's the agency doing about this?"

"Don't know at this point. My source is Tracy."

Kruger frowned, choosing not to tell Clark about the attack on JR's business the previous day. "How's she involved?"

Clark paused for a several moments before answering. "She's not sure. She received a PDF file in her private email account early this morning from the group. The message contained the legal files and an outline of their plans. According to the letter, more revelations are coming." Pausing for a moment, he waited for Kruger to respond. When none came, he continued. "The email recipients were a who's who of Washington, D.C., political reporters. All were addressed to personal emails, not their business email accounts."

"Great. What did you do with the email?"

"Forwarded it to Charlie Craft and then called Seltzer."

"Good, have Tracy forward it to JR. Here's the email to use."

Kruger recited the address from memory.

"What do you think is going on?" Clark asked.

"We dropped a hornet's nest on the bear's head."

"Do you think they'll keep our team involved?"

"If I have any say-so, they will. Remember, we report to the president."

"I keep forgetting."

Kruger smiled. "Plan on a conference call later this morning."

———

THE CONFERENCE CALL occurred at 11:20 a.m. at JR's office. Sandy drove in from his place at Lake of the Ozarks and Gibbs arrived an hour before. JR and Alexia did not attend as they busied themselves with damage control from the cyber-attack on Sunday.

After the meeting concluded, Knoll left for the airport and Gibbs asked Alexia to drive him. That way she would have a vehicle while he was gone. Plus, he wanted to spend a few more minutes with her.

Kruger stood behind JR's cubicle trying to find a non-flavored coffee pod.

"Don't you have just plain coffee pods for this thing?"

"I didn't get a chance to do my normal Sunday coffee buying at Sam's. We're running low, so look in the credenza. I have a couple of boxes hidden in the back on the bottom shelf."

JR's attention never wavered from his computer screen.

Following directions, Kruger found the unopened boxes of Ethiopian Yirgacheffe coffee pods.

"How the hell do you pronounce this name?"

"Beats me. Try it, it's good."

Shrugging, Kruger opened the box and placed one of the pods in the Keurig. He watched JR while the machine made his coffee. "How bad was the damage?"

"Not very. It did expose a few, uh…" JR hesitated for several heartbeats, "Vulnerabilities I didn't realize were there."

Kruger brought the now-finished coffee to his lips. The aroma was pleasant and he took a sip. Smiling, he nodded.

"You're right, this is good."

"Told ya."

"What about those vulnerabilities?"

"Without going into a boring thirty-minute lecture, let's just say they found a small hole in my firewall. Alexia fixed it. She's good, Sean." He turned and looked up at his friend. "Not sure where this relationship with Jimmie is going, but she seems more at peace with herself than when we first brought her here."

Nodding, Kruger studied the dark liquid in his coffee cup. "Do you trust her?"

JR gave Kruger a slight smile before turning back to his computer. "I only trust three people in the world. One is standing behind me, one is in Washington, D.C., pretending to be a big shot and the other one I married. But, yes, I am starting to trust her."

"She and Jimmie are going to start looking for land around Stockton Lake."

JR whipped around to stare up at the FBI agent. "Since when?"

"That's where they were yesterday when I called him."

"Huh."

"That was my response. I hope it works out for them."

"Let's hope it does. She's going to be a huge asset to this company."

Silence filled the second floor of JR's building. Kruger leaned against the credenza sipping his coffee while JR worked his magic with the computer. Five minutes passed without the two men speaking. Finally, Kruger asked, "How hard would it be to locate the members of Free America?"

"By locate, what do you mean, country or street address?"

"Both."

"Country is easy, street address, maybe." He stopped typing and turned once again to look at Kruger. "What do you have in mind?"

"Directive from the president."

"Uh-oh. What did I miss during the conference call?"

"The attack on your company was just one of hundreds. Several power grids were attacked, with Boston being the largest. They just got it back up this morning. There were a number of large banks struck. Money was transferred out, but they don't know how much at the moment. Turbines in Boulder Dam started to overheat, but were manually shut down before too much damage occurred. Air traffic control at Atlanta went haywire and almost caused two airliners to collide mid-air. Pilots prevented it. Need I go on?"

JR shook his head. "What did the president say?"

"He wasn't happy. The FBI will focus its collective attention on this for the foreseeable future. As will the CIA."

"What are we supposed to do, sit on our hands?"

Shaking his head, Kruger grinned.

"Nope, we…" He paused. "More precisely, you and Alexia are going to be the spearhead. Find them, JR. Tell us where they are. Once you do, Knoll, Jimmie, Joseph and I will figure out how to stop them."

"Wouldn't that be easier for the collective efforts of the FBI and CIA?"

"One would think so, but Roy doesn't want to wait. He believes you can find them faster."

Silence fell again between the two men. JR blinked several times as he stared at Kruger. "Hope he isn't putting too much faith in my abilities."

"He isn't. He knows you can do it. So do I."

———

"HOW LONG WILL you be gone, Jimmie?"

"Don't know. Week, maybe two."

Alexia grew quiet as she drove the Range Rover toward the airport.

"I will still be here," she said, looking straight ahead.

Gibbs smiled and looked over at her. "Were you thinking about leaving?"

She shook her head. "Not what I meant. I know we have not been together for very long, but..." She took a deep breath. "This place, you, everything about being here feels like home to me now."

He placed a hand on her thigh.

"Yeah, it's growing on me, too."

She shot a quick glance at him.

"I want to have children with you, James Gibbs. Do not get yourself killed. Okay?"

Suppressing a smile, Gibbs turned his head to study the passing scenery. An emotion he seldom felt washed over him. A small tear welled in his eye, which he wiped away with the back of his hand. Looking back at her he noticed, not for the first time, but with more appreciation, how pretty she was. A simple, honest beauty. He preferred simple and honest.

Once he felt he could speak without his voice catching, he said, "I have no intention of getting myself killed."

Chapter Forty-Two

WHEN ALEXIA RETURNED from dropping Jimmie off at the airport, silence permeated the second-floor cubicle farm. Normally filled with company associates, only JR remained. She quietly sat at her cubicle and booted up her laptop. Busying herself with work unfinished from the day and her back to the opening of the cubicle, she did not hear him lean against the wall.

"Are you okay, Alexia?"

She only nodded her head but did not turn to look at him. The back of her hand brushed a tear from her eye.

"Jimmie will be back."

"I know."

Silence again filled the empty room as JR studied the back of her head. Finally, he said, "I need to tell you something."

She stopped typing, turned, but did not speak as she looked at him. Her eyes were red from crying.

JR continued, "You and I have more in common than you realize." He paused, but she did not respond. "We both are very capable with a computer. That's a given. As you know, I also committed a computer hack that got me into serious trouble. Like you, when you escaped from Paris, I had to flee New York City. Now I'm here, as are you."

She still did not respond.

He continued, "When I got here, I was by myself for six months before I met Mia, Joseph and Sean. For some reason, and I am thankful for it, they believed in me." He swept his hand through air. "All of this became a reality because those three individuals cared about me and had faith. Without them, I'd be someplace I don't care to think about. You have the same opportunity."

She tilted her head slightly. "How?"

"Because that same group of individuals plus several more believe in you and they care."

She nodded, studied the floor between them and then returned her attention to JR.

"I only thought Jimmie cared."

JR smiled. "Yes, Jimmie does care, but Sean, Stephanie, Mia, Joseph, Sandy and I also care. We also believe in you and your abilities. You have the chance of finally having a permanent home here, if you want it."

He paused, "There is one more thing I need to tell you. When I found out you sold my identity to Orlov, I was furious."

She nodded, but remained quiet.

"Once I had a chance to think about it, I'm glad you did. Believe it or not, I've been paranoid about someone finding out who I really am. I came to the conclusion that it doesn't matter if people know my past. It's the past. I have a good life, with a wonderful wife and child. I have friends who care about me and a successful career. Thank you."

Tears trickled down her cheeks as she stood, walked to him and hugged him. Startled, he limply returned the embrace. It only lasted a few seconds before she disengaged and sat down again.

"I just want Jimmie and I to be together."

The smile returned to JR. "From what he told me, that shouldn't be a problem."

A smile came to her face. "He did?"

"Several times. There is something you need to know about Jimmie."

She stiffened.

"It's a good thing, don't worry."

She relaxed, "What do I need to know?"

"If you hear any rumors about him being what some people call a lady's man, don't believe them."

"What is this lady's man?"

"An American saying. It means someone who dates a lot of girls."

"Oh."

"Don't worry, Jimmie isn't really like that. Deep inside that tough ex-Navy Seal is just an everyday guy who wants nothing more than to have a normal life to share with someone special." JR pointed to her. "You're that special someone."

She sat a little straighter and a slight smile appeared. "He is not an everyday guy, JR."

"No, but that's how he sees himself."

"I did not realize it."

"Not too many people do. Now, we have a lot of work to do to help Jimmie and Sandy."

"What is that?"

"Find where all the members of Free America are located."

"How?"

"I'll show you."

———

304

PRESIDENT ROY GRIFFIN listened as each person at the table summarized the actions their department had taken since the cyber-attack earlier in the week. Except for a few questions to clarify the sometimes-vanilla responses, he maintained his silence. After the meeting, he asked FBI Director Paul Stumpf, CIA Director Dwight King, NSA Director Admiral Leland Berry, Homeland Security Director Paula Adams and Chairman of the Joint Chiefs of Staff General Bud Nelson to stay behind. After the room was emptied, Joseph sat next to the president across from the five individuals remaining.

Griffin started by turning to Stumpf and asking, "Paul, you said very little. Why?"

"Because, Mr. President, we don't know a lot right now. I'm not going to point my finger at another department, like some of your Cabinet members just did, when I don't know where to point my finger. It's that simple."

Griffin nodded. "I noticed." He turned to Admiral Berry. "What is NSA hearing?"

"Lots of chatter and lots of excitement about how successful the attack was."

"What about CIA, Dwight?"

"HUMINT is starting to come in confirming SIGINT..."

Griffin raised a hand, palm out. "English, please, Dwight."

"Sorry, sir. Our folks on the ground are starting to get confirmation of what our satellites seem to indicate. The locations of the hackers are spread out over western and eastern Europe, plus there are numerous locations around the Mediterranean Sea."

"Can you pinpoint any yet?"

"Not with any certainty."

"I see. When do you think you can pin down their locations?"

"Week, maybe two?"

Frowning, Griffin said. "They could move by then."

Turning to General Nelson, Griffin asked, "Bud, how soon could you have missions for Special Forces ready if we find the targets?"

"We practice this scenario all the time, sir. Once we know where, we can move quickly."

The president turned to Joseph.

"You know most of the key players with our allies in Europe," he said. "Can you coordinate with them once we know where the hackers are?"

"Yes, sir."

Paula Adams spoke up. "Sir, you act like we already know where they are. Do you know something the rest of us don't?"

Hesitating, he looked at Joseph who nodded.

"I am going to share something with each of you that goes no further than this room. Understood?'

Everyone nodded.

The president clasped his hands in front of him and laid his arms flat on the conference table.

"After 9/11, this government managed to increase spending, manpower and technology on national security to the point where one agency does not know what the other one is doing. You all saw this in action today. Twenty-two agencies fall under your jurisdiction, Paula. Yet not one of them has any clue how to find these cyber-hackers who are poised to strike again at any minute."

The room remained quiet. Paula Adams started to say something, then thought better of it. The president gave them a grim smile.

"With all the technology, resources and assets this government possesses, it can't find these criminals." He paused for effect and held up one of his hands and made a V with his index and middle fingers. "Two individuals sitting in a second-floor cubicle farm in the middle of the country found them."

There was a collective gasp at the president's words. Then

questions came from everyone but Paul Stumpf. He realized who Griffin referred to. The president turned his attention to Nelson.

"We will have locations pinpointed for you by midday tomorrow, General, so have your teams ready. Joseph will travel to NATO as soon as this meeting concludes to coordinate the strikes on locations in Europe. The United States will take care of the hackers in Algeria, Tunisia and Libya. We all have a lot to do. Thank you for your attendance this morning."

The room emptied except for Paul Stumpf and Joseph.

Smiling, the Director of the FBI said, "Sean's team?"

Griffin nodded. "They know the location of three hackers within the USA. I need the FBI to silence them before they can alert the others."

"Consider it done, sir."

Stumpf left the room and Griffin turned to Joseph.

"You have a lot of work to do," he observed.

"Comes with the job, sir."

"Yeah. Now I have to have tea and crumpets with the new ambassador from England." He paused. "Joseph, what the hell are crumpets?"

———

SANDY KNOLL WATCHED the darkened house in an economically-depressed part of St. Paul, Minnesota, from the front seat of a fifteen-year-old Cadillac Escalade.

Kruger sat in the seat next to him. "Thought you only drove Denalis?"

"I do, but one has to sacrifice at times for the team. Besides, this doesn't stick out in this neighborhood."

Kruger chuckled. "I suppose not." He glanced at his watch, fifteen minutes past 3. "Is Jimmie in place?"

Knoll nodded. "We'll join him when they're ready. He has

a tech guy checking with a snake camera. They're making sure no one's awake in the house."

A quick flash and then two longer flashes appeared from the porch of the house. Knoll made sure the overhead light was off and turned to Kruger. "Show time."

Kruger stepped out of the Cadillac and flipped a black hood attached to his jacket over his head. With his head down, he shuffled across the street to the darkened porch, Knoll following behind him. Once on the porch, his Glock appeared in his right hand and he flipped the hood back. He stared into the eyes of Jimmie Gibbs who was dressed in FBI assault gear.

The slender ex-Seal gave them a slight smile and in a low voice said, "You two ready?"

Both Knoll and Kruger nodded and lowered their night vision goggles.

He spoke into a microphone attached to his helmet. "On three. One... two... three..."

A muffled pop could be heard as directional-shape charges disintegrated the front door hinges. Two FBI rapid response agents rushed into the room, guns at ready. At the same time, a similar sized team at the back door breached it in the same manner. With Kruger, Knoll and Gibbs, seven FBI agents quickly swept into the structure, clearing rooms as they worked their way through the home.

Kruger swept his assigned area and came upon a dark room with a blinking light next to the window. A shadowy figure, visible in the green hue of the NVG, hunched over a laptop and frantically typed a message.

"FBI," Kruger yelled. "Hands on your head."

The figure took a brief glance at Kruger but did not stop typing. Without hesitation, Kruger raised his Glock and pulled the trigger.

Chapter Forty-Three

KNOLL AND GIBBS watched as the suspect, now in flex cuffs, was escorted to an FBI tactical van and driven away.

Kruger remained in the room with the laptop and consulted with JR on his cell phone. "So, what am I looking for?"

"I wish you hadn't shot the WiFi router," JR complained. "It would be so much easier for me to see if any emails got out."

"Sorry, I lost my head and panicked."

JR chuckled. "I'm sure that wasn't the case. What kind of email program is he using?"

"Looks like Gmail."

"Looks like?"

"Damn it, JR, it's Gmail, okay?"

"Figures. Easy to set up multiple accounts without a lot of effort. Go to the sent folder."

"I'm there."

"When was the last email sent? It will be on the far right side."

"Looks like seven-thirteen last night."

"Good, he didn't get an email out. Now, check the draft folder."

"I don't see one."

"Is there a down arrow with the word 'More' next to it?"

"Yes."

"Click on the arrow."

"Got, it. Okay, found it. There's the beginning of an email."

"Any information about the raid?"

"Looks like he only managed to start filling out who he was sending to."

"Good, that will give us emails we can trace. Anything in the subject line?"

"No."

"Okay, check the time stamp on the far right."

"Same time as our raid."

"He didn't get a message out, Sean. You guys are good to go. Get that laptop to me as quick as possible. No telling what we will find on it."

The call ended.

Knoll leaned against the door jamb and asked, "What's the verdict?"

Kruger glanced over his shoulder at the big man and smiled. "Nothing got out. It's still in the email draft folder."

"Smart, shooting the WiFi router."

"Lucky shot."

"You weren't trying to hit him?"

Kruger shook his head. "Nah…" He stood and faced Knoll. "How would you feel if you were typing an email and someone shot you?"

Knoll chuckled. "It'd suck."

"Let's get this laptop to JR. No telling what he'll find on it."

THE LAPTOP SECURED from the hacker's house revealed its secrets gradually. JR and Alexia were finally able to confirm the rest of the Free America members' locations.

The computer hacker looked up at Kruger, who was yawning. "You look like shit."

"Yah, well, so do you. What'd you find?"

JR gave the FBI agent a quick smile and handed him a sheet of paper.

"Locations with GPS coordinates. Thank you, Google Earth."

Kruger stared at the page. He lowered it and smiled at his friend.

"You never cease to amaze me."

"Just part of the service."

CONGENIAL MEETINGS between party leaders in ultra-partisan Washington, D.C., occur occasionally, particularly when the nation faces a crisis, 9/11 and the Great Recession being the most recent. A different crisis faced the new president and Congress. Since the revelation of sixty members of Congress hiding criminal or sexual assault charges behind the veil of attorney-client privilege, fifty resignations and ten censure votes occurred within the ranks of Congress. Replacement members had yet to be appointed by their respective state governors, so legislation ground to a halt with majorities suddenly in question.

However, with the devastating cyber-attacks occurring almost simultaneously with release of the Rothenburg and Sandifer legal files, the country stood on the precipice of a total collapse of public trust in government. Protests, rallies, sit-ins and political pundits denounced the handling of the crisis by members of Congress. Cries for investigations and additional resignations arose from individuals seeking to take advantage of the chaos.

Into this backdrop, President Roy Griffin gathered top congressional leadership for a meeting, a meeting that would ultimately cement his place in history as one of the great presidents of the United States.

———

AS WAS HIS HABIT, Griffin listened to the whining of Senate Majority Leader David Clayton without interruption. FBI Director Paul Stumpf sat quietly next to the president.

"Mr. President, it is the complete and total failure of the FBI, CIA, NSA and all the other departments under Homeland Security that caused this crisis. What are your plans to correct this mismanagement of our country's security?"

Griffin smiled as he tapped a pencil on a notepad in front of him. Looking Clayton in the eyes, he said, "First, I have accepted the resignation of Paula Adams, effective immediately and assigned retired Four-Star General Alton Patterson as interim Secretary. That is, until Congress can confirm his appointment." He looked around the room, but no protests seemed to be forthcoming.

He continued, "Second, with all due respect David, you are wrong. The failure of Homeland Security to prevent this crisis was a lack of vision by Congress and the previous administration to place a competent individual in charge. Ms. Adams is a fine person, but she lacked the background and vision to deal with the complexity of the department."

House Minority Leader Darrel Williamson said, "The Senate rushed her appointment, just like they did most of Bryant's picks for his Cabinet."

The president raised his hands. "Darrel, we're here to solve a problem, not pass blame. There is plenty of that to go around. Let's keep focused on what we can do now."

Williamson glared at the president for a few moments then softened his expression and nodded.

"Mr. President," Speaker of the House Sheila Davidson pointed at Paul Stumpf, "what is the FBI doing and why didn't they stop this attack?"

"I'm glad you asked, Sheila." Griffin turned to the FBI Director and nodded.

With a smile, Stumpf passed out five folders, one for each of the leadership, one for the President and one for him to refer to. "The FBI has been investigating the individual who financed these attacks for almost six months," he announced.

Clayton pounded the conference table with his fist and his face grew crimson. "Why didn't you stop the attacks if you knew about them?"

Griffin raised a hand. "David, let Paul finish."

The elder senator from the state of Illinois sat back, crossed his arms and glared at Stumpf.

The FBI Director continued, "We learned of a group calling themselves Free America several weeks ago. Following a money trail, created by a Russian oligarch named Dmitri Orlov, allowed us to discover the existence of this group."

Senate Minority Leader Jefferey Ramirez frowned. "That name sounds familiar. Where have I heard it?"

"Senator, Dmitri Orlov was the Chairman of the Board for three banks seized by the FDIC several weeks ago. They all failed a surprise stress test."

"Now I remember."

"We believe that event was the catalyst for the cyber-attack by Free America."

"Why do you say that?"

"Because we can trace over fifty-two million euros transferred by Orlov into the coffers of the hacker group."

All four members of congress widened their eyes. Stumpf continued, "Because this Free America group maintained operational silence until the attack, we had no idea where they were located. That is no longer the case. Members of our Cyber Crime department located individuals within this group inside the continental United States immediately afterward. The FBI Rapid Response Group, utilizing coordinated raids last night, raided all three residential locations and seized equipment and individuals involved in the crime."

No response came from the members of Congress, only silence.

Griffin picked up the narrative: "Because of these raids, the FBI can identify the exact locations of the remaining members of the hacker group. They are overseas. Most are in Europe, which our NATO allies will handle. The problem with the locations not under NATO control is they happen to be in three countries on the southern rim of the Mediterranean."

Clayton put his hand on his forehead and muttered, "Oh, dear god."

"Tunisia, Libya and Morocco."

Sheila Davidson frowned. "Are the governments of those countries involved?"

Stumpf answered the question. "They do not appear to be."

Ramirez turned his attention back to Griffin. "What do you need from us, Mr. President?"

"What I need from Congress is the authorization to use our military Special Forces to seize these sites and detain any individuals involved."

Clayton stared at Griffin with an astonished look, as did Sheila Davidson. Both looked at each other and seeing the political value of the request, they both turned to Griffin and said in unison, "Yes sir, Mr. President."

After the members of Congress left the room and Paul Stumpf busied himself putting files in a briefcase, Roy Griffin turned to him and asked, "Do you think they bought it?"

Stumpf gave the new president a sly smile. "They didn't have to buy it. They saw political gain in approving your request. You'll get the authorization."

By midnight, President Roy Griffin received authorization from Congress to go to war against Free America.

Chapter Forty-Four

AT EXACTLY 12:07 A.M., the Cessna Citation X touched down at the Springfield Branson National Airport. After completing his landing, the pilot immediately taxied the plane to a well-lit private hangar. The doors opened as the aircraft approached. Inside the hangar, a dark gray Chevrolet Suburban with blacked out windows could be seen parked next to the northern wall. As the plane entered the hangar, its twin turbine engines spooled down and the hangar doors closed. When the plane came to a complete stop, two large exhaust fans kicked on to ventilate the interior of aviation fuel fumes.

Two men stepped out of the Suburban. One was large, the sleeves on his FBI-emblazoned polo shirt stretched by the size of his biceps. The other man, slender with an athletic air about him, waited for the cabin door to open on the Cessna.

Four men, all dressed in orange jumpsuits, all shackled and all with hoods over their heads, were escorted down the plane's airstair by U.S. Marshals.

The larger of the two FBI agents recognized one of them. U.S. Marshal Toby Weber smiled and shook the man's hand.

"What's it been, Sandy? Two years?"

"At least."

"Time flies."

"It does. Any trouble on the flight?"

"Only the Russian, kept mumbling about wanting a lawyer. He started to agitate the others, so we gave him a mild sedative. He's groggy, but conscious. Shouldn't cause any problems for you."

Weber handed Knoll a clipboard with numerous pages held secure at the top. "Transfer of custody paperwork."

Knoll nodded, skimmed the documents and looked up at Weber. "Got a pen?"

When the documents were signed and returned, Weber handed Knoll a 9 X 12-inch white envelope with the seal of the U.S. Marshal's office stamped on it.

"Tell Kruger he owes me. I hand-walked that through DOJ yesterday."

Accepting the envelope, Knoll nodded. "Thanks, Toby."

Almost as tall as Knoll, Weber was a no-nonsense U.S. Marshal with short gray hair, a deep Texas tan, round face, piercing green eyes and broad shoulders. The last time they worked together was in Houston, Texas, during a hostage rescue.

Weber pointed to the four men as the other U.S. Marshals arranged them in the Suburban. "The three hackers haven't said a word since we took custody of them. One kind of whimpered when we put the hood over his eyes, but the others, not a sound."

"You ever been to the Federal Center here?"

"Couple of times. Why?"

"You know a quick way to get them inside without a lot of fuss?"

"Yeah, want me to drive?"

"Thought you'd never ask."

Four hours later, with the three former members of Free

America and Yuri Popov secure inside the United States Medical Center for Federal Prisoners, Weber was driven back to the airport where the Cessna remained in the hangar, refueled and ready to depart. Knoll watched the plane take off and turned to Jimmie Gibbs.

"Now the fun begins. You gonna grab some sleep here in town or go back to Joseph's?"

"Alexia's been working sixteen hours a day at JR's since this mess started. I got her a hotel room close to his building. I'll crash there." He glanced at his watch. "She's probably already back at JR's."

"How you two doing?"

Gibbs gave Knoll a sly smile. "Pretty damn good."

Knoll grinned.

———

AT PRECISELY 10 A.M., one of the hackers entered an interview room situated in the Federal Center. He was still dressed in the same orange jumpsuit he arrived in earlier that same morning. He looked haggard and weary. His hands and feet were shackled and attached to rings in the floor and tabletop, his freedom of movement limited.

Kruger, followed by Knoll, entered the room. Knoll leaned against the door and gave the young man a menacing scowl. Kruger sat across from the prisoner and opened a manila file folder. He read quietly for five minutes as the hacker started to sweat, but remained quiet.

Looking up, the FBI agent said, "My name is Sean Kruger. I'm a Special Agent with the FBI and my colleague is Special Agent Benedict Knoll." He pointed to the pages in front of him. "This report tells me you've not been very cooperative."

The hacker stared at Kruger, but said nothing.

"I see, the silent type. Let me tell you what we know, then maybe you'll be more talkative."

Again, his answer was silence.

"Your name is Edwardo Gates, born in New York City to a single mother from Puerto Rico. She gave you the father's last name, but you've never met the man. Your mother worked two jobs while fellow Puerto Rican friends, whom your mother lived with, helped raise you. You served a two-year stint in the army with one deployment to Afghanistan and an honorable discharge. On your return to the states, you attended Rutgers on a scholarship and graduated with a computer science degree. You worked for Google for three years, then suddenly quit. Now you're sitting in a Federal Prison with a possible life sentence staring you in the face. What did I get wrong, Edwardo?"

"Leave my mother out of this."

Kruger cocked his head. "When was the last time you spoke to her, Edwardo?"

The man shook his head.

"Did you know she passed away this past spring?"

The young man's eyes widened and he sat a little straighter. His expression changed and he narrowed his eyes. "You're trying to trick me." He paused as he stared at Kruger. "I have nothing else to say."

Shrugging, Kruger pulled out a folded newspaper page and opened it so the hacker could see the obituary.

As the man read the article, his shoulders slumped again and wetness pooled in his eyes. "I didn't know."

"Why did you join Free America?"

In his unguarded state, Edwardo said, "To avenge the way my mother was treated in this country."

"How was she treated?"

"Like a non-citizen."

Kruger did not respond. He simply let the man talk.

"She used to tell me stories of Puerto Rico, the food, the culture, the simple way of life and how much she missed it. She came to New York City with a man she met in San Juan who promised her a high-paying job and to become his wife. Once she became pregnant with me, he disappeared. There was no high-paying job and the guy was married. As a single mother, she never made more than minimum wage in a city with one of the highest costs of living in the world. She was never given a chance and could not afford to take us back home."

"So, you joined Free America to change the country?"

"Yes."

"Did you know who funds the group?"

The man shook his head.

"Why that particular group?"

"Because we were all Americans looking for a way to change our country for the better."

Kruger pursed his lips. "How many members of Free America do you think there are?"

"I do not know. If I did, I would not tell you."

Nodding, Kruger clasped his hands together on the table. "Of the thirty members we've identified, only three are Americans. The rest are located in European cities and three countries in northern Africa. The group is funded by a Russian named Dmitri Orlov, an oligarch who used to be a KGB officer prior to the fall of the USSR. Trust me, his intent for the group is not to change the United States for the better."

Gates stared at Kruger for a dozen seconds. A slow smile appeared. "Nice try, Mr. FBI. I don't believe you."

"That's fine, because I think your self-proclaimed patriotism is bullshit. You were motivated by greed. It's as simple as that."

The prisoner tried to stand up, but the shackles prevented

him from raising more than six inches. "Don't you dare question my love for my mother and this country."

Kruger shook his head. "If you loved your mother so much, why didn't you know she was gravely ill?"

"I was busy."

"Once again, bullshit. Some of my colleagues interviewed your mother's friends. She hadn't heard from you in over three years, Edwardo. Want to try again and tell me the truth or do you want to spend the rest of your life in some dark hellhole in Colorado?"

"I want a lawyer."

"Can't have one."

"Why? I'm an American citizen. It's my right."

Kruger stood and smiled. "Not if you've been declared an enemy combatant and a terrorist. You have no rights according to the Patriot Act of 2001."

He turned, nodded to Knoll and the two agents left the room.

Knoll chuckled as they walked down the hall. "Think he'll figure out you're as full of shit as he is?"

Returning the chuckle, Kruger looked at his friend. "Let's hope not."

THE INTERVIEW with Yuri Popov proved to be more productive. The Russian was led into a different room. He was unshackled, but still wore the same orange jumpsuit. Kruger and Knoll were waiting for him. After he sat down across from Kruger, he said, "What do I need to do to not be sent back there?"

"Tell me everything you know about Dmitri Orlov and his organization."

"How can I do that, Agent Kruger? If I help you, I will be

arrested and sent to a much worse hellhole when I get back to my mother country."

"We can always put you into a general population prison. Let your embassy know where you are. Maybe the same thing that happened to Peter Yanovich will happen to you."

Popov closed his eyes. "What happened to Peter?"

Reaching into his inside breast suitcoat pocket, he retrieved two pictures and laid them on the table between he and Popov. He pointed to a picture of a large man entering a coffee shop. "Recognize this man?"

"Yes, it is Boris Volkov."

"That was taken by a security camera in a Starbucks in Arlington, a few days ago." He pointed at the second picture. "Do you know the guy Volkov is talking to?" The picture was of two men hunched over a table in conversation.

The Russian shook his head. "No."

"You sure?"

Popov glared at Kruger, his forehead furrowed. "Yes, I am sure. Who is he?"

Tapping the picture on the image of the other man, Kruger gave Popov a grim smile. "He was arrested on a drunk and disorderly charge later that night and remanded to the same sheriff's jail as Yanovich. He stabbed Peter to death the next morning."

Popov took a deep breath and let it out slowly. "I want a deal."

"Thought you might." Kruger opened the white envelope with the seal of the U.S. Marshal's office and extracted a sheath of papers. Placing them on the table facing Popov, he sat back and folded his arms over his chest. "That document is from the United States Department of Justice offering to place you in the Witness Protection program in exchange for your full cooperation."

Silence filled the room as Popov stared at the documents.

He blinked rapidly, his stare shifting from Kruger to the papers several times. Finally, after five minutes of silence, Popov said, "What do you want to know?"

———

IT WAS APPROACHING 6 P.M. JR's eyes, blood-shot with fatigue, stared at the computer screen. He did not hear his wife approach his cubicle. Still needing crutches to get around, she managed to pull up a chair and sit down next to him.

In her Texas drawl, she said, "JR, why are you still here? You've been at this since yesterday without sleep."

He did not look at her, but nodded. "I know. I'm missing something. Alexia and I have located all the members of Free America and I know the raids are planned. But once that happens, what stops Orlov from starting all over again? It will set him back, but it won't stop him."

She placed a hand on his shoulder. "JR, a long time ago, my Pappy used to read me stories about the Texas Rangers."

JR frowned and looked at her with a puzzled stare. "I'm not following you, Mia. What has this got to do with stopping, Orlov?"

"Let me finish. After the Civil War, the southern states were devastated. A lot of folks who had nothing, decided to settle in Texas to start a new life. One of the bigger problems they faced were Mexican bandits coming across the Rio Grande and raiding their settlements. The Rangers were in charge of protecting them. Pappy claimed his great-great granddaddy, Roy Brown, was a Ranger. I never doubted him and enjoyed listening to stories of his exploits."

"Mia, is this going anywhere?"

"Yes, be patient."

JR nodded, placed his elbow on the desk and supported his head with his hand.

"Anyway, Roy Brown had a problem with a certain Mexican bandito named Cortez. He and his men were terrorizing settlers, trying to make a go of it west of what is now Austin. The Rangers could never catch Cortez, but they captured or killed the men he rode with. The bandito would ride back to Mexico and recruit more men and return. Finally, Roy Brown thought of a solution. He asked for a meeting with the leader of northern Mexico. They met at the Rio Grande. Roy had a group of rangers with him and the leader had protection as well. To make a long story short, Roy convinced the leader that the bandito was stealing more than what he was reporting. After Roy Brown's visit, Cortez, the bandito, disappeared and was never seen again."

Blinking, JR was quiet. "Who was the leader Roy Brown spoke to?"

"The legend is he spoke to Emiliano Zapata."

Smiling, JR nodded. "So, Roy Brown convinced Zapata that his loyal bandito wasn't that loyal."

Mia nodded.

"We've already hidden a lot of Orlov's money." He paused and smiled. "So, if we conveniently let his friend in the Kremlin know where that money is…"

"Very good, JR. I believe you have the skills necessary to make that happen."

Chapter Forty-Five

KRUGER STOOD next to Bentley Thatcher, a member of the Royal Canadian Mounted Police, inside the CATSI security gates monitor room at Toronto Pearson International Airport. Thatcher held a photo of Boris Volkov given to him by Kruger. This was the first time either man had worked with the other. Thatcher, familiar with the legend of Sean Kruger, found the real individual readily likeable.

When they first met, Thatcher's demeanor indicated he was less than pleased to be a subordinate to an FBI agent from the States.

Kruger put him at ease immediately. "Sergeant Thatcher, I am not here to interfere. I'm here to assist with identification. The suspect we are looking for has violated numerous Canadian statutes as he has in the United States."

As the men shook hands, Thatcher tilted his head. "Not what I assumed, Agent. I was led to believe you would request immediate extradition."

Shaking his head, Kruger smiled. "No, sir. I am merely here as a courtesy. The DOJ feels Canada will have better luck prosecuting this individual than the United States. This is your bust, not mine."

The smile on Thatcher's face grew.

In the third hour of their vigil Kruger pointed to a large man entering the security queue, his passport and boarding ticket in hand. "That's him, Bentley."

Thatcher nodded and spoke into a handheld radio. "Heads up, lads. Suspect is in the queue. Large man, brown overcoat draped over his arm with a gray suit. Line three. Let him pass through and then we'll have a chat with him."

Kruger heard several "rogers," "got it," and "about time" from the other members of the RCMP waiting around the security gates. Volkov passed through the gate without incident until he emerged from the security area. As he moved into the terminal, he noticed three men and two women converging on him. His head swiveled as he looked for an escape avenue. None appeared acceptable. With growing concern, Kruger watched as Volkov grew more agitated with the perceived threat.

He said, "Bentley, tell your people..."

Before he could complete his warning, Volkov slid behind a mother holding a young child's hand and wrapped his arm around her throat. He screamed, "Back off, or I'll crush her neck."

By this time, Thatcher and Kruger were out of the security office rushing toward the increasingly disparate scene fifty feet from the security gate. The young boy cried as his mother's eyes bulged and her face grew crimson as pressure on her air passage increased. She tried to scream, but she did not have the air to do it.

Five RCMP trained their Smith and Wesson 5946 sidearms at Volkov as he held the woman and faced them. When Kruger and Thatcher arrived, Volkov used his free arm to pull the woman more in front of him, creating a smaller target. Since Volkov was already covered by the RCMP, Kruger did not draw his weapon. Instead, he stood next to one of the female Mounties and said, "Give it up, Boris. Popov is talking and Orlov won't help you."

Volkov screamed and increased the pressure on the woman neck. Her eyes rolled up inside her eye sockets and she went limp.

A single gunshot rang out. The exposed side of Volkov's forehead disappeared in a pink cloud of mist and the unconscious mother sank to the floor.

Thirty minutes later, the woman Volkov took hostage was en route to a local hospital with a crushed larynx. Her chance of survival increased dramatically when a traveling doctor did an emergency tracheotomy.

"Who fired the shot, Bentley?"

"I'm surprised you didn't hear it. It was the female officer you stood next to."

"Kind of wondered why my ears were ringing. Thought it was the adrenaline rush."

A grim smile appeared on Thatcher's lips. "I should discipline her, but she did save that mother's life."

"How is the woman?"

"Emergency room. We will know shortly."

Kruger offered his hand to the sergeant, "Sorry to cause all the trouble, but I need to get back to D.C. and brief a few people."

"It was a pleasure meeting you, Agent Kruger. Next time, come as a tourist."

The FBI agent replied with only a grim smile.

———

PRESIDENT ROY GRIFFIN and Joseph Kincaid listened to Kruger as he recapped the events of the past several days.

"Twenty-five of the known Free America hackers are in custody, two are dead and three were not at their residences when the raids occurred. Interpol is searching for them as we speak."

Joseph tapped a notepad with a pencil and frowned. "What about Popov?"

"He signed the Witness Protection agreement. He's giving us details on Orlov's ultimate plan."

Griffin stiffened. "What is it?"

"Relatively simple. When he was dealing with Robert Burns Sr., he discovered there were a lot of politicians who had less-than-perfect backgrounds. By buying Rothenburg and Sandifer, he had access to who those politicians were. At first, he wanted to blackmail them, but with the sheer number of important individuals involved, he decided exposing them would create more havoc."

The president stood and started to pace. "What was Free America all about?"

"Popov didn't know for sure, or at least he won't admit he knows But he did speculate it wasn't really Orlov's idea. It was forced on him by his friend in the Kremlin."

Joseph tapped his fingers on the side table. "Why did he feel that way?"

"Don't know, but I can guess."

"Indulge us."

"It was a back-up plan if the first one didn't work. Orlov panicked and released both at the same time. From what I have seen, it didn't work too well either."

Griffin stopped pacing and turned his attention to Kruger.

"It did, but not in the way he intended. Congress is actually working together on this for a change. There is bipartisan agreement we need to step up our cyber security and they finally admit the Russians have been trying to interfere with our elections for almost a decade."

"Good."

"What's next for your team, Sean?"

Kruger gave the president a sly smile. "JR's working on a little surprise for Orlov. Once he tells me it's been delivered, I'll take Knoll and Gibbs and fly to Paris. I want to be the one to tell Orlov about it."

President of the United States Roy Griffin smiled.

―――――

"HOW LONG WILL YOU BE GONE?" Alexia watched as Gibbs packed his duffle bag.

"Not sure, Alexia. Sean didn't say."

"I want to come with you."

Jimmie Gibbs raised an eyebrow. "Thought you couldn't step foot in Paris."

"Alexia Montreal can't, but Alexia Martinez can. Besides, I want to get married in Notre Dame."

Gibbs smiled and crossed his arms over his chest.

"You do? To whom?"

"You silly. That way I will be Alexia Gibbs, wife of a handsome FBI agent and soon-to-be mother."

His smile turned to a frown. "Excuse me?"

She laughed and embraced him. "I'm pregnant with your child, Mr. James Gibbs."

He returned the embrace.

"Not sure what to say at the moment. This is unexpected. It's great, just unexpected."

She raised her head and looked him in the eyes. "Are you telling me you don't know how babies are made?"

He laughed and hugged her tighter.

―――――

"IT WAS ACTUALLY MIA'S IDEA."

Kruger looked at his friend with a quizzical expression. "Huh."

JR shook his head. "Is that all you can say?"

"At the moment. So, what did you do?"

"I transferred all the money we skimmed on the transfers, plus thirty million Euros from an account in Dubai. All that money now resides in a bank in Hong Kong."

"So?"

"The owner of the Dubai account resides in Moscow."

"Who's the owner of the account in Hong Kong, or should I guess?"

JR did not respond right away. "You heard about the Free America hacker in Stockholm that wasn't home when they raided his house?"

"Yeah, he's the last one still at large. Interpol is searching for him."

Shaking his head, JR smiled. "They won't find him. He doesn't exist."

"What do you mean, he doesn't exist?"

"I made him up."

"How did…"

"Easy, Sean. I needed someone associated with Orlov to make the transfer. Someone who could be blamed with what appeared to be ties to the banker."

"So, who's going to tell the owner of the account in Dubai?"

"When you get to Paris, let me know. I'll make sure he gets the message."

Chapter Forty-Six

WELL-HIDDEN by the crowd milling around the street vendors across from Orlov's office building, Kruger watched as the banker exited and turned to the northwest on Quai de Montebello. Stopping in the small café on the ground floor of his building, he bought a coffee in a tall paper cup and continued his walk toward Rue de la Cite.

The number of midday tourists making the trek to and from Notre Dame Cathedral made the sidewalks crowded and the going slow across the Seine. Once in the courtyard of the ancient church, Orlov walked to his favorite bench and sat down.

Kruger followed, staying behind Orlov as they approached the center of the courtyard. A quick survey of the area found Sandy Knoll standing in the middle of a crowd of tourists at the cathedral's entrance. Gibbs maintained a twenty-yard distance behind Kruger making sure no one disturbed the meeting about to occur.

While Orlov stared at the statue of Charlemagne, Kruger appeared next to him and sat down several feet from the banker. Orlov turned to see who arrived and recognized Kruger immediately.

Without a change in expression, the Russian returned to looking at the statue. "You have been a resourceful adversary, Agent Kruger. Congratulations."

Kruger sat with his hands in his leather jacket and remained quiet.

"What do I owe this visit to, Agent? I am sure you did not fly across the Atlantic to just sit next to me."

"No, I didn't."

"Well?"

"Actually, I wanted to bring you up-to-date on the results of your—uh—activities in the United States."

"How thoughtful."

"Yes, I think so."

"So, tell me, exactly what were those events and what were the results of these so-called activities?"

"Did you know that all members of Free America are either dead or in custody in various jails around the world?"

The Russian blinked rapidly several times, but did not change his expression. "Not sure who you are referring to. I have never heard of this Free America group."

"Ahh…." Kruger nodded and pulled a folded piece of paper from his inside jacket pocket. "For someone who has never heard of them, you certainly were generous to them. Since the sixteenth of June of this year, you've transferred over twelve million Euros into their operating account at the Credit Suisse Bank in Geneva. Want to see the bank records?"

He held the paper, now unfolded, so Orlov could see it.

Orlov glanced at the paper, turned his attention to a tourist boat moving upstream on the Seine, then turned back to Kruger. "You have me at a disadvantage, Agent. You say I know something about events I know nothing about. How do I defend myself against these false accusations?"

"No need to defend yourself. I am merely pointing out facts. You don't have to say anything. Just listen." Kruger's tone sharpened and he narrowed his eyes while he made the next statement. "The cyber-attacks carried out by Free America accomplished one thing, although I doubt it was what you expected."

"What did I expect?" His eyes were now cold as they stared at Kruger.

"You expected them to push the citizens of the United States into a panic and cause Congress to once again fall into dysfunction. It did, at first, at least until we determined where the attacks were originating. Once it was known who instigated them, President Griffin received a mandate from Congress to stop the interference. Our technology sector is working overtime to build new safeguards against cyber-attacks. A friend of mine's company is right in the middle of this endeavor."

Orlov snorted. "Fantasy."

"Is it? Special Forces from four European countries and the United States identified locations and stopped your hacker buddies."

Orlov stood and stared down at Kruger. "I am done listening to your delusions."

"SIT DOWN."

The Russian frowned, but returned to sitting.

"We discovered a security camera shot of Boris Volkov talking to a man who later murdered Peter Yanovich while he was in custody at the Arlington County jail. Volkov' tried to fly out of the Toronto airport, but unfortunately met with an accident."

Orlov stared at his coffee cup, but did not raise it to his lips.

Kruger continued, "You made one huge mistake, Dmitri."

"And what might that be, Agent?"

"You sent the Frenchman to try and kill my wife and me. The big mistake he made was also hurting the wife of the friend I just mentioned. It became personal to both of us. Not smart at all."

"Please tell me when you are finished telling me these delusional accusations. It is becoming quite tiresome."

"I understand certain individuals in Moscow are questioning your effectiveness and loyalty."

Silence was Kruger's answer.

"Know where that came from, Dmitri?"

The Russian stared across the Seine at his office building but did not answer Kruger.

"My friend."

Orlov glared at Kruger with his face turning crimson.

"You see, cyber-attacks can go both ways." Kruger glanced at his watch and then back at Orlov. "The problem is, my friend is better than those amateurs you hired."

The sound of screeching tires could be heard from across the river. Orlov's eyes widened as he watched three cars skid to a halt in front of his office and three men from each car rush into the building.

Kruger stood and pointed toward the newly-arrived cars on Que de Montebello. "If I had to guess, those gentlemen are probably here to escort you back to Moscow."

Orlov also stood and stared Kruger in the eyes. "What have you done?"

"I didn't do anything. You see, my friend in the cyber security business is also one of the best hackers in the world. He made sure all of your screw-ups were revealed to your friend in Moscow. Who, by the way, now thinks you are a thief. I doubt he is very pleased with you right now."

Orlov turned away from Kruger to attempt an escape and ran straight into the chest of Sandy Knoll, who growled, "Going somewhere, Dmitri?"

The Russian recoiled from the encounter and tried to step

around Knoll. His attempt stopped when the retired Special Forces Major grabbed his arm.

Kruger looked across the river as the nine men emerged from Orlov's building. One hurried to the driver's window of the first car and gestured toward the cathedral's courtyard. "Uh-oh, Dimitri, looks like they know where you are."

Orlov struggled to free himself from Knoll's grip, but the big man held him in place.

Jimmie Gibbs, now at Kruger's side, chuckled. "Looks like I get to practice my Russian."

Kruger's mouth twitched as he watched the three cars speed across the Rue de la Cite bridge and skid to a halt in the circle drive in front of the courtyard. The nine men emerged from the cars, leaving a driver in each. All were dressed in dark business suits and moved with the practiced precision of trained military men as they spread out in a semi-circle to confront the four men near the concrete park benches where Kruger's party stood.

Gibbs turned to Orlov and said, "These guys look pissed, Dmitri. Sucks for you."

Kruger barely suppressed his smile as he watched the senior member of the group approach ahead of the other. He was Kruger's height, blond with dark blue eyes, slender face and an air of authority. When he was ten feet away, he pointed at Orlov and spoke in Russian.

Gibbs nodded and replied in the same language.

The leader smiled and motioned for his men to stand down.

Gibbs turned to Kruger and explained, "He told me they were here to help Mr. Orlov find his way back home and for us not to interfere with their task. It wasn't quite that friendly, but you get the point."

"What did you tell him?"

"I told him we were there to make sure Dmitri waited for them. That's when he smiled."

"I noticed." Kruger turned to Knoll and nodded.

The big man released Orlov's arm and the banker stood still, a defiant look spread across his face. He began speaking in Russian, but before he could finish his speech, three young men appeared by his side and started walking him toward the waiting cars. The Russian who Gibbs had spoken to returned his attention to the three Americans and gave them a quick bow, then turned and followed Orlov to the cars. A minute later the cars disappeared into the Paris traffic.

Kruger turned to Gibbs and asked, "What did Orlov say there at the end?"

"Something about being a Colonel in the FSB and reporting only to the president. I don't think they gave a shit."

"Apparently not." Kruger looked around. Tourists wandered the courtyard as they flowed in and out of the historical cathedral. "Once again, we find ourselves in this beautiful city having an afternoon spoiled by Dmitri Orlov." Out of the corner of his eye, he caught a glimpse of a familiar woman standing on the steps of Notre Dame. She smiled when he looked at her. He turned to Gibbs.

"I thought Alexia didn't like Paris."

"She loves Paris. With her new identity, she can move freely around without worrying about being arrested."

"Huh."

Knoll chuckled, "Tell him the real reason she's here."

Gibbs waved at her and then turned to Kruger.

"She wants to get married in Notre Dame."

Smiling, Kruger looked back at Alexia. "To whom?"

Knoll laughed and Gibbs shook his head.

Epilogue

JOSEPH LEANED against the wood railing facing all the activity occurring on his large backyard deck. He held a crystal highball glass with ice and twelve-year-old Glenfiddich. As he took a sip, he watched JR, Jimmie Gibbs, and Sandy Knoll standing next to a large charcoal grill attending to steaks, chicken and burgers. JR's son and Sean's children ran in the yard playing tag. Mary, Mia, Alexia, Linda and Stephanie stood in a huddle, laughing and gossiping. A smile came to his face as he realized this was his family. A group of people he loved and enjoyed being around.

Sean Kruger walked up and leaned against the railing next to him. "How long do you and Mary plan to be here?"

Joseph glanced at Kruger. "A week. Unless some crisis occurs. Why?"

"Just curious."

Nodding was Joseph's reply. The two old friends surveyed the activities on the deck. As the first warm weekend since winter, it was a perfect Saturday afternoon to gather and be together in a social setting. He looked at Jimmie Gibbs and then at his bride, Alexia. He turned to Kruger. "When is Jimmie and Alexia's baby due?"

"Sometime in late July."

"She doesn't resemble the woman you first brought here at all."

"No, she doesn't. She's no longer the gaunt person we found in the Mexican apartment. The weight she's gained looks healthy on her, she smiles and laughs more, adores Jimmie, loves being around children and continues to be a valuable asset for JR's company."

"Good. I'm glad it worked out for both of them."

"So's Jimmie."

Joseph smiled. "How's Stephanie doing?"

"No ill effects from the accident. She's more aware of what's going on around her and a more defensive driver." Kruger smiled. "I believe she finally realized my constant reminders about being cognizant of her surroundings were a noble endeavor and not harassment."

Joseph chuckled. "I haven't had an opportunity to talk to Mia. Is she doing okay?"

"Seems to be. She's like JR, doesn't talk about it much."

"I noticed she has a slight limp."

"Occasionally, only when she's been on her feet too long. Doctor told her that would eventually disappear." He turned to Joseph. "What about you? Are you and Mary coming back soon? You're six months into your one-year commitment to Roy."

With a grim smile, Joseph nodded. "Yes, I know. Mary and I miss this place and the solitude. But…"

"Uh-oh, the dreaded, 'but'…"

"It's complicated, Sean. Griffin is making a difference. Even he's surprised. He's got a new Cabinet with competent men and women, plus Congress is working with him."

Chuckling, Kruger sipped his scotch. "How long will that last?"

Returning the smile, Joseph answered. "Who knows? It could fall apart tomorrow."

"You didn't answer my original question."

"To be honest with you, we don't know. Mary is involved with the First Lady in several women's advocacy councils. I have this funny feeling we will be there longer than a year, maybe two. I really don't know. It's up to her."

"What about this place?"

"I spoke to Jimmie about it."

"And?"

"They asked permission to convert one of the upstairs bedrooms into a nursery."

Kruger smiled. "I take it they will be staying."

Joseph nodded. "For a while. They bought land near Stockton, did you know that?'

"No. Good for them."

"They're going to build. From what Jimmie told me he inherited a little money when his father passed and is going to use it to start construction."

The two old friends fell into silence as they watched the activity on the deck. After several comfortable moments of quiet, Joseph said, "The President is very pleased with the work you're doing."

"Tell him I'm glad he's pleased."

"Are there more threats out there like Orlov?"

"We think so."

"How bad?"

"Hard to tell. After Orlov was taken back to Moscow, all the internet chatter went silent. JR thinks they are retrenching and trying to determine their next steps."

"That's scary."

Kruger nodded. "Yes, it is."

Joseph turned to Kruger again. "How much longer are you planning to do this, Sean?"

The right side of Kruger's mouth twitched.

"Right now, I'm not traveling much. I like that. As long as the travel is limited, I'll stick around. Why?"

"The president asked me to find out. He wants your team to start looking into other threats."

Raising an eyebrow, Kruger looked back at Joseph. "Such as?"

"The increasing number of lone gunmen attacking random public gatherings."

"I thought that was our original mandate."

"It was, but after we disbanded when Bryant became president, the mandate disappeared. Roy is concerned about the increasing number of mass shootings. They're becoming more frequent each year."

Kruger sipped his scotch, but did not respond.

Joseph continued. "Any ideas?"

"No, but with Alexia working for the company and JR taking a less active role, he'll have more time to think about it."

"Probably be a good idea to put several proposals together."

Frowning, Kruger looked at Joseph. "Okay. Do you know something I don't?"

"The President is tired of saying his thoughts and prayers are with the families and not having an answer for them. He wants a definitive action plan."

"What's Congress going to say?"

"As long as it doesn't include taking guns away from people, they will approve anything."

"That ship sailed a long time ago, Joseph. Taking guns away isn't the answer. Being able to identify vulnerable individuals and then providing mental health care may be one way, but it's not the only solution. Will Congress approve funds?"

"We won't know until the president asks them."

"Is that why he wants the proposals?"

Joseph nodded.

"Guess I'd better get busy."

Get a FREE prequel novella from J.C. Fields

vinci-books.com/ghost-in-the-mirror

Some shots echo forever.

Twenty years after executing a Desert Storm mission that continues to haunt him, former Marine sniper Michael Wolfe has retreated into the shadows.

But when FBI Special Agent Sean Kruger investigates a series of expert assassinations targeting military officers, Wolfe's name keeps surfacing.

Next in the Sean Kruger Series

vinci-books.com/seankruger6

A murdered friend. A ticking clock. A final case that cuts too close.

FBI profiler Sean Kruger is thrust into a chilling investigation when his close friend is murdered.

Turn the page for a free preview…

The Dark Trail: Chapter One

The first glimpse of dawn lightened the eastern sky as Deputy Director of the FBI Alan Seltzer tied the shoelaces of a brand-new pair of New Balance athletic shoes. He rose on the balls of his feet to make sure the shoes were as comfortable as the day he'd bought them. They were.

Satisfied, he exited the kitchen into the garage, hit the button for the automatic door opener and retrieved his five-year-old Cannondale carbon-frame racing bike from its place of honor, a space-saving bike rack on the east wall. The bright yellow cycling jersey and padded biking shorts fit his slender frame snuggly, a reminder he was still in good shape even though his fiftieth birthday would occur in a few weeks. After fastening the straps of his boldly colored bike helmet under his chin, he guided the bike into the ebbing darkness and punched the code on the keypad to lower the door.

With it closing behind him, his eyes were immediately drawn to a dark-colored Ford Explorer sitting in front of the house across from his. A vehicle parked on the street in this neighborhood, while not illegal, remained a rare occurrence.

He noted the unusual event, but it did not cause his sense of concern to heighten.

As he mounted the bike to start his daily routine, he remembered not kissing his wife before leaving the bedroom. Something he rarely missed. The thought of going back inside was quickly dismissed as he glanced at his watch. He was already behind his morning schedule.

Riding a bicycle ten miles a day and more on weekends helped him stay fit and gave him the solitude to contemplate problems connected to his high-pressure job. It was his favorite time of day.

Obtaining his current position had taken hard work and perseverance. As the first African American deputy director, he was responsible for keeping the various divisions working smoothly and overseeing high profile investigations. Notable predecessors of his position included men like Clyde Tolson and the infamous Mark Felt, who just before his death in 2008, confessed to being Deep Throat for the Washington Post reporters during the Watergate scandal.

The problem on his mind this morning was a particularly disturbing pattern he'd discovered within numerous FBI and municipal police investigations over the past five years. He'd told no one and was preparing to take his findings to the director the following day. If the director gave the go-ahead, he would assign a specific agent within the FBI to take over the case.

The special agent he had in mind was Sean Kruger. They had been classmates at the FBI Academy and had obtained agent status on the same day. Even though their career paths were different, they'd remained close friends throughout the years. Alan had become a rising star within the ranks of management and Kruger had established his reputation as the agency's top profiler. This being the reason he wanted Kruger to lead the investigation. If he was correct, there was a new serial killer on the loose and the FBI would need Kruger's skills to find him.

As he rode, and contemplated this problem, he noticed the dark SUV following him in the rearview mirror attached to his bike helmet. A note of concern crept into his consciousness as his morning ride entered a particularly beautiful park several miles from his home. Parts of the park were fairly isolated and his path would soon lead to one of those sections.

He heard the SUV rapidly approach on his left and pass too close for his liking. This caused him to slow his pace. As the vehicle raced ahead and skidded to a stop, it blocked the road ahead. Applying the brakes, he slowed his bike to a stop as his concern grew. No one emerged and he could not see the driver inside the vehicle due to the dark tint on the windows.

Wanting to avoid a confrontation, Seltzer prepared to turn the bike in the opposite direction and ride away.

At this same moment, the SUV's front driver side door opened and a man emerged with a suppressed pistol in his hand.

Seltzer did not have time to react as the pistol spat four times. The impact of each bullet forced him away from his bike as he fell to the pavement. Surprise and denial were the last emotions he felt as his head struck the asphalt. The last image he would ever see was his killer walking toward him. As blackness engulfed him, his body exhaled for the last time.

The assailant walked toward the fallen bike rider. A thin skin colored balaclava obscured his facial features as he approached his target. Standing over the prone man, he pointed the suppressed Glock at the individual's head. As he smiled underneath the balaclava, he pulled the trigger one more time, sending a bullet into the fallen man's temple.

Satisfied, he returned to the SUV and drove away.

Twenty minutes would pass before an early-morning jogger came across the body of FBI Deputy Director Alan Seltzer and called 911.

The Dark Trail: Chapter Two

The sound intruded into his dream. At first it was just an annoyance, then, as he swam toward the surface of consciousness, he realized it was his cell phone. Sean Kruger instinctively reached for the device on his nightstand. As he accepted the call, he glanced at the digital clock radio next to the phone: 5:32. Phone calls at this time of morning were rarely good news.

"Kruger," he croaked as he struggled toward alertness.

He listened, raised himself to sit on the side of the bed and cradled his forehead, his elbow on his knee. "When did it happen?"

He grew quiet as he listened.

Stephanie Kruger stirred beside him and rose to one elbow.

"Ah, geez."

She placed her hand on his back and he turned to her with an empty, distant stare.

After listening a few more moments, he said, "I think that's a good idea, thank you. Call me when you know more details."

The call ended and moisture welled in his eyes. "Alan Seltzer was executed this morning on his morning bike ride."

She sat up in bed, her eyes wide. "What do you mean, executed?"

"Someone shot him four times in the chest from a distance and then fired a round pointblank into his head. That is an execution."

"Oh, my gawd, Sean. When?"

"About an hour ago. That was Paul Stumpf. When the EMTs found his ID, they called the FBI Headquarters, who patched it through to Paul. He's on his way to the scene as we speak."

"What about his wife?"

"FBI agents are at the house now. Apparently, Alan was the only target."

She reached over, drew him into an embrace and whispered, "I'm sorry."

He returned the hug as a tear trickled down his cheek. "Paul wants me in DC to head up the investigation."

"I thought you were on a special team."

"Not anymore."

She closed her eyes and they embraced tighter.

By ten a.m. more details concerning the murder of Alan Seltzer emerged. Forensic evidence from the crime scene told FBI investigators a large vehicle had screeched to a halt, blocking the road. The bicycle and body had been found twenty-five feet from the skid marks. Four spent shells had been found in this area with one shell a few feet from the body. A security camera, positioned in the center of the park, captured the incident, although the distance caused the image to be grainy.

The video allowed the technicians to identify the vehicle as a dark five-year-old Ford Explorer. A similar truck was found abandoned in the parking lot of a Falls Church, Virginia

Target store late the same morning. An Arlington police report identified the vehicle as stolen the night before. FBI forensic technicians pored over the SUV at their lab located at Marine Corps Base at Quantico, and by late evening, found no evidence as to the identity of the assailant.

At 5:14 p.m. central time, Kruger received an email outlining his new assignment as the lead investigator into Deputy Director Alan Seltzer's murder. He was to report directly to FBI Director Paul Stumpf at Headquarters the next day.

"How long will you be gone?" Stephanie sat on the bed as she watched Kruger pack his suitcase.

"At this point, I would say indefinitely. I just don't know, Steph."

She nodded. "We'll miss you."

He looked up and gave her a grim smile. "This is not what I want right now."

"I know." She paused for a moment. "When's your flight?"

With a glance at the digital clock on his nightstand, he said, "Bureau plane will be at the airport around seven, which will put me into DC by ten eastern time. I have a meeting with Paul at seven tomorrow morning."

"At least you don't have to fly commercial."

"No, the agency is making this a high-priority. I don't believe any requests for manpower will be denied either."

"What did JR say?"

"He fussed about it for about half a second and then agreed to accompany me to DC. He's meeting me at the airport. That way if he gets a chance to come back early, he'll have a car."

She took a deep breath. "I'll go over to Mia's after you leave."

JR Diminski, now an official member of the FBI Cyber Crimes Division, stared out the window next to his seat as the Gulfstream 550 slipped through the night sky. He turned to Kruger, who sat across the aisle. "I'm sorry about Alan."

Kruger nodded. "I'm thankful his kids are grown. They can help his wife get through the next few days, weeks and months."

"I've never met her."

With a smile, Kruger turned to his friend. "I really didn't know her either until we took a cruise with her and Alan the first year Steph and I were married. The two wives developed a close friendship during that week. Stephanie will join me once we know when the funeral service is scheduled."

"So, we aren't on the special task force anymore."

Kruger shook his head. "The task force has been suspended until further notice, by order of the president."

"What about Sandy and Jimmie?"

"They'll be joining us in DC day after tomorrow."

"Good." JR returned his attention to the window.

After an extended length of silence passed between the two friends, JR said, "Any ideas where to start?"

"I'm going to look through Alan's bureau and personal files. I want you to do a deep dive into his office and personal computer. I'm told the bureau has all of those items locked away waiting for us. My first inclination is to assume he stumbled onto something he wasn't supposed to, and it cost him his life."

"You don't think it was random?"

"No, I'm positive it wasn't random. The fact someone stole a Ford Explorer and ambushed him in the area of the park with the least amount of CCTV security worries me. This was carefully planned and executed. We'll start there."

JR nodded.

At 6:45 the next morning, the J. Edgar Hoover building was abuzz with activity, most of which centered around the investigation into the murder of Deputy Director Alan Seltzer. In the midst of this maelstrom of activity, Sean Kruger and JR Diminski entered the conference room next to the office of the Director of the FBI. Milling around the room, Kruger saw Scott Lambert who was the Executive Assistant Director for the Criminal, Cyber, Response and Services Branch, Dr. Teri Monroe, Executive Assistant Director for Science and Technology Branch and numerous individuals he did not know. He also saw Joseph Kincaid, the current National Security Advisor for the President of the United States. JR made a beeline toward him while Kruger talked to Lambert and Monroe.

As he shook her hand, Monroe said, "I haven't spoken to you since the Randolph Bishop affair. It's good to see you, Sean."

"Good to see you too, Teri. Congratulations on your promotion."

With a shrug, she blushed. "I don't get to do things I enjoy any more, like working with agents such as yourself."

Kruger gave her a smile. "How's Charlie Craft?"

"He's now one of my assistants."

"When you see him, congratulate him for me."

"You can do it yourself. He's been assigned to this investigation."

"Good, I haven't had the pleasure of working with him for a while."

Turning to Lambert, Kruger said, "It's been awhile since I last saw you too, Scott. Wish the circumstances were better."

"I agree."

Their conversation lasted a few more seconds before Kruger noticed JR and Joseph approaching. After shaking Joseph's hand, the older man leaned over to speak quietly to Kruger.

"When was the last time you spoke to Alan?"

After blinking a few times, Kruger replied, "I hate to say this, but it's been several months. Why?"

Joseph took a deep breath. "Look at his personnel files. My nephew told me about a theory he had but didn't have enough evidence to take it to Paul yet."

"What was it?"

"I'm not going to taint your perspective. You'll find it."

At that moment, Paul Stumpf entered the conference room and sat at the head of the table. Everyone found a seat and the room grew quiet.

"Thank you all for being here early this morning. This will be a short meeting. There are a few organizational matters we need to attend to." He looked around the room; everyone remained quiet, waiting for him to proceed. "First and foremost, the individual in charge of the investigation into Alan Seltzer's death will be Special Agent Sean Kruger."

Everyone nodded and shot a glance at Kruger.

"You will give him your fullest cooperation at all times, no delays or push backs. Is that clear?"

Again, everyone nodded.

"Now that we have that settled, Dr. Monroe, would you present the findings your team found yesterday?"

Teri stood and walked to a laptop at the opposite end of the conference table. She pressed the side of a mouse and a screen on the wall lit up with a still image. She said, "This is a security camera view from the First Virginia National Bank near Alan's home. Pay attention to the left side of the screen." She clicked the mouse again.

From the left side, a bike rider could be seen pedaling hard as he crossed the fisheye lens' focal range. Two seconds after the cyclist disappeared, a dark SUV followed the same route. She paused the video when the Explorer was halfway across.

"We believe this is the SUV involved with the shooting."

She pressed the mouse again. The scene jumped to another view of a residential area. "This is a view from a doorbell camera on a home two blocks from the park. Note the Explorer is following closer in this view."

Everyone in the room watched as the bicycle moved from the left to right of the screen, the Explorer now only twenty or thirty feet behind the rider. When the short video finished, Teri pressed the mouse. "The next shot is disturbing, but necessary to watch. Our technicians have cropped the shot and enhanced it as much as possible."

She clicked the mouse again. There was not a sound in the room as the events unfolded in front of them. From the right side of the screen, the Explorer passed the bicycle and suddenly stopped, blocking the road. The rider slowed the bike and attempted to turn around. At that moment, the door to the SUV opened and a figure emerged.

She stopped the video. "We apologize for the poor quality of the video, but beyond this, enlargement pixel count is compromised." She started video again.

A figure emerged from the SUV and pointed an elongated pistol at the bike rider. The cyclist collapsed to the pavement and the gunman walked slowly toward the fallen man. Once he stood over the body, he pointed the pistol at the prone figure's head. An audible gasp sounded throughout the room. At this point the gunman turned and walked back to the Ford and drove away.

Teri ended the video and faced the group. "Preliminary autopsy indicated Alan was already dead before the fifth bullet was fired at pointblank range." She sat next to the laptop.

A hushed silence fell over the room as Stumpf let the effects captured on video sink in. After several moments of silence, he continued, "This was not a random act of violence. This was an execution of a senior member of the FBI. We all knew Alan. We all respected Alan and considered him a friend.

He was also a valued member of this organization and I will not allow whoever did this to go unpunished."

Heads nodded around the table.

Stumpf stood. "I want to see Agent Kruger, Agent Diminski, and Joseph Kincaid in my office. The rest of you know what needs to be done. Dismissed."

Grab your copy...
vinci-books.com/seankruger6

About the Author

J.C. Fields is an award-winning author living in Southwest Missouri. He is an associate member of the International Thriller Writers, a member of Sleuth's Ink Mystery Writers, and serves on the board of the Springfield Writers' Guild.

The Sean Kruger Series has won numerous awards. His first four novels have been awarded the Literary Titan Gold Book Award, *The Imposter's Trail* was awarded Best Mystery/Thriller at the 2017 Ozark Indie Book Fest, and in 2018, Readers' Favorite awarded *The Fugitive's Trail* a silver medal in the Fiction - Suspense genre.

Acknowledgments

I continue to marvel at the amount of support I receive as a writer. As the number of novels increases, so does the need for a support system. Before I published my first novel, *The Fugitive's Trail*, there was only myself pounding away on my laptop at odd hours of the early morning and on the weekends, stealing as much time as possible in my office. It is only when an author decides to publish his work that he discovers the need for assistance.

To those individuals who have assisted along the way, I say thank you and tip my hat. Some of you have been here from the beginning, and others have joined as the need arose.

Sharon Kizziah-Holmes, owner of Paperback-Press, has been there from the beginning, believing in my work and maintaining her enthusiastic support.

The members of the Springfield Writers' Guild continue to offer suggestions and advice as my catalog of titles increases.

As my development editor, I cannot thank Emily Truscott enough. She continues to offer excellent suggestions and gently keeps me from bruising my ego when I need to change something critical, like the title. Thank you, Emily; your suggestion was perfect.

Alisa Trotter is the newest member of my support team. Thank you for your fine-tuning of the manuscript; it is amazing what one final read-through will find.

Paul J. McSorley, what can I say? Paul has become an integral partner in creating the audio versions of my novels. He is wonderful to work with and has become THE voice of Sean Kruger.

And again, last but not least, my wife, Connie. She is and always will be my life partner and largest supporter, even while tapping her foot outside my office with a, *we're late, are you done yet?* glare.